BREATHLESS

Translated from the Swedish by
Deborah Bragan-Turner

BREATHLESS

Anne Swärd

VIKING

VIKING
Published by the Penguin Group
Penguin Group (USA) Inc., 375 Hudson Street, New York, New York 10014, USA

USA | Canada | UK | Ireland | Australia | New Zealand | India | South Africa | China
Penguin Books Ltd, Registered Offices: 80 Strand, London WC2R 0RL, England
For more information about the Penguin Group visit penguin.com

Originally published in Swedish as *Till sista andetaget* by Svante Weyler Bokforlag, Stockholm

English-language edition first published in Great Britain by MacLehose Press, an imprint of Quercus

LIBRARY OF CONGRESS CATALOGING-IN-PUBLICATION DATA

Swärd, Anne.
[Till sista andetaget. English]
Breathless / Anne Swärd ; Translated from the Swedish by Deborah Bragan-Turner.
pages cm
Originally published in Swedish as Till sista andetaget in Stockholm by Weyler in 2009.
ISBN 978-0-670-02654-8
I. Title.
PT9876.29.W38T5513 2013
839.73'8—dc23
2013007099

Printed in the United States of America
10 9 8 7 6 5 4 3 2 1

Book design by Carla Bolte

ALWAYS LEARNING   PEARSON

To Nadja

To Samuel

In memory of L.

BREATHLESS

SUNSHINE HOURS

Every day she sat in a deck chair on the veranda, counting the hours of sunshine, drinking ice water, dozing. Trying not to think about cigarettes. The sweet smell of fresh tobacco, the smooth taste of smoke, the delicious rustle of a newly opened packet of Silk Cut, and the sensual warmth that filled the mouth. Pregnant with a giant apricot, that was how she looked. Her taut, rounded stomach was covered with down and had a springy resistance when the father-to-be and his brothers poked their filthy fingers at it. It smelled of sun-warmed, harvest-ripe fruit. How they wanted to take a bite, but she stopped them: No! Not quite ripe yet. Three more weeks in the sun. *Three weeks?* They had been patient an eternity, how could they stand more of this waiting? But she pushed him and his brothers away. They would have to be content to watch and wait. For a little while longer the magic fruit belonged to her alone.

She sat there and saw her stomach darken, swell, stretch in a high dome toward the light. Rejoiced in the last luxuriant warmth of summer, tried not to think about cigarettes and the future and him. The other one. For love is a folie à deux, she had read somewhere. And now she knew it to be true from her own experience, and the worst thing was that all it took was for both of them to be slightly crazy—together, the whole thing became utter madness.

Her infatuation had grown until it lost its softness, and her stomach likewise. She looked on them both as if they belonged to someone else: the lunar mountain that rose up above her hips, and the ravine of ill-starred love, so deep she couldn't see the bottom. Pull yourself together, she said to herself. Get a grip, get a grip . . . don't think about him. But whenever she tried not to think about him, there he was in her thoughts.

Love is something one is stricken with, like a fever or bankruptcy. No, it was a fever that laid waste to her body, however hard she tried to cool it down on the outside. Love has no laws, veers between lovers as it pleases. She hated him. Loved him. Loved him so much that she hated him. His mere existence was bad enough—so close that some nights she thought she would go mad. Indeed she was not sure—perhaps she had already.

The stone walls of the house had the warmth of the entire summer stored up in them, and it was impossible to breathe inside. Instead David had made a bed for them in the corner of the veranda that was shaded in the morning. They slept close together on a mattress to the sound of the sparse night traffic on the highway in the distance, the rasping calls of the tree frogs from the overgrown dam behind the house, now and then a freight train and a solitary nightjar over the field. Even in her dreams she tried not to think about the other one. It didn't work, however hard David held her to him. She had exercised willpower before—when she went down into the cellar to fetch beer, even though she was terrified of bats and knew that they were hanging from the low ceiling—but this was so much more difficult, her will not strong enough to resist the thought of him.

At night David's arm around her stopped her floating away, out into the cold dark universe, her stomach like an inflated helium balloon. But during the day she sat alone, proud and dignified, and wanted to be left in peace. Shooed him and his brothers away when they sniffed around her like dogs, as if they believed she was the bearer of a secret, when in fact anyone could tell what was on its way: an apricot, king size. She was becoming incredibly big.

The due date passed by days and weeks. The bulging fruit grew more and more overripe. Her navel, which once had been a little white bud, spread into a rose of gossamer skin and turned brown in its innermost folds. Her legs, which she could no longer see, filled with water, and a river delta of veins branched out, distended, snaking down her inner thighs.

Björn, grandfather-to-be on the father's side, gave her Tiger Balm to rub into her swollen ankles, but she couldn't reach down. She allowed him to do it for her, as the act of tenderness it was. Like Farah Diba on her peacock throne, although her own feet hardly smelled of virgin milk; they were black and cracked after a whole summer barefoot. Idun, grandmother-to-be on the father's side, had sent off for the latest firm molded bras from Swegmark mail order. She had never really bothered about bras before, but was informed by the future grandmother that from now on she had no choice. It wasn't just her stomach that was growing, had she not noticed?

"Will you stay like that afterwards?" David said and nodded toward her new and different charms.

"I should hope not," she said, having no desire to carry them around for the rest of her life and satisfied with the manageable size they had been hitherto.

In her strange state she was above all trivialities. Heat, hunger, boredom, agitation, flies—none of the bothers that usually irritated her could trouble her now. She had never given birth before and so she wasn't apprehensive. It was natural, she thought. Animals do it more or less en passant, and she had always thought of herself as an animal, a fox, lithe and instinctive. She had decided that when it was time, if she could manage it, if it didn't go too quickly, she would conjure up the picture of the vixen giving birth alone in the cool darkness of its lair.

The longer an apricot hangs on a tree, the easier it falls. Björn had three apricot trees trained against the sunny side of the house, and at this particular time in late summer the fruits were so distended, so sweet, so ripe, so ready that just a look was enough for them to loosen and land in one's hand. Things happen when the time is right. Even a skeptic could be convinced of that.

While she waited she took pleasure in the last warmth of the year, gathering it up as one gathers one's strength, without knowing how badly one is going to need it.

It was a protracted delivery.

When the killer-whale baby finally rolled out of its mother after three days, she stared at the result with shock. The child looked nothing like a shiny rose-pink apricot covered with golden down. More like an Eskimo. The feeling that it had been worth it—the months of waiting, the body's drastic transformation, the fear that took hold with the very first contractions, the reckless drive to the maternity clinic in thick fog, the unspeakable pain, the feeling that she was the last living soul on earth and lying there all by herself in a strange delivery room in a deserted hospital and giving birth as best she could although she had no idea how, and the lies afterward when everyone declared that she hadn't been alone even though they had no notion how alone she had been—the feeling that it had been worth it didn't emerge straightaway.

It should have been a boy. Someone who looked like the father. Because he was the one who had made something start to grow inside her, uncontrolled, then at least what came out should have exhibited certain similarities to him, the originator. But no, first it was a girl, second . . . hair as dark as if it had been dipped into a bottomless lake.

Later, when it was the new papa's turn to inspect the harvest's yield, he stared too. The girl resembled no one, least of all him, but not her mother either. He didn't utter a word, overwhelmed by the seriousness of the moment or perhaps by disappointment. All the others on both sides of the family were various shades of Nordic blond. The nurses didn't react until they saw the child in her father's arms, but it had happened before, what with all the new foreign workers in the area. And sometimes babies were born with coal-black hair that discreetly fell out after a few weeks. After all, it was man's ability to adapt that meant he survived.

The obstetrician washed his hands somewhere in the background, and maybe he was thinking once again that his job really was grunt work rather than craftsmanship: women who screamed and kicked and calved as if there were nothing human left in them. Like this one.

"It was a big stomach for such a little one," he said, without turning around to reveal whether he meant the mother or the child, probably both.

The mother recovered, but there was something frail about the child. It wasn't really a perfect baby—rather pasty, rather weak, growing feebler as the days passed, the blood count too low, a clear case of anemia. Against her black hair and dark glistening eyes, her skin had a bluish pallor. The pediatrician thought they should give her a transfusion, but the mother didn't want him to stick needles and tubes into the little mite, and so he reluctantly gave the child a few weeks to improve.

Jaundice at the clinic and a ban on visiting. The two families stood in the hospital grounds and waved when the mother lifted up her daughter on the balcony. A pale, dark-headed infant was all they could see at that distance. Everything in miniature apart from the eyes, unless it was just the color, dark sea green, giving the illusion that they were huge.

Maybe it wasn't a miracle, but it felt like it—the situation improved. Even though the birth certificate was just a piece of paper, it did verify that her daughter existed, this wan little thing lying under the hospital blanket and squinting out at the dazzling September light. It was to be Angela Rafaela. "Eh?" the new papa said doubtfully. But it had already been decided, and once the thought was formed it could not be withdrawn. It ought to have brought bad luck. Angela Rafaela after the archangel Raphael with his powers of healing, because here was a child who had healed herself, and there was reason to believe that some higher authority had had a hand in it. Or perhaps just the tip of a wing, but it had made all the difference.

"She has to have a name that people can pronounce as well," the new papa's mother said.

"Okay. . . . *Lo*," Mama said, irritated. Was that simple enough? She was clutching at anything and the name Lo—Swedish for lynx—had just popped into her head.

"Angela Rafaela Lo Mård? That sounds crazy," Papa said.

That people would just call her Lo Mård hardly made things any better.

How could anyone think he had the right to interfere? She had no intention of taking back the name she had just given—that would be tempting fate, like sucking the life out of the tiny nostrils.

"David, it's already decided," she said. "Next time you can give birth and choose the name." While she had been sitting in the deck chair, nurturing the baby inside her all summer, she had been reading the erotic diaries of Anaïs Nin, whose full name, Angela Anaïs Juana Antolina Rosa Edelmira Nin y Culmell, was unabashedly long.

But at least Grandmother was satisfied that the name they would use would be Lo. It was easy to remember, and that was the most important thing about a name, after all.

I was baptized on the Feast of the Guardian Angels in October 1969, a year of hope with a slight hubris in the air. The moon wasn't quite so far away. It shone with the same desolate light, but now that it had been touched by men it seemed less remote in the planetary darkness. The year of the moon landing was, according to my father's mother, the last year that man could still surpass himself in anything other than stupidity.

My first memory is of a bright light shining straight at me. I always thought it was the sun, but it must have been the lamp in the ceiling seen from below as I was passed from arm to arm in a kitchen full of people. So many arms and yet I didn't feel trapped. Such a strong light and it shone just on me. The adults warmed their hands on me, sniffed at my neck to drink in the aroma of new life, kissed me one after the other as if I were a holy relic in a shrine.

No one could understand how I had come to be, in what dark corner of the large house it could have happened, the house where my parents and their brothers and sisters lived like one family. They just had to get used to the idea. My young uncles and aunts pulled me from all sides. I wasn't supposed to have been there, but now that I was, dreams and hopes were spun around my dark head, something of which I was fortunately unaware. I wasn't to trouble myself with anything other than existing. A ship so overloaded with expectations was to be a vessel too oppressive for a small child.

Tender roots in the new earth, in the rich black soil, so unlike the barren ground they had moved away from. My small roots would bind them to the place where they still didn't feel at home in their own right. Someone had to be born here so that the others could hang on to the birth certificate's clear proof of their belonging. The adults must watch closely over me so that no harm should come. Protect, nourish, raise, make me housetrained, set one or two extendable boundaries and look the other way when I overstepped them. As soon as I was big enough I would slip away to escape the affection. I needed it to be there, just as long as I could stand still long enough to accept it.

Born under a lucky star, according to the story they told me. Someone pointed out the Lynx constellation in the Northern Hemisphere. I loved standing out in the yard with Papa's brothers when they were in that mood, magnanimous, when they would look at shooting stars and dream of getting away—back home— where they really belonged. Sometimes they could be depressed and lighthearted at the same time, and then the starry sky was the only thing that helped. Every now and again they were in high spirits and acted as if they were from the Ministry of Silly Walks. On those evenings the stars didn't matter to us.

If I wasn't happy as a child, I didn't realize. The short-term happiness that darts between trees is perhaps the only kind there is. I was happy as long as I could run free, happy in my puppy fat, happy when I was lying under the bed eavesdropping on my young aunts who spent a whole summer talking about nothing but sex, happy when Papa's youngest brother, Rikard, chased me through the arboretum, even though I knew it wasn't as much fun when he caught me. I never saw that happiness was so brief, because it came at such short intervals that I hardly noticed the gaps.

About the time on the veranda, about the art of not thinking about the forbidden, I still knew nothing.

"Beware of love," Mama said as she sucked the poison out of my swelling foot, spat a long yellowish jet into the grass, and rinsed her mouth with milk.

Love and snakes.

Love, snakes, and the highway.

Love, snakes, the highway, the lake.

Bats.

High-voltage power lines.

Horror films.

"What about dogs?" I asked.

"Them too."

"Nothing else?"

She raised the ax. "More?"

"Yes."

"Undercooked chicken. Bacteria," she said and swung the ax with all her strength so that the pieces of birchwood shattered. The strength in her arm muscles was not to be trifled with.

"And vole fever," she added.

"Vole fever doesn't exist down here, Mama. It's only farther north."

"And the rest. Watch out for the rest," she said.

I wrote it all down in the green Chinese silk book with the ferrous smell of melting snow and blood between its pages. The book for beautiful things and dangerous things—I just didn't yet know which was which. Fear is something you have to learn, if you aren't born with it, Mama said. I had to be protected from myself because I didn't have an ounce of fear in my body.

"You would go along with anyone at all without something inside you telling you to stop. Do anything you like, get into real trouble." That wasn't true. I never got into trouble.

Mama tried to teach me what fear was.

Papa tried.

Both my grandmothers and grandfathers tried.

All my aunts and uncles.

And Lukas.

No, maybe not Lukas. But the others tried.

Yes, Lukas did as well. Trust your fear, he used to say.

BRUSHFIRE

One dry, aimless day in an infinitely long summer, a brushfire broke out beside the railway that carved through the landscape. A landscape already scorched by the sun, my landscape, open and gently sloping down toward the lake.

It burned in the field of barley and along the railway embankment, smelled of singed weeds and tar, white-hot rails, blackened barbed wire. Insects and field mice burned. The earth burned. The blackthorn bushes crackled, the turkey sheds smoldered and screeched. Something was changing, a feeling of security melted away; a different mood would take its place.

The news spread as fast as the fire. It was in the middle of the factory holiday, and most people were at home and rushed up from all sides. When the whole village was standing ready along the edge of the field it looked like a civil defense exercise, were it not for the terror in people's eyes. The flames advanced rapidly in all directions with the help of the wind. Allowed to run its course, it would soon reach the houses. The fire brigade took its time. It was a much drier summer than usual in the middle of harvest, and perhaps there were fires in several places at once. But we couldn't wait, as the fire wouldn't wait. Mama and Papa's mother started to break off large branches along the embankment for all the helping hands. Cooperation and working together were needed now—just like the old days, one of the elderly people said.

Everyone in my family was there, and I wanted to be there too. At first they tried to push me out of the way, but soon it was all they could do to keep the fire in check and they were no longer aware of me. I ran back and forth with water like all the others. Saw Mama go dangerously close to the worst of the fire, saw Papa's brothers help to smother the flames with military blankets and tarpaulins. Two tall women, my father's sister and my mother's, walked along the embankment in men's high Wellington boots, stamping out the embers. Papa's father Björn and Mama's father Aron worked side by side with quick, jerky strides, like brothers in identical overalls, but Grandfather Björn was taller by a head, as enormous as the bear he was named after. They wanted to show that they were just as capable of work as their sons, and they had begun to create a firebreak in the field so that the blaze would lose its hold. I saw Mama's mother standing on the side of the hill cradling an empty zinc bowl, as if she didn't know why she was standing there. As if someone had tricked her into thinking that she could direct the teamwork from up there, just to keep her out of the way. Papa had burned his hands and was being bandaged up by Mama's brother, who ruthlessly ripped wide strips from Papa's favorite shirt to protect his damaged palms. My mother's sisters were members of the long chains of people passing water out of the nearest houses from hand to hand.

The fire spread along the side of the hill as if it would never be halted. Working against the wind, we tried to limit the disaster, until at long last we heard the sirens approach.

It was dangerous to get in the way of the hard jets of water. Everyone drew back—all except one, a teenage boy I had already noticed as the only one to get nearer to the fire than my mama. At times he looked almost as if he were standing in the flames. When everyone else had taken a step back he continued his monotonous firefighting. Mama shouted a warning to him, but he took no notice. She managed to shove him away from the flames, but he went straight back. She grabbed hold of him tighter and screamed something at him in the voice she always had when she was afraid. When she hit him, he didn't react, just pulled away and carried on. She took hold again and shook him, as if she were trying to wake him out of a spell. He broke loose again, but his strength was gone and he sank down onto the charred grass as if all the energy had emptied out of him in an instant.

From mania to inertia in seconds. Black from his hair down to his gym shoes. I had never seen a dead person, but he didn't look alive. Smoke could poison you, I knew—during the last autumn storm Mama and I had helped Papa's father clean up in the arboretum after the wind had been through it like a tornado, and when we burned the branches the smoke made me sick and I threw up half the night.

Papa's father led Mama away through the crowd. I went closer to the unknown boy to see if he was breathing. His chest inside the sooty T-shirt seemed to be gently rising and falling, but for safety's sake I sat a little away from him. If he stopped breathing I would call Papa, who'd once breathed life into a child who had died—a girl caught in the weir next to the factory. Papa said that he had seen my face in hers as he gave her the kiss of life. Mama's sisters said that certainly my papa had brought *that* girl back to life, but once long ago he hadn't been able to save the one whose name we couldn't mention in case Mama's mother heard it, the youngest, the one who fell through the ice. Even so, Papa was the only person I knew who could wake the dead.

After a very long time the stranger opened his eyes and with difficulty he sat up. I should have left, but when he looked at me I couldn't. Papa had given me a carton of milk that was good if you had inhaled smoke. I took a couple of sips and gave the rest to him and he accepted it without a word and downed it in one.

When I asked him which of the people there were his family, he said that there was no one. I couldn't think of a single person in the village who was missing; all of them had come out of their houses to help.

"Don't you live here?" I said. He nodded and indicated toward the lake. There was no house there. He was just pointing over an empty field. I stood and screwed up my eyes in the sun. Had there been a house there that had burned down?

"Can't you see it?" he asked. I sneaked a look at him to see if he was pulling my leg. Strained my eyes, stared at the place he had pointed to, but there was nothing there.

If that was where he lived, why had he tried to fight the fire here and not from his own side? It was as if he had tried to put out the fire in the wrong place altogether. I explained which people in the crowd were my family—all except for Mama, not wanting him to know that she and I were related. I had never seen Mama like that before, never seen her hit anyone, except for once when she was alone in the cold-storage room with someone—I didn't manage to see who, probably Papa—the incident so bewildering that I all but forgot it.

His eyes widened at each mention of the twelve I identified as my kin.

"What about you? Do you live on your own?" I asked.

"No, of course I don't live on my own," he said, not looking at me. "I'm only thirteen." He spat into the grass, black and red.

But I didn't think that was so.

He gazed out over the field, as if he wondered himself where his house had gone, but he seemed to be in no hurry to rush home and make sure that his family was okay.

"What about you, then?" he asked. I'm sure it was obvious, but

I still couldn't tell the truth. Papa used to say that I was older than I looked. Mama didn't agree at all. I was just quite small. "How old?" the boy said again, measuring me as he looked. Not much to measure, I hadn't even reached the age of seven. Instead of answering I asked him where he lived—truly. Then suddenly I felt his hard hands take hold of me. I lost contact with the ground without warning, rising right up until I was taller than him, and there . . . far down the slope, sheltered from the wind and people's view by high trees, was the house. Beyond my horizon, far beyond the limit Mama had set for me to roam around on my own, almost down by the water's edge, the widening of the river, round like a lake, silver blue, with two narrow streams that meandered farther north and south.

He set me back down on the grass. I straightened my sleeveless dress that had ridden up and gotten creased and had the marks left by his black hands. Felt my face tighten with soot and heat.

As soon as the worst of the disaster had been averted, speculation over what had caused the conflagration began. Or who. Arson, Mama believed. Sparks from the train line, Papa said. Dry grass that spontaneously ignited, Mama's sisters thought. Arson, Papa's father agreed—it had begun to burn in several places at once; natural fires seldom follow such a rapid pattern. Mama's father thought it might be a bit of everything: it was a fire summer, a snake summer, a summer of parched and overheated emotions. I said nothing and no one asked me what I thought.

The danger wasn't over. The ground glowed with sealed-in heat, for the fire could creep along the roots and stay alive for days and restart at any time. Watch had to be kept on the field all through the night. The thirteen adults who under normal circumstances looked after me would have been too preoccupied or exhausted to bother whether I was in my bed or not. The rest of the night I sat with the unknown boy near his house wrapped in a heavy saddle blanket that smelled of propane and old stallion, filled with new, unfamiliar feelings.

The fear that the underground embers would suddenly flare up again kept me awake. His presence as well. Was he one of those you had to be wary of? I wasn't sure. The fire, the dark, the tiredness, the stinging in my eyes, the sense that I had to look after myself now, that no one would protect me so far away from my usual territory. Independent overnight. No one would recognize me when I came home, *if* I ever came home. It seemed unreal that I had had a family at all. I felt so grown-up, so far from home, that I lost sight of my old life, the house, the arboretum, the cars in the yard, the tall white birch, my hiding place. Where this endless night would lead I had no idea. For the first time in my life I was alone with someone I didn't know, nestled beside the forbidden lake where, it was said—I knew this even though I wasn't yet seven—people from the village had deliberately gone under. One or two from the neighboring village too.

Where he lived was still the only thing I knew about him, in the house where no light was turned on the whole night. He went into the garage and found a blanket for me when he heard my teeth chattering in the darkness, but he didn't go into the house, despite hunger, despite thirst. I didn't know what his name was, only how his hands felt when he lifted me up off the ground, the smarting of the tender skin of my armpits, a cold tingling in my stomach. He didn't fetch a jacket for himself, never felt the cold, he said, sat on his heels, huddled up, and smoked as if he didn't have enough smoke inside him already.

The only things I had smoked before were chocolate cigarettes, and even that I had done in secret. But when he offered me a cigarette, I couldn't say no. What would he think, that I was a child?

I didn't want him to light it for me, just sat there, tightly wrapped up in my blanket like a stuffed cabbage leaf and carefully held the cigarette in my hand. Thought I would save it, as a mark of . . . something. It was the fact that he had asked me that was important.

This was something I would always remember. The only thing I wanted to wipe from my memory was the sound of the birds on fire, but that was hard when the smell of them hung over the field. The turkey sheds were already in flames when Mama managed to open the padlock, and the birds that were still alive flew out like blazing torches and set fire to the barley where they fell.

The whole village was shrouded in a stench of the charred remains of living creatures. The pain in my lungs helped to keep me awake. To sit with a stranger and say nothing and feel cold and keep sneaking a look at him and then at the glow of his cigarette and know that our job was so important that we had to make sure that the whole village didn't catch fire made everything easier to bear. Including the longing for home I felt when I saw the bats silently swoop after insects above the lake.

He didn't ask what my name was. I told him anyway.

"That sounds like a boy's name."

"No, it's the name of a beast of prey," I said.

"Yes, yes. I know. I know all about beasts of prey," he said and looked at me skeptically when I related what Mama had once told me. That one autumn when the ice froze earlier than usual up in the north, where my family came from, a she-bear walked out to one of the rocky islands and went into hibernation. When she woke up in spring the ice was gone and she was caught in a trap. Men went out in boats and looked at her in awe. In those days a bear was an exceptional sight up there, and she was a magnificent specimen. Then they shot her, because they were hungry that spring after the war, and everyone knew it was the same bear that had killed my great-grandfather, so his family received the biggest share of the meat.

"A bear's not a beast of prey," he said.

"I know, but that was the bear that killed my great-grandfather who gave Papa's father the name Björn. And it was Papa's father who gave Mama the name Karenina. And Mama who gave me the name Lo."

"Oh, right," he said, and looked at me quizzically. "Are you going to smoke it or can I have it back? It was my last one."

"I'm going to," I said, "but not at the moment."

Lukács Zsolt. That was what he was called. Or rather, Zsolt Lukács—a misunderstanding that occurred long ago when he arrived here at the outset with his father. As far as he knew his father had written his name down on a piece of paper for the day-care staff the first time he left his son with them, not realizing that in Sweden the given name usually comes first. When he picked up his son later the same day everyone called him Lukas.

And Lukas it remained. It was a funny story, but he didn't tell it as if it were funny. He didn't mind the mix-up, he said. Lukács had been his mother's surname, that was why he liked it. And when he pronounced it in Hungarian it sounded like lo-cat.

A number of times during the night he had to go off and throw up after all the smoke he had inhaled. He had gone nearer to the fire than anyone else, displaying a defiance that reminded me of that dangerous look in Mama's and Papa's eyes when they threw themselves into the surf at the sea. Again and again into the waves, into the flames, as if each time were the last.

He knows all about beasts of prey, I thought, as I watched him dry his mouth and sit down again. I realized that he was the one who had started the fire. I didn't understand why. Sitting on the burned-out field on the lookout for signs that it was starting up again, I was suddenly aware that he hoped it would.

The sandy field, the heat under the soles of our feet, the smell of burned flesh when we ran. If the fire hadn't started, I would never have encountered him. When I returned home that morning I knew hardly any more about him than before we had met. Not much was said during the night, but the fire had burned all the way between our two houses, and that had altered everything.

At home in the dawn, blue with cold and altered, everyone still asleep. I slowly washed my hands with Grandmother's lily-of-the-valley soap; the rest of me was so black I would probably never be clean again. Creeping down into the bed between Mama and Aunt Marina, I tried to steal some of their warmth under the blanket without waking them with my ice-cold hands and knees. I wanted to face both of them, couldn't choose, and lay on my back instead. Mama's sleep was troubled, and she tossed her head back and forth so that her long hair became more and more tangled on the pillow.

When the family assembled on the veranda for a very late and silent breakfast, I behaved as if nothing had happened. Papa's hands were wrapped in clean new bandages. He fumbled and grimaced and swore as his mother and Mama's sisters had to help him with his coffee and porridge. He looked as though he enjoyed being waited on from two sides, his father teased. No one else said anything, the subject of the fire having been exhausted long before. All that remained was to eat in silence and then to go down and gawk at the devastation.

I couldn't tell them that I had met someone who had offered me cigarettes, and had seen the sun rise from another world on the other side of the field. I was hurt that no one had even noticed my absence. But belonging to everyone in a way meant belonging to no one—at night I often wandered around between the beds and any one of them could have thought that I was sleeping with one of the others.

Just as the guilty return to the scene of the crime, all the villagers returned to the burned-out field. Perhaps it had all been a nightmare, but no, it looked as though war had rampaged along the field of barley and the railway line. The wind had died down and the sour smell of smoldering vegetation hung stubbornly over the black landscape. No one spoke, as there was nothing to add, except possibly a cautious word of thanks directed obliquely upward, that at least the fire had been halted before it reached the houses.

The boy who had said he was called Lukas was there as well. He stood slightly aside and hung on his rusty bicycle, with a look I didn't really comprehend. I glanced back, but didn't go up to him, stayed with Papa's brothers and counted charred electricity poles along the embankment. Growing up, I could see, meant not saying all you knew.

The rain finally came, a day too late. A grime over everything that had burned. The impression that something had threatened the village gave a feeling of solidarity in misfortune, even if it didn't last.

BOY'S EYES

We lived at the edge of the village in a district with no name, where beauty and wilderness began. The sloping fields of grain and the sky, the forest of bats and the power station. And the lake that wasn't a lake, just as our village wasn't a proper village in that it didn't have its own name. It was an unwanted growth or maybe a free zone with its own laws, or lawless, depending on your point of view. We lived at the place where three silver trails ran together— the river, the railway, the highway—where the world began or ended. That also depended on your point of view. Lately I have started to think that nearly everything depends on your point of view.

The secret about him I had to keep better than any secret I had kept before. I had never learned the secret about secrets, apart from what I hid under Mama's wardrobe where she never vacuumed: a worn-out hunting knife, a bottle of Paco Rabanne, the steel guitar strings I couldn't resist unscrewing from Rikard's guitars, a porn magazine with pressed butterfly wings and chewing gum wrappers. And now the cigarette as a relic among the others in the dust.

Until now I had been able to go from one to another of the family's thirteen adults and pour out everything I wanted to without anyone tiring of me. Now I had fallen through the rabbit hole into a world I couldn't speak about. Lukas had said that that night was a baptism of fire. I didn't know what this meant, but he said it as though I would clearly understand. How he said it was all that mattered.

A few days after the fire, I walked down the gravel track to his house by the lake. Through the trees, with leaves as dry as sloughed snakeskin, I caught a glimpse of him with someone I assumed to be his papa. He was at the top of the roof, his papa down below on the step, appearing to give his son an order, though I didn't hear what. I went closer, accustomed to bringing a smile to the faces of adults. The indifference in the man's eyes when he turned made me feel uneasy in the ensuing silence, a quiet so stark that I could hear the snakeskin leaves rustle. Lukas shot me a quick glance before he turned away. I spun around and walked up the hill toward home without looking back.

   People around here are different, hard to make out, Mama's father used to claim. And that wasn't a good thing—to be different— it was preferable to be the same. Like us in our family. It was true that Lukas had said they weren't from around here either, but they were from another foreign place and differed in another way.

Boy's eyes, boy's hands, boy's smell. I wasn't afraid of him. The feeling was more like the one brought on at the lake. Bottomless. So swampy you never knew if there was something under your feet or not. Not exactly frightened but disturbed by the fact that from the very first day at school he stood in one corner of the enclosed yard and looked at me as if I had something he wanted. It was obvious he didn't intend to come up to me and take it, like the older boys, with a modicum of force. Not him. No threats from him— he just watched. As if he had all the time in the world to wait. His eyes were like suction cups—not moist and warm, but reserved and insistent. I kept far away from the spot he had earmarked for himself, but his gaze cut right through the schoolyard. He was alone like me. No, more alone, so alone that no one even quarreled with him. He didn't look as though he kept to the wall because he was afraid of ambush, just that he had laid claim to the patch and sat on the back of one of the benches looking at nothing in particular. Or at me.

A few weeks later, when he happened to be behind me in the lunch line, I noticed that he still smelled of smoke. It was hard to believe it could be from the railway fire, but I hadn't heard talk of any other since that one. Mama's mother had bathed me of it in heavy-handed fashion and then thrown out my clothes, so impossible was it to get rid of the smell of sulfur pervading them. But then, she often flung things out and bought new, in thrall to a phobia of everything that didn't smell immaculately clean. She used to scrub Grandfather Aron in a hot bath every afternoon when he came home from the leather factory. Clean clothes were lying ready for him on the bed, and then it was time for the afternoon shave, a custom that lived on from the past, from the north where he always had to have a protective layer of stubble when he went out into the harsh cold of the morning.

"You have a strange accent. Where do you come from?" Lukas had asked me toward the end of the night of the fire. He spoke a husky, soft, slow Skåne dialect that poured like maple syrup in the darkness between us. Outside the family I had hardly met anyone before starting school, but I knew there was one world at home and another beyond. At the grocery Papa would pretend he understood, while mumbling to me that he didn't grasp a word of it and how long did you have to live here before you could understand this impossible language? Mama didn't pretend. She said "What?" after every sentence until they became irritated with her and thought she was making fun of them. I didn't understand everything either, but it wasn't me they were talking to, so it didn't matter.

"Ripberget," I said. True, I had never lived there, but all the same that was where I came from, and my language too.

"Dialect," the boy corrected me. "You don't speak a language, you speak a dialect."

"Okay, but it's a different country anyway. Twelve hundred miles away," I said, making a sweeping gesture somewhere toward the field.

"Me too. Twelve hundred miles. But that way," he said, pointing in the opposite direction.

Snow patches, wind-exposed slopes, cloudberry ants, burned forest land, ore fields, bare mountain above the tree line, clearwater lakes. These I had heard about since the day I was born. "Clearwater lakes, if only I could describe them to you, but you can hear in the words how pretty they are, Lo?" When I closed my eyes on Papa's knee I saw them quite distinctly, one lake behind each eyelid, as clear as crystal.

"Grilled whitefish," Mama said. "Over an open fire down by the water. Better than anything you can ever dream of if you've never tasted it." If I really concentrated hard I could taste the sooty flavor.

"In summer you can sometimes see bears roaming around in the big expanse," said Papa's eldest brother. "Most often alone. Bears are solitary creatures."

"Soli-what?"

"Lone wolves," Mama explained. "Like your grandfather." I opened both my eyes.

"Is that why he's called—"

"No, no, your papa's father got his name because his father was killed by a she-bear just before he was born," Papa's mother said.

"And bog myrtle vodka," Mama's mother interrupted, and blew

her nose into the tissue she always had up the sleeve of her cardigan. "Bog myrtle vodka and bleak fish under the birch tree by the river," she went on. "That's my dearest memory from home."

She pointed to the silver birch casket where she kept this memory. I opened the lid.

"But it's empty."

"I know," she said, nodding, and did not care to explain further. It was typical of her to say strange things that you had to try to understand as best you could.

"The cabinet's empty, the emperor's naked, and all of you are homesick!" Papa's father's voice was heard suddenly from the hammock. We had hoped that he was asleep, but he never slept. And he hated nostalgia. Ripberget and Laxberget were just romanticized translations of Kiirunavaara and Luossavaara, as they said at home. Homesickness, as persistent as piles—he blamed all on that. It was one thing to move house, Papa's mother objected, but to move your roots was quite another.

"The dark, the cold, the unemployment, the mosquitoes? Is all that to be forgotten now?" Grandfather asked. A feeling of disquiet spread around the table on the veranda. Papa stood up and left, and his brothers contented themselves with staring at their plates. Grandfather pierced me with his eye over the edge of the hammock. "Don't listen to them, Lo, it's pure hogwash, we come from a land where no one can stand still. You get eaten alive. Swarms of mosquitoes suck your blood until you lose your reason, if you ever had any. As long as you keep moving you can survive, but any man who has to stop to eat, have a pee, sleep . . . God help him. Set birch bark alight in a tin bucket and lay it in the grass, that's the only thing that helps. And not even the thickest grass smoke works on those bloodsucking monsters. No place for sensitive folks, Lo, no place for the likes of you and me."

I didn't know who to believe, if the Promised Land were here or there or somewhere else entirely. According to Papa's father it was here, in the warm south, in the land of rich earth and short winters. He was never heard to say he wished he were back there, like the others. I was happy too, but that, Papa assured me, was because I had never seen anything else.

It couldn't only have been the never-ending winter darkness or the unemployment or even the mosquitoes that had made them move. There must have been something more. Perhaps the girl whose name we couldn't mention, the youngest one who drowned. If her name couldn't even be mentioned, how could they continue to live in the place where it happened? To see that water each day and not know if it was a lake or a grave they saw. Everything must have lost its beauty after that, or at least have borne a bitter tinge, nature's cruel indifference.

After the fire, silence soon settled over our village once more. Everyone retreated to his own side of the overgrown hedges. It wasn't like at home, Papa's mother let it be known, where garden boundaries didn't exist and you went to see people when you felt like it, went in without knocking, helped yourself to something to eat, and lay down for a rest on the kitchen sofa while you waited for the owner's return. All my pictures of what the family called home had been painted by someone else. A ptarmigan is a bird that can be snared in the snow and eaten, with a wild and bluish taste—that I knew. But I didn't know what it looked like when it was flying or how the snare worked in reality, if they were caught by the neck or the foot and which was worse.

His dark eyes turn blue when it's cold. But I don't know that yet. The night of the fire was a state of emergency, and since then I have just seen him at a distance. The age difference should be enough to keep us apart. He is almost an adult, at least not a child, not in my eyes.

The very first afternoon that I'm going to walk home from school by myself, he coasts up beside me on his man's bicycle, slightly too large for him, so close that I think I can smell the smoke from the fire again. Instead of increasing my pace I slow down, walk so slowly that he finds it difficult to keep his balance on the bicycle.

I don't reply. He doesn't ask anything either.

I don't know where he wants to go, only that I shouldn't go with him.

I walk slower and slower until he wobbles right into me. The handlebars tilt straight against my face, the pain so sharp I can't even cry. I'm normally paralyzed at the sight of blood, but this time I just clench my teeth, struggle to my feet, and start to limp away. It's raining, and my shoelaces, my favorite skirt, and my minuscule ponytail are soon hanging down. I hear him come after me on his bicycle, which has a new squeak, and he says something about sorry and damn well didn't mean it and wait. When he catches up with me he takes hold of me around the waist and lifts me up roughly onto the crossbar.

"Hold on," he says. As if I had any other choice. He has already started pedaling.

Your life flashes before your eyes when you die, Papa has said, though how should he know that? As we sway through the traffic at top speed, the voices of my family flood through my mind. The boy rides twice as fast and half as steadily as Mama does. I close my eyes and get ready to throw myself off, but I stop short at the last minute. At this speed . . . I would kill myself. After an eternity he brakes so hard that the gravel scatters. I want to look and yet don't want to see where he has brought me and what is going to happen there. Not until I hear a familiar dull chopping noise do I open my eyes.

I should just run in and not say that it was his fault, because then it would be too bad for . . . I can't hear if he says "you" or "me." His voice is drowned out by another that is shouting my name. Mama with the ax. Striding through the grass and wearing an expression that warned she was expecting the worst.

"Is *she* your mom?" he says in a strangled voice and takes a step backward.

Did he really think he would be able to drop me off at my house unseen?

Mama stares at my bloodstained T-shirt, then at Lukas, and then back at the blood. Holds me so hard as if she believes she can stop the red that is oozing from my mouth in a copious mix with saliva. Papa's father has appeared behind her and examines my mouth decisively. Says that it's only a bite, admittedly right through the lip, but only a bite nevertheless, and a bite means that the teeth are fine. Children bleed a lot, they have to, he says, so it cleans the cut and prevents blood poisoning. Mama is not listening, just glowering darkly at Lukas as if she thinks it was he who bit me.

"Take it easy," Grandfather says. Then, turning toward Lukas, who is already on his way, "You! Hey, you're going nowhere. I want to talk to you." But there is something about him . . . the way he just defies Grandfather, throws his leg over the bicycle and sets off down the hill while Grandfather stands there, disarmed, glaring after him.

My mouth is throbbing and bleeding and has a thick taste of iron. I feel sick. Not so sick that I need to throw up, but still I bend over the burned September grass and force out a bit of school lunch so it splashes up over Grandfather's feet. It has the desired effect: they stop watching the boy, let him disappear while they look after me. Streaks of blood mingle like red worms in the gray fishy sludge.

I squeeze out a few tears as well, which fall on top with ice-cold precision.

So cold that I do not recognize myself. That feeling again of not being able to touch the bottom, of having gone so far out into the lake and only imagined that I had something under my feet.

No, and again no.

Keep away from him.

Do what we tell you, do just what we tell you, this is not negotiable.

Up until this point I had lived surrounded by love without rules. Never a no, and then all of a sudden as many noes as there were adults in the house. The freedom to roam and do as I wished was abruptly over.

At night I can't sleep, my thoughts running in circles like flies until exhaustion takes them. Evil under the surface, winged devils, sunken laughter, the accustomed paths through my territory suddenly full of cracks. But I'm not afraid of them. What scares me is the attraction they hold.

He is taller than me by two heads. He can cover my hand with his so it disappears. His wrists are twice as wide. Is this the problem? I don't get a proper answer from Mama. On the other hand, I can spit much farther than he can. Mama's sister Katja, my instructor in technique, has taught me how to spit and how to kiss. When it comes to holding breath underwater, it is a tie. It is true, when we are standing in the sun, I disappear completely in his shadow, and he can pee much farther—I don't stand a chance in that. Or when we arm wrestle. But he doesn't make a big deal about it. There are more differences than similarities, but it's the differences that please us.

I shouldn't have repeated the crude stories to Mama, who

immediately suspected where they had come from. About the nightingales who sing at their most beautiful when they have had their eyes poked out.

Lukas doesn't treat me as a child. He doesn't take it into account.

"I have something I want to show you," he says one day, pointing toward the forest of the bats on the other side of the lake. For me the forest is still just a dark silhouette farther away than I've ever been. A boundary, beyond which I can't imagine what is waiting. He looks at me as if he has set a trap out there or discovered a secret grave or an abandoned fox cub we can tame.

"Come on." I am stubborn, but Lukas won't give in. "You'll like this, I promise." I don't think much of his promises, but I let myself be persuaded in the end. I'm able to ride on his bike rack until the greenery becomes too dense; then we hide the bicycle behind a blackthorn thicket and continue on foot. I follow his white T-shirt through the almost impenetrable foliage, a guide leading the way across the rugged terrain of pungent giant caraway and scrubby bay willow. An oppressive heat that forces your eyes out of their sockets. Sometimes I lose sight of him and I have to stop and listen.

Halfway we have to pass through the dead part of the forest. I've never set foot here before, even with him. Lukas comes to a halt, before taking a first step in among the silver-gray trunks. A sense that the ground under the leafless trees is poisoned. I grip his shirt and hold on tightly as I follow him. The naked elms, ghostlike in death, will be easy victims if there's a bad storm. Lukas nimbly dodges the huge skin-colored moths between the stumps. I stick close behind him to shield myself. Even before we have made it through I start thinking that we have to go back as well, before darkness sweeps in over the lake.

After the dead forest the vegetation becomes thick once again, a sweet and indefinable scent of wilderness. In the midst of the undergrowth is a large enclosure with guinea fowl, forgotten. No one seems to have passed this way for a long time. Lukas wants to release them, but he can't open the iron grille. Scared by our presence, they flap against the wire netting in a hopeless attempt at flight. We move on and there it is, overgrown and camouflaged by nature—the house Lukas found when he was trying to keep out of his father's way. The pearl fisher's house. He needs me. Someone small and flexible has to climb in through the broken window to open the door from the inside. I shake my head.

"Yes, Lo."

"No way." Not for anything.

"Sweets?"

I hesitate. Is there anything I wouldn't do for sweets? Negotiation has begun. Lukas lifts me up at the window and it looks like a horror film in there. Curtains of cobwebs, a rank smell of mold, darkness locked in long ago. I refuse.

There's a dead body in there. There must be. Otherwise how could the key be on the inside? Lukas can't answer that. Instead he brings out a bag of cough drops, prepared for me to be awkward. Still no. Not so difficult—cough drops taste horrible. He takes a piece of bubble gum out of his other pocket. I shake my head firmly. He holds out a whole handful. Nope. Then he produces the entire bag. When it comes to bubble gum, I am weak, and why shouldn't he take advantage of that? However much I go on about it, Mama never lets me have any because it always ends up getting stuck in my hair. I snatch the bag, and with my mouth full of bubbles I begin to wriggle in through the opening Lukas has lifted me up to. I scrape my back and whimper, but Lukas just pushes me forward. Too late to change your mind now, he says. I've already stuffed three pink pieces of gum into my mouth, so now I have to keep my side of the bargain. As soon as my feet hit the ground I hurry to unlock the door and let him in. The cobweb curtains sway. I stay close to the open door, chewing and blowing nervous bubbles, pretending to keep watch while Lukas checks around. Things we have never seen before and cannot fathom what they are. Things we do not know if we should be frightened of or not. It takes awhile before we realize that the odd-looking bits of trash hanging from the ceiling are dead bats that never woke up from their winter sleep.

It smells like another country in there. Not that we have ever, apart from Lukas's first dim recollections, been in another country. But we imagine it would be like this.

The house is small and dark like the innards of a clam and has been empty for so long that the hinges have rusted up and creepy-crawlies have taken over. The amount of dust, like a thick layer of radioactive fallout, indicates that no one has set foot in here for a very long time. There are traces of scampering mice and outspread wings of owls in the dust on the floor, drifts of droppings, moths and dead wasps along the walls.

Everywhere are these remarkable things on dusty cluttered shelves. Tiny skeletons of animals we don't recognize, a lacquered box with razor-sharp knives, beautifully ornate chopsticks. Ancient crumbling herbal cigarettes that according to Lukas were some sort of drug. That doesn't stop him smoking them, the sweet stench of the exotic sapped by lying forgotten for decades, but still powerful enough to intoxicate, at least enough to make him spew in the sink.

There are so many strange things to smoke, so many foreign places to make your own. This is a place made for hiding away, a refuge from curious eyes. Despite the mummified bats on the ceiling, we go there. Despite the giant ghostlike trees of coral in the windows where the spiders have spun new webs on top of old. And under the floor, no, we can't even begin to think about what lies under the floor. The pearl fisher's forsaken loves, Lukas says.

We've heard about the pearl fisher. No one seems to have known

him, but everyone knows the stories. How he journeyed to Japan
to try his luck in the pearl waters there, only to discover that the
Japanese pearl fishers were all women. So much for his macho ad-
venture.

We try to make the space our own in a cleanup operation. We
sweep in a frenzy, haul out the heavy rugs and wash them in the
lake, and then the Japanese quilts, which float like marbled paper
in an oil bath before they fill with water and sink. Clean out the
flues to the stove as well as we can and test it with a fire, unaware
that we are sending smoke signals to the entire village from our
secret den.

This place unnerves Lukas, and yet he wants to come here. The
derelict house has something going on in its walls, something
crawling and breathing, but nevertheless this is where we head all
the time.

Every morning I wait for him at a different spot we have decided
on the night before, according to an ingenious system no one
would be able to discern a pattern in—just as the points in a constellation resemble nothing unless you already know what they're
supposed to represent. Sometimes I wait under the wrong tree or
behind the wrong greenhouse, dovecote, garage, in the wrong out-
of-the-way spot by the lake. But he always finds me in the end. The
village is not very big.

Below the pearl fisher's house we can bathe without being seen,
concealed by a dense thicket of waterside trees. The land around
the lake is covered in a thick growth of bay willows, water plan-
tains, and wild angelica shielding us from view on all sides. As long
as no one comes up close we won't be discovered. You have to be
careful not to become entangled in the plants growing wild underwater. They seize hold of your legs and hold you down under the
surface. The water snakes. The slow-swimming adders.

Mama is looking out of the window. She has done this the whole time we have been sitting in the empty classroom that smells of glue, book dust, mother's sweat.

"There must be a mistake."

"I don't think so," the teacher says coldly.

I say nothing. Through my effort to sit still I can see out of the corner of my eye that the door is ajar. There is a way out, at any rate.

"A misunderstanding," Mama tries again.

"The only misunderstanding here," the teacher says slowly, "is Lo's."

Difficult to sit still on the sweat-slippery stool, but I try at least not to look provocative, because provocative is what the teacher calls me and is something she can't stand. When I asked Papa what it meant, all I could grasp was that it was something you shouldn't be.

"Not at your age," he said. "You can wait awhile for that."

"We've never had a first-year playing truant before. But this"— the teacher performs a peculiar wriggle of her upper body in an attempt to adjust her bra unobtrusively—"young lady does it like a fully fledged high school student."

Mama's gaze rests somewhere out in space. I look at the teacher, who in turn looks at Mama. No one's eyes meet, and it's best if it stays that way.

"I think Lo has totally misunderstood what compulsory school attendance means. Do you know what compulsory school attendance means in Sweden?" Without taking her eyes off Mama, she directs the question at me. I shake my head. "No. There you are. Just as I thought."

"But for goodness' sake, she's only seven," Mama objects weakly.

"That's what I'm saying," the teacher replies. "If you play truant like this at the age of seven . . . then it can only get worse. There are *statistics* to prove it."

Accusing blue eyes in the stale air of the classroom. I look at the teacher who looks at Mama who looks at a crow who is sitting high up on the frame of the swing.

"You and your husband had better make clear to your daughter what's important. Otherwise there's no point in her making an appearance here for the rest of the term. In the autumn perhaps we'll let her start the year again."

The crow lifts its tail, shits, screeches, and flies away.

"Well," says Mama, as if this were a sign, "in that case we'll go. Come on, darling, I've got an appointment at the hairdresser's in a minute." But no one is going to escape so easily. The teacher wants to talk to Mama alone. "Lo stays here," says Mama, not wanting to be left alone with the teacher.

"No, she does *not*," says the teacher.

All that remains is for me to leave.

That Mama has already lost is obvious by her humiliated silence. I slide off the sweaty plastic seat—another reason to escape from the classroom with its bad vibe and stagnant air. Lukas is probably prowling around outside like a criminal. He's the one they are going to talk about now. He's the one who has made me into a fully fledged truant at such a tender age. That's the last thing I hear the teacher say before I race along the corridor and out to freedom.

Lukas is idling away the time on the fence between the playgrounds. The older children are not allowed to enter the area for primary children, so he's sitting there without letting his feet touch the forbidden ground. The tractor tire smells of burned rubber. I spin around and around on it until the heavy chains creak.

"Come on," he says, but I've just finished spinning and can't stand up. When I bend my head backward the clouds above me are sucked together in a swirl.

I know that they can see us through the window. You're going to get into so much trouble, I'm thinking, and maybe I say it aloud, because Lukas suddenly looks as though I've struck him across the mouth, although it was meant as a warning and not as a threat.

"Who hit you?" I usually ask when I can see that it has happened again. One shouldn't ask, but I'm just a child and so I do. Lukas, on the other hand, is old enough to know that it's best not to answer. Anything you say can be used against you. At school no one seems to have the courage or the desire to touch him, so it's not difficult to figure out where the bruises come from.

"Lukas is twice your age, why aren't you with your classmates?" the teacher had asked while we sat waiting for Mama, who was late for the meeting.

"But they're *children*," I exclaimed.

"Yes, but little one, so are you." Perhaps. But I've never seen it that way. The first thing I felt when I came to school was shock—thrown in among my peers, in the midst of a pack of wild dogs, all snapping at each other's legs.

Lukas was old enough for seventh grade that year, but he had been moved back two years, a hard nut to crack. They couldn't put him in the special class for maladjusted children because he wasn't a troublemaker—it would have been easier if he had been a troublemaker. Fighting at recess, cheeky to the teachers, if he had had any obvious problems, difficulty sitting still, for example. But no, he has no trouble whatsoever with that. Sits absolutely still on the bench, doesn't move a muscle, regrettably he doesn't move his pen either and never puts up his hand. Can't learn a thing. At home, perhaps, but what he learns at home is of no use when he comes to school.

When Mama eventually comes out, her curry-colored toweling tank top is sweaty under the arms and her eyes are dull with migraine. She takes an unopened pack of cigarettes from her shoulder bag although she stopped smoking long ago. A single glance summons me to her. Lukas has slipped into the shadows and cannot be seen. Not a word from Mama as we pedal home, she in front, slipping slightly from side to side on the seat of her jeans, as the bicycle is adjusted for Papa's mother. Mama is tall, but Grandmother is taller. And I am small and at the moment I'm trying to make myself smaller. From now on I have to toe the line, do as I am told, no more no less, not cause more awkward meetings. Next time it will be the headmistress, the teacher has warned.

Crisis meeting in the kitchen. Everyone has to be there except for me. Unaccustomed to closed doors, I wail and kick at it until Papa's brother Rikard, who as a rule is always on my side, comes out and picks me up in both arms, carries me away, and flings me onto the television sofa.

"Stay!" he hisses, as if I've been transformed into a dog. If that's how he wants it, I think, and try to bite his hand, but Rikard pushes me over as if I were weightless.

"Don't move an inch," he warns, "and I never want to hear that Lukas's name again." I've never seen him like this before. Sitting still out of sheer surprise, I feel the blood pounding in my ears.

Mama is also changed. A different tone. The difference between blank shots and live ones.

"I love you, Lo, but not when you lie."

"I don't lie!"

"Not when you lie, I said." She punishes me in the worst possible way—by withdrawing her love. Doesn't comfort me when I begin to cry.

"You should beware of lies, they are dangerous. Little caterpillars that lie never get any wings."

"I'm not a caterpillar!"

"No wings, Lo, just think about it."

Lukas had arrived in the village the year before I was born. He could remember almost nothing about his life before this, and what I had done with my time before I met him—that part of my life had already faded from my memory too.

"Why are you so dark? When all the others are so fair?" he asked. "Where do you really come from?" He thinks it's unfair that he is the one called darkie, when I'm the dark one of the two of us. In summer his hair is bleached until it is nearly blond, so it's just his eyes and his name and the fact that everybody knows. My origins are just as distant as his, but only on a map. It's not completely true that all the others are fair—in every class there are children belonging to the Greek workers, with names as long as the night freight train. But those children have each other. They're obvious, belong together, keep together.

Our home is not here, but a conviction we help one another to sustain. Because neither of us knows what it looks like where we really belong, we can imagine those places however we want. For Lukas, born on the outskirts of Budapest, a few hazy details emerge out of context. A blue glove, warm bread, a fox in a trap, blood in the snow, one or two words from a nursery rhyme or a swear word, he is not sure. Unsorted, unusable moments, a sensation in the stomach, mouth, nose, not really a smell or a taste, just a vague feeling.

At his house they never speak about what they've left behind.

The two have no language in common. His papa has mastered only rudimentary Swedish and Lukas even less Hungarian, just the very simplest of phrases. Amid such silence between them at the dinner table, they hardly know each other, father and son, two wastelands.

Lukas doesn't go near my house, knows that he's not welcome. Instead every day is filled with lies for his sake.

Beware, Mama says. Boy's eyes, boy's hands, boy's smell. Love and the other lies. Especially love, whose poison is like a snake's, goes straight to the heart with no time to cause pain, and suddenly you're lost. I always wondered who she had cherished with that sort of love.

KARENINA

My mama with seashells in her ears, no makeup, her long body constantly moving, sweat glistening at her armpits, narrow waist, broad bottom, flared Lee jeans, strappy platform clogs. I loved her as a capricious wind that comes and goes to suit itself. It was Rikard who taught me to cycle, Marina who taught me to swear, Lukas who taught me to swim and roll cigarettes, Katja who taught me kissing and long-distance spitting, Grandmother Idun who taught me to paint my lips and click my fingers to "My Funny Valentine." Mama taught me nothing. Not even to look out for all the things she was afraid of.

She didn't turn me away, but was merely out of reach the whole time, even when we were together. A perfectly normal mother except that she smoked Silk Cut that you could only buy on the ferries over to Denmark. Papa was also quite normal apart from the fact that he could walk on water, however thin the ice was.

Together they made up a sacred circle of four: Idun and Björn, Anna and Aron. Grew up together, always lived together, before the children, with the children, with the tar-boiling, haymaking, forest, mine, railway. When my parents and their brothers and sisters were teenagers and Papa's father had the idea for the long move south, the two families did even this together. Everything they owned was packed up in the same way they lived: mixed together and shared, secure and cramped.

They bought the place unseen—the house by the undulating Skåne field, the largest they could find that was fairly reasonable.

The houses were twice the price of those in the north, which Grandfather Björn took as a sign of what a promised land the south really was. Not cheap, but promised.

And so it came about that all their savings were suddenly tied up in a place they had never even seen. In addition they had been obliged to take out a loan so big that Grandfather Aron couldn't sleep at night. He had never been in debt to anyone before, had been brought up that way and thought of it almost as a sin. To buy a house unseen, that was madness . . . madness, according to Grandmother Idun. She was usually the one who made the decisions, but not this time, otherwise this wouldn't have happened. The idea that they should move was Björn's, the man she loved for his ideas, but he didn't usually carry them out. This time was different, he said, the children's future.

Before they packed up their joint vanload of furniture and set off on the twelve-hundred-mile journey south, someone had to go on ahead and reconnoiter. The house had to be renovated, but they didn't know how much needed to be done. None of the sons could take time off to accompany Björn, so instead it was my mama, Katarina, who volunteered. Björn was doubtful, but Grandmother Idun persuaded him. Katarina was as strong as their own boys, and besides she was the most practical of the youngsters. It was just a case of setting her to work; she was used to lending a hand.

Idun had spoken. And so it was.

The train across the country took a day and a night. Neither Grandfather nor Mama had traveled so far before. He had been involved in laying tracks, but had never actually made a train journey anywhere. And neither of them had the faintest notion that where they were going to move was so tremendously far away. He had wanted to travel alone. Why had Idun insisted? They sat in silence all the way down to the Västerbotten border, then Mama fell asleep, fortunately. With her head against his shoulder, which embarrassed him slightly, but at least he was relieved that the silence between them had a natural cause.

The house was far from what he had imagined. If this was what they called "in need of renovation," then they had entirely different standards down here. A cellar of standing height rather than a crawl space. Extremely well insulated with proper synthetic material, not just air gaps and sawdust. Björn went from room to room and breathed in the feeling of newness. Modern materials and kinds of wood that smelled different. A dining room—that was a phrase to savor—redolent of punch. Big enough for them all to be able to eat together for the first time, as long as they bought a larger table. Wall-to-wall carpets in the bedrooms so numerous that they would not have to sleep more than two to a room. The ground floor the size of a small cathedral. Practical ceilings, high enough even for Björn, Idun, and their tall sons. Massive double-glazed windows that let in so much light, not what they were used to: temporary secondary windows that always fogged up in winter.

Björn opened the window onto the garden and flicked out the flies lying sluggish and well fed on the sill. He had never seen fatter flies. And there it was, the arboretum, the reason he had fallen for this particular house. The impressive collection of exotic trees—at least they were exotic to him, born beyond the tree line. They spread out coquettishly in front of him. A Garden of Eden. Paradise.

Katarina following at his heels, just as dumbfounded, went to stand next to him at the open window. He wanted . . . to say something, but he was speechless. It wasn't like him to be so weak and sentimental. Perhaps because he had taken off his shoes and was barefoot like a child. When he'd had the chance for the first time in his life to experience the feel of a fitted carpet between his toes, he'd unlaced his boots and let his big white feet sink into the unresisting softness. He really did want to say something, something that was worthy of the situation, but he couldn't. And it didn't help that she stood there so close to him, her sandals kicked off too, her hand raised. She held her slender brown hand before her like a delicate and exotic leaf, as if she were trying to touch the magnificent arboretum from a distance. He hoped she understood what a kingdom he'd lain at her feet.

This was what all their children deserved. They hadn't grown up in luxury and affluence—far from it—but the future was theirs, he promised her. As far as he knew, all the children had originated in the warm flour-smelling bakehouse, at the side of the house that the families had rented together for many years. So was it chance or delusions of grandeur that made them choose regal names for their firstborn? But who has a greater right to cherish dreams than those who possess nothing, and hadn't he and Idun always dreamed of being able to give their eldest son, Erik, all this? And Anna and Aron had undoubtedly held the same hope for their Katarina.

There she was now, Katarina, like a vestige of the old in the midst of the new. It must have been to do with the change in the light. Something that rendered her a little like a queen, looking out over the new landscape as if in two minds whether it was worth conquering or not. An ice queen, coldly distant, or maybe just exhausted after twenty-four hours on the train. Her scent of birch and melting snow. Surrounded by the unfamiliar, she smelled of home.

"Queen Katarina." He laughed. She hadn't been following his thoughts and gave a start at his laugh. Watchful, looked at him as if she thought . . . that he was flattering her? Or the opposite, that he had caught her red-handed committing the mortal sin of pride— standing there, hand raised to the mirage beyond the window as if imagining that all this was hers and hers alone. Did he want to bring her back down to earth with his sarcastic "queen"? She lowered her hand, but as he glanced at her, her distinct profile was no less majestic.

"You know who you're named after, don't you?" he said. No, she didn't know. Didn't know who he was talking about, even though she had spent several years longer at school than him, serving no purpose at all.

"Russia's greatest ever ruler, Catherine the Great. A conqueror." She mumbled something inaudible in reply, still suspecting that he was making fun of her, that he'd picked up on her weak point, her vulnerability, and he wanted to put her in her place so she didn't get ideas. Conqueror? Why did he call her that?

It wasn't time to go to bed, but she had unrolled the mats and the old military sleeping bags on the floor, to serve as their beds until the furniture arrived on the van. And she'd been out and bought something for them to eat and candles and a pack of beer at the grocer's shop, which was almost closer to the house than the outside privy was back home. While they ate, Björn continued to talk about Catherine the Great, and she resisted the urge to ask him to listen to her instead. She had things to say too. She just hadn't found the right words yet.

This tsarina, who had clearly made a big impression upon him, had conquered vast territories on Russia's account. She'd had three children by three different men, presumably none of whom was her husband—she'd simply had him assassinated after he'd been crowned regent and then took the throne herself and reigned for another thirty years over her huge empire, Björn related, opening another beer.

They'd come to a promised land, everything would be better here, he assured her, as they sat in their makeshift sleeping quarters with the military sleeping bags. It was just like during the war, only without the war. What did he mean, "everything," she wondered? She didn't think there was anything wrong with their life at home. What were they lacking?

"Light, warmth, and hopes for the future, Katarina, for a start . . ." A winter in Skåne is as short and mild as a holiday—without the temperate winter there would be no arboretum.

"What's an arboretum?" she asked.

"It's a tree universe," he said. "A universe of trees." That evening they went in for the first time, among the tall trunks that made even Björn look small, despite his stature.

They fell asleep and awoke in a different state of happiness, but with the same feeling of elation. He rose quickly to see if the arboretum was still outside the window. It hadn't been a dream. The trees were where they should be, all the different species he'd never seen before and whose names he didn't know.

The house needed no work, so they could take some time off, relax, bask in the sun until the others came down from the north. The only thing they had to do was to buy a scythe to cut the grass and a good book on trees so that they could guide the others around the grounds, point out sugar maples, black poplars, empress trees, everything that was now theirs. Björn had thought they'd bought a house at great expense, but now it turned out they'd acquired a paradise for next to nothing.

Jubilant, he lifted the newly awakened Katarina as if she were a slender birch pole and waltzed her around the room with long jerky steps.

She weighed nothing. A tiny waist like Idun's before the five children. He could have danced with her until darkness settled over the fertile fields of early summer, if she hadn't been so dizzy that she crumpled into a laughing heap on the floor. A princess on a pea in a punch-scented dream about a proper house. Her clearwater gaze.

He felt young himself, was laughing too. It had been a long time, but he couldn't help it when he looked at Katarina sitting with glowing cheeks, shy all of a sudden, even though she was the boldest of the four girls, more like Idun than her own mother. Her blue skirt had ridden up in the careless movements of the dance, and she tugged at it. Such recklessness. There must be something in this new world that was making them like this. Intoxication that went straight to the senses, bypassing reason. The air was already pulsing with cow dung and buttercups, while at home winter was barely over. If anyone could see them now, they would think that the buttercups, the cow dung, the change of air, idling about like this, sleeping like vagabonds until late in the morning, the shift from late winter to early summer, all of this had gone to their heads. Decompression sickness. The danger of stepping too quickly into the light. Giddiness. Blinding.

He was unaccustomed to it. Perhaps that was all. He'd never been alone with any of the girls, and now they were almost adults, especially Katarina, at seventeen the eldest. A young Idun, tall, strong, lucently fair, her skin like birch. Powerful arms. Strong neck. Cold eyes. Like morning water, he thought. The sensation of waking up too quickly when you plunged into her gaze. He had always sobered up when he looked into Idun's eyes. But Katarina's eyes didn't have the same effect on him, they made him confused, not clear-headed.

Idun was the same as ever, only not quite so translucent, and her strength had passed into a kind of heaviness. He didn't lie when he said that he loved her more with every child. But differently. Because Idun *had* changed, as if each child were a whole new experience. He didn't share this feeling. For him it was just more of the same.

There were days when he wished that he remembered. He'd asked her, "Do you remember?" and Idun had smiled wryly and said, how could she ever forget? And then he'd been too ashamed to ask her to share her memory with him. However hard he tried, he couldn't recall their first meeting—the crucial moment. Perhaps there was no crucial moment, but he imagined something, yes, against the light in a cloudberry meadow.

He remembered her forever. She'd always been there, as natural as breathing. You didn't think about it all the time, but you couldn't survive without it. Sometimes he wished he could recollect how it had been when he first fell in love with her. There were days when he really needed that memory.

Why are you telling me all this? Katarina thought, but she allowed him to continue: buttercups, cow dung, change in the air, light. Something made him see her differently, she knew. Indeed, seeing her at all was different. Speaking to her. He'd never done that before. She had the feeling that he walked around the many rooms of the new house looking for her as soon as she was out of sight. And when he disappeared into the arboretum for a long time, it was she who searched for him, she who went through the trees calling his name, as if she really missed him.

In order not to feel completely useless waiting for the two families, they refined the dream before the others arrived, made a few small repairs that were in fact unnecessary, took care of the vanload of furniture that had been sent on ahead. Together they sat on the veranda in the evening and enjoyed the calm before the storm, the absence of mosquitoes and the presence of each other, the unfamiliar smells from the arboretum of balsam poplar and eucalyptus.

"If your love is unrequited?" she said one evening when they had unrolled their sleeping bags and were just about to go to sleep. Her voice rose cautiously at the end, making the words a question. He looked at her in astonishment. What in heaven's name did she think he knew about all that? She'd fallen silent and blown out the candles in the beer bottles, their only source of light here where, in contrast to home, nights in early summer were dark.

"Well, then you take the name Karenina like in a Russian novel about impossible love . . . and then you put up with it . . . until it passes," he said.

Put up with it until it passes? Was that all he had to say?

Put up with it until it passes . . .

Didn't he understand? Was that really the only thing he could advise her to do? He knew nothing about Russian novels. Had just happened to see the copy of *Anna Karenina* that she was reading in the evenings and picked up the name from the back of the book. He knew nothing about anything. Unrequited love included.

BREATHLESS

To your last breath, Lukas said. It was September, and all the most important things that have happened to me have always happened in September.

Lukas's eyes were black as river pearls. When it was cold they turned blue, the Japanese rice cooker dirty pink, the mosquito net gray from many summers' insects.

There was a strong smell of angelica in the late-summer air. The flies that had lapsed into a coma during the hottest weeks had come back to life and become annoyingly intrusive. And they buzzed around Lukas in particular.

"To your last breath," he said, but I wasn't so sure.

"It's dangerous," I said, a pointless objection, a lame protest.

He just shrugged his shoulders at my warning.

I didn't intend to stop him, nor to go with him.

"You'll have to do it yourself," I said.

"Sure. You'll never be a real man, you're too cowardly." Mild scorn in his voice.

Maybe so, I thought, maybe he's right. Or I simply didn't have enough desperation within me. This water was too deep for me— even though anyone could see how much the lake had shrunk in the summer heat. Anyway, I didn't want to be a man, I wanted to be a woman. This was what I thought but didn't say.

I disappeared into his shadow. He'd shot up that summer and I hadn't kept up with him. He'd had an erection for several days, he said. It was as if something had locked, a mechanism that had gotten stuck, impossible to bring down. Now he had it in his head that it would help to swim across the whole lake underwater, hold his breath and count, focus on survival. He looked at me inquiringly, but to be honest I had no idea whether it would work. Perhaps it was good to give his blood something else to do instead of collecting in one place in his body, causing problems. But he had to do it himself. With my tiny leather pouches for lungs I'd sink like a stone halfway across. And his problem was hardly going to go away because *I* held *my* breath, was it? If we shared the same bloodstream, maybe. It was what he wished for, that we two should be one. We weren't, just as our village wasn't a proper village and the lake wasn't a proper lake, only a place where the flow of water swelled and the river spread out, deep like a lake.

I had a rough idea how it worked, even though I didn't have one of my own. It wasn't mechanical, as Lukas seemed to think. It was blood that made it stand straight out in his blue boxer shorts. Or possibly an evil spell as punishment for paying it too much attention. Some things don't thrive on attention—that was what he used to say to me.

I glanced at it, as if it were an overexcited puppy that someone had played with too much. "Don't think about it, it'll go."

"I can't *not* think about it. I can *only* think about it." He had flies around his mouth, and something in his eye made me feel uneasy, made me scratch away at old insect bites just to distract myself from the feeling of impotence—not my own, but his.

He took his hands away from his crotch and pointed. "Will you feel it? It's sick."

I shook my head.

"To hell with it, then," he muttered. "Maybe you don't believe me . . ."

I did believe him, perceived his desperation. I was ten years old and yet I knew more than he did about certain things, despite his sixteen years. Unlike Lukas, I had someone to ask. He had to discover everything by himself, and sometimes played up his incomprehension to diminish the age difference between us.

"Can't it be emptied?" I asked cautiously.

Lukas pulled an exasperated face. "I've tried that."

"That's not what I mean. I mean empty it of blood."

He shook his head in distaste and consternation. "Blood's all connected up together in the body, just one system, like, one single lot of blood . . . You can't empty one part of your body without emptying the rest. You'd bleed to death."

For all I knew he might be right, but his own tactic sounded just as dangerous: to swim the whole length of the lake underwater without coming up for breath once. You can breathe in your imagination, he maintained, right up to your very last breath, for there's always a last breath, even in your mind.

"It hurts, don't you understand!"

I lowered my gaze and stared at the problem. Hurts as in a sore that he has picked at?

He gave a murderous look and reached out for me just as I turned my back to him, groped in the air a second too late.

"The only sore I have is you," I thought he said, but perhaps I just imagined it. He often said that I imagined things, and now I had reached the house and opened the door that was hanging askew on its single hinge. The pearl fisher's house, our hiding place. A well-kept secret tucked away in the thick greenery by the lake.

The day had been doomed the moment I opened my eyes, and had only gotten worse. Chatter, laughter, squabbling, Grandmother Anna's clatter in the kitchen, Mama's chopping, Grandfather Björn's voice penetrating everything, my aunts' music, cars in the yard, all the familiar noises, and every now and again something unfamiliar that could make me prick up my ears and sneak closer—these were the normal sounds in our house that never slept. But this morning only quiet—a sound all its own—as when a prevailing wind suddenly abates and the silence is so palpable it can be heard. I had fumbled for Mama and Aunt Marina on either side of the bed, although I was aware they couldn't be there because I couldn't hear them breathe.

Hello, here I am all by myself in bed and it's my birthday, I wanted to shout, but to whom? I waited for the morning light to travel over the cloudberry-patterned wallpaper. When it seemed that my humiliation was complete, I rose to look for them, confront them, demand congratulations, banana cake, restore order. From room to room in the large house I went, not finding a living soul. At last I heard faint sounds outside the open kitchen window, voices muted as if they were each talking into a plastic bag.

There was a gloomy atmosphere around the garden table. I had never been to a funeral, but knew it must feel like this, the air heavy to breathe. I saw in Mama's face that something was very wrong. She had never been good at hiding things, and now, red with weeping, her legs curled under her on the cane chair, she wasn't even trying to. I hadn't seen Mama's face like this since Papa left us the year before. She was smoking, although she had stopped long ago—no one would forget the dramatic finale when, to prove that smoking was over forever, she'd thrown out every ashtray we had in the house, including the blood-red crystal one she'd been given by Papa's father. An exaggerated gesture, and what was it worth now? Still, it is possible to smoke without ashtrays, and this she did. The saucer before her was piled high, despite the early hour. Papa's sister Marina had also lit a cigarette without any protest from her mother, and Mama's brother Isak was sitting on the back of the chair with his dirty boots on the seat, another offense no one objected to, murmuring:

"It's awful. Fucking awful, and that's a fact . . ."

I lurked on the windowsill, a wretched circus monkey in front of a miserable audience who wouldn't even look at me. What about *me*! I wanted to shout. But the sight of Mama filled me with a knot of anxiety that only she could evoke. Instead of saying anything I leapt through the air and landed crouched on my heels in the middle of the table. It was intended as a pleasant surprise, but Mama didn't even raise her eyes. I didn't notice how the others reacted, because I only had eyes for her, all my attention directed to her half-closed eyelids and smoking mouth. She was the center of the distress, there was no mistake about it, and it reminded me of something I didn't want to be reminded of on any account.

Rikard shooed me off the table like one of the irritating flies in the September heat. Mama lit another cigarette as Marina in one deft movement drew me to her. She held me hard and in a practiced maneuver lifted me onto her lap, even though I'd shot up too that summer, all arms and legs, and could hardly fit on her knee any longer.

"Is it something to do with Papa?" I whispered in Marina's ear. She blew the smoke past my face and brought her lips close up:

"No, for once it's nothing to do with your papa. But you must leave your mama in peace today."

"What about the cake?" I pleaded, and she laid a finger on my lips. It stung like a nettle.

"We'll sort it out, hush, don't be such a baby."

It began to feel like the garden of death, but I didn't know who had died. No one answered my questions, as if I too were talking into a plastic bag and the questions stayed inside it. If you were invisible, you might as well disappear. I went inside and packed the essentials, the secrets in the dust: the hunting knife, the steel strings, the porn magazine, the aftershave, the cigarette, still unsmoked since the night of the fire. The bicycle that Papa had left behind was far too big—I had to ride at a slant under the crossbar, and although it was downhill all the way along the gravel track between the fields of stubble, it was very difficult to pedal.

I used to imagine that the lake was an enormous eye, the only visible part of an even more enormous underground creature. This beautiful, terrifying giantess Hyrrokkin would one day rise up and surprise us all, distort our perspective, dislodge woods, factories, roe deer, houses, and fields of corn, which would collapse into the crater where her body had lain, and she would just walk away. She belonged to a different and a better world, like Lukas and me. She'd just rested here awhile and would leave devastation in her wake.

It was Papa's father who had told me the story about Hyrrokkin. He was interested in mythological women, particularly the demonic ones with extraordinary powers: Jezebel, Lilith, the sisters Fenja and Menja who made the sea salty. He liked to watch Mama when she was chopping wood too, her shirtsleeves rolled up and her hair Medusa-curly with sweat, a cigarette in the corner of her mouth when she thought no one could see her. Hyrrokkin meant smoke, Grandfather said, and I had seen smoke rising out of the earth at dawn, especially over her eye when it was turned to ice in winter. Now she was tucked up under the ground, invisible except for her mirrorlike eye. You could bathe in it if you dared. It was not for the fainthearted.

Her eye was gazing right at me, with a beguiling look that enticed me even from afar. Almost no one ever bathed here. There were rumors about people who drowned themselves and people who were drowned. I was so young that I had only vaguely heard them, but I had been warned numerous times about the lake—like everything else Mama warned me about, I didn't let it seriously affect me.

After a while Lukas entered the pearl fisher's house, where I was stretched out on the bed waiting for him to think better of his underwater tactic. I was far more concerned about him diving right into Hyrrokkin's eye than about his hard-on, which after all couldn't last forever.

He found my hastily packed canvas bag next to the bed.

"Have you run away from home? Couldn't you have brought something to eat?" he said as he rummaged through the contents, flicked through the porn magazine, and then fished out the holy cigarette from our first meeting. Before I had time to open my mouth, he picked up a lighter and lit it . . . it burned like tinder.

"And what the hell are we going to do now?" he said and blew the smoke hard at the ceiling.

I shrugged my shoulders. "Dunno. It's my birthday, but why should we worry about that?"

"I mean, what are we going to do about this?" In a forced manner he indicated toward his stubbornly swollen prick—there were many words for it, but "prick" was the ugliest and most ridiculous and Lukas said it all the time, which gave me the impression that he didn't like it.

After searching among the books under the bed I found an old medical book that I had looked in many times before. I blew off the dust and opened it at a page with pictures that looked as though we could be on the right track. Lying on my back, I read it silently to myself first and then out loud for him:

"Erectile dysfunction." I raised my eyebrows questioningly, but Lukas was stamping up and down on the spot and appeared not to have heard of it.

"Priapism?" I carried on.

"Uh, I don't understand a single word of this stupid language. Get to the explanation."

"Urological emergency," I continued. I had always been a good reader, even when I had no notion what it was about.

"But skip that bit, get to the point—farther down, farther down . . ."

I let my eyes skim over the text. Lukas's mouth was twisted in torture, as if his condition from one moment to the next had become untenable.

"Prolonged and painful erection not caused by sexual arousal. The causes for this condition may include: leukemia, psychoactive drugs, anabolic steroids, recreational drugs such as alcohol and cocaine, protracted sexual activity, a burst artery in the scrotum . . . scrotum?"

"Yes. Don't know. Haven't a clue." He looked pale and signaled to me to continue.

"Bite from a black widow spider, tumor, carbon monoxide poisoning, spinal cord injury, or lacking diagnosable cause. The problems are due to blood trapped in the erectile tissue. An erection lasting more than four hours is deemed to be a medical emergency."

Lukas was no longer complaining; he nodded at me to read on.

"Four hours, it says. How long did you say it's been like this?"

"Days, on and off."

"*Days?*"

"Yes, for a while it seemed to be getting better, but then it got worse again."

"But listen: the condition requires immediate medical attention, to prevent scar formation that could result in permanent inability to maintain an erection." I looked at him as he stood in front of me, legs wide apart, with the face of a maniac.

"Immediate medical attention, it says here. Doesn't that mean . . . today?" I traced down the page with my finger, searching for the answer:

"Treatment involves draining the blood by inserting a needle into the penis."

"Aagh!" Lukas looked as though he were trying to cast off something that had scalded him, but his hands were empty and it was a pitiful, disembodied gesture.

"The area is numbed with local anesthetic and the blood is drawn off from—"

"No thanks!"

"—from the erectile tissue until the swelling goes down."

"Can you stop!"

"Wait. There's an alternative: ice can be put on the perineum to reduce the swelling. Perineum? What's that? Well, you can put ice on it anyway. Climbing stairs is sometimes effective, as the exercise can send the blood flow to other parts of the body."

"Shut up now." He groaned and sank to the floor, but I kept on reading:

"In serious cases prolonged accumulation of the blood can lead to necrosis, spontaneous tissue death, gangrene. Fully developed gangrene cannot be cured. In cases of dry gangrene the affected tissue falls off of its own accord. In cases of wet gangrene the affected area must be amputated, i.e., a surgical removal of the penis, known as penectomy."

Lukas's face turned pale green, and with his hands at his crotch he stood up and backed out of the room, moaning.

Stairs and ice—he had no choice.

Lukas was not welcome in our home, preferably not to be seen at all in my vicinity. But there were no stairs at his house and no freezer with ice either, so we had to get into my house unseen. While I made sure it was safe, he started to race up and down the steep stairs between the cellar and the floor above.

"This feels like"—he looked as though he would be prepared to have it amputated after all—"a sadistic joke," I caught him saying on the way down.

"But is it working?" I asked impatiently.

No one trusted him before, and now he was running up and

down our stairs half naked and could be discovered at any moment. Still, it was this or a needle in his penis—that was the choice. I saw his lean suntanned back disappear up the stairs. A back I knew so well, and yet it often seemed so unfamiliar, as changeable as his face. When his height increased, out of control, last spring, his body had not managed to adjust its proportions. He was in disharmony with everything, as if there were no longer enough room in his body, as if he had stretched out rather than grown. Become a tall thin shadow of himself, almost worse than Papa the summer before he left.

"How does it feel?"

"Sore."

"But has it gotten softer?" I asked next time he passed me as I stood on guard on the landing. He thrust his hand down to see.

"Has it hell."

Ice was now his only hope. If the stairs were hard work, the ice was humiliating. Lukas was doubtful, but in the absence of ice cubes I had already fetched two bags of frozen mushrooms and stood in the food cellar with them dangling from my hands. He took off his trousers, but I told him to put them on again, that it would be cold enough without putting them directly on his skin. It would be no consolation if he brought it down and it suffered frost-bite in the process.

"Okay, but I'm doing it myself," he said dismissively. He jumped onto the freezer, frowning with pain, and accepted the packets of mushrooms.

It was probably the thought of amputation that helped him to endure—that and shame and ignominy, as well as pain. The cold appeared to aggravate his suffering instead of relieve it. Like cures like, was Rikard's standard response when something had to be remedied. He had for a long time wanted to be a boxer, but he had such thin skin, his eyebrows couldn't take it. The boxer knows nothing of the dancer's pain and the dancer knows nothing of the boxer's discipline, he claimed; you should respect what you don't understand. Like now, how it was feeling for Lukas. I could see that it was hurting, diabolically, but perhaps that was a good sign, if Rikard's cure logic was correct. We didn't have time to think it over, we just had to try and see.

Time passed and still nothing happened, and then, to speed up the proceedings, Lukas pulled down his shorts and put the deep-frozen bags of mushrooms right on his crotch.

With that, Marina arrived.

She was suddenly standing there in the cellar doorway, carrying an armful of hammock cushions rescued from the unexpected cloudburst, staring at us. The rain had made her mimosa-yellow cotton top see-through—one of her breasts was larger than the other—and I was struck by how remarkably like Papa she was, apart from the breasts. I'd never noticed it before, but with her medium-length hair now wet and pushed back off her face she was so like him that I gasped.

Mama was upset when Papa left, but his sister Marina was the one who was angry. How she shrieked at him in the kitchen. Marina's screaming was the most terrifying of all the things that happened at that time.

Now with a violent push she threw the cushions aside and snatched for a weapon. That turned out to be a vacuum cleaner wand, an old-fashioned chrome model, lethal. Without a word she raised it up toward Lukas, in attack or in defense, it was impossible to say. The bags of frozen mushrooms slipped from Lukas's hands onto the stone floor with a muffled sound. His shorts were still hanging around his ankles as he sat and tried to take in what was happening: the chrome wand, the expression on Marina's face . . . If I could have moved, I would have pulled them up, but I was just as transfixed.

All the evil energy in the room was directed toward Lukas. She didn't even look at me, just made a vague gesture that I should move away from him. But I couldn't.

"I haven't done anything," he said. You only put soap on hands that are dirty, as the saying goes in my family. Marina . . . I saw the chrome pipe gleam in the light from the fluorescent strip when she swung it around in the air to build up speed. She was going off the rails, she must be. Hyrrokkin had drawn herself up to her full height.

Instead of covering his penis, which was still standing straight up, Lukas raised his arms to cover his face. As if he seriously did think that she would hit him. She would never do that. Even if she *was* losing control. *Not Marina* . . . The thought ran through my head the second before she did it. Hard. Right at Lukas's face with an awful thud. A shrill sound like the call of a bird of prey escaped from my lips. He groaned softly. If he hadn't been so used to protecting himself at home, the blow would have knocked him to the floor. The sound of the metal against his forearms was excruciating.

While she was reloading her chrome pipe he finally seemed to grasp the seriousness of his predicament, jumped down from the freezer, pulling up his shorts on the way, and, crouching, started to move toward the open door, to the garden and freedom. The torrential rain outside almost drowned his voice as he rattled off what sounded like a stream of accusations and apologies. Marina was standing in his way. *Let him go,* I was thinking, *just let him go . . .* afraid of what he might do otherwise. But she looked more furious than scared, blocked the doorway, raised the shining chrome pipe toward him again. Capable of anything at all, it seemed, as if she really were someone else.

When he, with the speed of a fighting dog, grabbed hold of the vacuum cleaner tube, I saw the fear in her eyes. Marina had never been hit before; Lukas was used to it. When the shock of the surprise attack had subsided, she would soon lose the assailant's advantage.

Mama's sister Katja had explained about the use of sound cannons—they were as effective as water cannons to disperse rioting crowds—and now I climbed up on the freezer and yelled as loudly as I could in an attempt to defuse the menacing situation. Lukas had just succeeded in wrenching the weapon out of Marina's hands and lifted it up toward her to gain free access to the door when Papa's brother Erik appeared in it with Katja immediately behind him. Without waiting to take in what had happened, they overpowered him. Suddenly it all unfolded like an unreal film: Lukas on his knees on the concrete floor with Erik on top of him, a hard kneecap in the small of his back. It looked horrible and quite unnecessary, as Lukas was completely still.

"Are you okay?"

Marina nodded in reply to Erik's question. I wanted to say that it was *she* who had hit *him,* even though it was Lukas who happened to be holding the weapon when they came in, but I dared not open my mouth. When everything was quiet in the room, a musty odor of half-thawed mushrooms mixed with moldy winter apples and caustic soda from the adjoining laundry room filled the air.

The chrome pipe was a side of Marina she had never revealed before.

"Take him up to the kitchen," she said, and without demanding a word of explanation Katja and Erik obeyed her command. Lukas offered no resistance when they yanked him away.

Leaning against the freezer, Marina gasped for breath. She looked as though she was trying to find herself again, after she had been lost, or perhaps she had actually for a while been changed into somebody else. A stranger had possessed her body—that must have been what happened.

"Lo . . ." she began, but broke off and started to pull at her top that was so yellow it almost smelled of mimosa. It was so hopelessly out of shape that she couldn't straighten it. Lukas had pulled it to one side when he tried to disarm her. One of the seams was torn and it had the mark of his hand on the front between her breasts. "You're coming with me. Now!" she ordered and dragged me up the stairs.

Mama was sleeping. We had to tiptoe around the house and there was no opportunity for a noisy interrogation in the kitchen.

"What's wrong with Mama? Who's died?" I asked.

"Jean Seberg," Erik said. Who? Was it someone we knew? But he wasn't listening. He stood by the sink holding Lukas in a harsh grip and said that we were going to take this matter to Lukas's father. And *that,* he intimated, was just the beginning.

No, not Lukas's papa, not Gábriel. To drag him into it . . . my family had no idea.

There was one other place where I belonged, a place I could disappear to whenever I wanted. A snow kingdom far away, vast, imposing, silent, desolate, wild. A landscape where there was only one season with a short interruption for a summer soon over. Completely different from here, where the past was overlaid and obliterated by the oppressive scent of growth, stagnant heat, flies, the lake's jade-green eye staring unceasingly at us.

Escorted by Papa's brother Erik and sister Marina, we walked in deathly silence down the gravel track to Lukas's house. The late-summer sun was going down over the fields, on the day that never had been a birthday. I thought all along that Lukas would run off, because Erik was no longer holding on to him, but sooner or later he would have to come home, so what was the point?

The person they said had died—the whole time I was thinking of her as the only one who could have saved us from this. If the others, like Mama, had been more concerned about her death and less about Lukas and me, we would have gotten away with it. They would not have had the energy to turn everything upside down as if disaster had befallen us in our food cellar.

No one in my family apart from me had ever been in Lukas and Gábriel's house. I tried to say that it was no use talking to Lukas's papa as he couldn't speak Swedish, but they thought I was trying to help Lukas out of fear. I was—but not because I was afraid of him. I was afraid of what was going to happen to him. *Anything you say can be used against you.* Lukas must have had that line in his head, because he didn't say a single word in his defense.

"Say something!" I whispered to him.

"It's better," he mouthed and nodded in the direction of his crotch.

"Something else. To them. Lukas . . . Please . . ."

But he just shook his head.

It had passed, his stubborn erection, but what help was that when one problem just led to another? To be caught red-handed, instant evidence—that was all my family was waiting for. Proof that he was anything but an innocent friend, that what had seemed fairly harmless about him when he was thirteen had grown into something dangerous now that he was sixteen. We had been eyed with suspicion the whole time, never able to relax, our games an act that took away the pleasure, took the playfulness out of playing. If neither of us let go, we would both sink. *To the last breath*—I recalled the phrase now. It came from a film that ended with one person betraying the other. I had never really understood why.

Gábriel stood in the doorway and watched us approach.

"I'd like to live in Mexico. I hear it's so lovely," I whispered, to ease the tension. Lukas laughed. A clipped dry laugh. Erik gave him a shove, as if to emphasize that soon he wouldn't be laughing, he could be sure of that.

The bruises on Lukas's body were the only testimony to his father. Otherwise he was seldom seen, sometimes on his way to or from work with his bicycle, or when he made repairs to the house, prone to rot—it was so close to the water that the floors were always damp, just like in the pearl fisher's house. Once in a while he would sit on the wooden porch and watch the kites or turn on his radio, tuned in to wavelengths we didn't understand.

"I'm a real scumbag . . ." Lukas whispered out of the corner of his mouth as we slowly neared his house.

"What does 'scumbag' mean?" I whispered back.

He laughed again and received another irritated push, this time from Marina.

"You damn well *won't* laugh, do you hear?" she hissed.

In the final scene of *Breathless* the man is running, shot in the back, the bloodstain spreading across his white shirt, until he collapses. She is behind him—she who has informed on him to the police, in spite of love. It is silent when he falls, just the look on her face as she bends over him, watching him die in the street. "I'm a scumbag," he says, before closing his eyes with one hand and drawing his last breath. "What did he say?" she, bewildered, asks the policeman who has just shot him. "He said, 'You're a scumbag,'" says the policeman. Then—her empty gaze into the camera—"What does 'scumbag' mean?" before she turns away and the screen turns black.

What the final scene was actually about, I couldn't understand. Loyalty, guilt, but how they related to each other . . . Now at any rate I felt like her, traitor and executioner in one, as if it were I who was hauling Lukas up the steps where Gábriel had just opened the door and looked questioningly at his son. How do you measure silence? It was so quiet you could hear the clouds moving above us—until Gábriel said something in his own language. Lukas's hand made a vain gesture toward the cigarettes in his pocket, something he often did when he felt under pressure, but he was only wearing those threadbare shorts. He looked like he was freezing, holding his arms around his body.

"What did he say?" I whispered.

"I don't know. He always talks like that when he's angry," Lukas said under his breath so only I could hear.

"Do you sleep with a lot of men?"

"Not so many."

"How many?"

I hold up seven fingers. "How about you?"

"Me?" Lukas sounds surprised at being asked.

Gestures quickly with the fingers of one hand . . . twenty-two.

The bedroom scene in *Breathless* was my favorite. It was best to do it with the hat and the cigarette too. We had to manage with Grandfather Björn's old Stetson. Jean Seberg playfully tried on Jean-Paul Belmondo's gangster hat, while he lay on the bed smoking. Lukas said that I had Jean Seberg's dimples. Her eyebrows as well. And something about the way I looked. "Sixties rebellious youth," it said on the video case. Without really knowing what it meant, we acted it out as faithfully as we could. Lukas's role was an antihero, it said. This thought appealed to him, a hero who was anti-everything.

"I'd like to live in Mexico. I hear it's so lovely. When I was little Dad would always say, 'We'll go there next Saturday.' But he'd always forget," I mimicked.

"I bet it's not great at all in Mexico. People are such liars." (Lukas's turn.) "It's like Stockholm." ("Stoekkoelm"—he was imitating Jean-Paul Belmondo.) "Everyone who's been there says: the Swedes are terrific, I had it three times a day. But I went there and it isn't true—they're not like they are down here—and they're just as ugly as Parisian women."

"Swedish women are very pretty," I objected.

"No, no, perhaps a few of them, but not all. The only towns where all the girls are beautiful—without being gorgeous, but charming, like you, where fifteen out of twenty girls have something special—aren't Rome, Paris, or Rio de Janeiro, but Lausanne and Geneva."

Jean Seberg, Mama's favorite actress. She was the one who had died. On a street in Paris. No blood, no audience. For real. Lukas and I had borrowed *Breathless* from Mama's collection with a handful of other films and watched it on the rental set at Lukas's house. Saw it so many times while his papa worked his shift at the factory that we could not fail to learn the lines. *"Do you sleep with a lot of men?" "Not so many." "How many?" Seven fingers . . .* One time I wanted to swap and say Lukas's lines, but he wasn't inclined.

Following an overdose of sleeping pills Jean Seberg was found in the backseat of her car after she had been missing from her apartment for eleven days. Eleven days. The car had been parked the whole time on a busy Paris street without anyone noticing her—how could that be possible? How can you live in a town like that? *Were* there even towns so big that somebody could lie dead in a parked car for nearly two weeks without anyone walking past and wondering? Had no one seen her, or did no one care?

Mama had heard a report of her death on Swedish radio on the morning of my tenth birthday, so I hadn't imagined the funereal atmosphere in the house.

A son. Her farewell letter was written only to him. Not to any of her many husbands—it doesn't matter how many of them there were—the letter was still only written to her son: *Diego, my dear son, forgive me, I can't live any longer. Understand me, I know that you can, and you know that I love you. Your mother who knows you. Jean.* I knew just enough English to understand her parting words. "Forgive" and "understand me" and "I love you" were not the most important—the most important were the last words . . . "Your mother who knows you." It was so unbearable to think of him, so sad, and at the same time—a twinge of jealousy when I considered that my mama would never have written that to me.

Almost anything at all can look like a crime if you consider it in a certain way. A dead woman on a backseat, Lukas and I in the dark cellar. They condemned him without a trial, forbade him to go near me. We didn't see each other for two days. No one allowed me to slip out. Papa's brother Erik declared that he was going to keep tabs on every step I took, every step Lukas took as well—somehow or other, even having forbidden Lukas to come within sight of our house. After Erik went back on the day shift he had no hope of carrying out his mission. I would escape and Lukas would search me out again . . . However hard they pushed me, I was never going to betray him like Jean Seberg betrayed Jean-Paul Belmondo in *Breathless.*

INNOCENCE

Whenever I travel by train he comes to me. A haze that rises in my memory. Trickles out even if I attempt to seal it off with sleep or conversation. Perhaps a visit to the restaurant car with a glass or two of wine and a book that would usually sweep me away from this world. I don't know how he can sense that I'm on a train, but he does and that is when he appears. The railway separated our houses, the endless night trains, the slow freight trains pounding toward morning. Every time I go by train I travel back into memories, childhood, through summers and winters, skirt lengths, hairstyles, chewing gum that has lost its taste. I shut my book—not worth trying to read now. The sky is ablaze with yellow and a color I can't name. I am crossing from loneliness into loneliness. Loneliness is only a lack of companionship that one must grow accustomed to, until it becomes a companion in itself.

Traveling by train at night is a journey toward light, conveying so much sleep across Europe. At daybreak I go out into the narrow corridor. The compartments are in line, like airless pigeonholes for eight people. I stand there with the morning smokers and the old folk in crumpled suits and shiny synthetic dresses, who, like me, always wake in the hour before sunrise: the suits, the frumpy dresses and me—a small, sleepy, tragic troop.

I like being alone among other people, exactly as I am in the stifling compartment with room for a large family or eight strangers.

Opposite me a newly breastfed baby is sleeping. I can't hear her breathe, but I can feel the gentle rhythm of peace surrounding her in the dimness. And the mother, slowly falling asleep, between deserted villages and sparse forests, the roe deer of dawn here and there in the mist. Hungarian, Slovak, Polish countryside, they all merge together after so many hours on a train: the child on the seat, Lukas's face, the coral landscape, sunken ships whose hulls resemble the hollow chests of gigantic whales with ribs eaten clean by shoals of silvery krill. The skeletons radiate light even in the darkest deep. The reflection of all one has left behind, with or without regret.

If I dip my hand into the tangled threads of memory, the first thing I come to is the fire. The fire that perhaps has spread farther in my recollection than it did in reality. The fire, and in it Lukas.

It is a summer of extreme heat. Forest fires have broken out in eastern Europe. An electrical storm has caused hundreds of fires that are left to burn unattended. After the driest spring for over a hundred years, enormous stretches of land are now burned out. The lack of rain combined with dry thunderstorms has created a smoking inferno.

The pediatrician I slept with last night in a room facing the busy street has still not come down for breakfast. Not that we slept much. No doubt he will spend the whole day in bed, exhausted. In positions I didn't even know existed, I tried to relax and be compliant and not succumb to nausea when he turned and twisted me this way and that. I felt like the white foam on the dark surface of a wave heaving and swelling beneath me, my skin an almost sickly white against the blackness of his. In the background the pulsing of R&B. *That's how you like it, huh? That's how I like it, babe.* If only life could always be like this, fitted together like a supple pair of hips: *Huh? Yeah* . . . He was heavy, and though I typically have a weakness for the boyish sort, it's still good to go to bed with someone you can really feel.

"Do you often go with strange men?" he asked.

"Not so often."

"How often?" I held up seven fingers. The speed of my reply made him laugh. Seven hundred . . . was what he seemed to think.

Now, on the speaker in the dining room: Marlene Dietrich's seductive voice that must have been left from the night before—it is not suitable breakfast music. I keep an eye on the door where guests, hungry and sated, come and go. Is he going to miss his conference today? Yes, at any rate he will miss breakfast. Should I wake him? No, I'm not his wife. He had no wife, he said. But he liked married women. Innocence made him melancholy.

Lust for men and fear—perhaps they are feelings within me that cannot be separated. It is men who have to be distinguished one from another. But how does one know? How does one see? The signs? Don't suspect someone without cause, but making a mistake can lead to disaster. It is easier with all the other things Mama warned me about: highways are all dangerous, it's possible to drown in every single lake, snakes can be divided into poisonous and nonpoisonous. But men . . . you simply have to live with the uncertainty. As I recall, she didn't warn me about strange men or unprotected sex, like other mothers did. Just about love.

I resolve to place my trust in someone, then try to see him in that light. Without trust one is dead, or might just as well be, but too much trust also carries the risk of not surviving long. Men who can't take a no, men who have never taken a no, or men who have decided never again to take a no—they will do whatever they like with the next girl who says no.

The television reports of the fires last night made me restless. I went out after dark, the town feverish with Friday evening, hunting season, high heels, whites of the eyes glowing, smashing glasses. I don't like this frenzy, actually, prefer daylight, normal days in normal places, chance meetings when one least expects them. But every so often I feel like being wild with rouge plastered on my cheeks. Slip into a bar convinced that someone is sitting there waiting for me.

It was pleasant talking to an American, to be able to speak without thinking. It started with one glass that soon became two and then three. I threw caution to the wind and the barriers came down and all my secrets spilled out, unimpeded. Perhaps because he didn't seem to be listening very carefully—he wasn't going to correct me if I contradicted myself, demand explanations, would just listen and forget. Appeared to have heard all the stories before, from his position behind the bar in an Arizona desert, I imagined, where he stood pouring out mescal and listening to the world's troubles. And I could see what he thought of me . . . a poor lonely lady of the night, all dressed up and nowhere to go.

His features were sharp like a cock-of-the-rock, as if his blood were a mixture of all races, until he became everything and nothing, free. A man who can ride but can't swim. A man who can score a bull's-eye at any distance but can't distinguish one woman from another under his nose. Grand Canyon, Lake Como, I thought when I saw him. Oakland, Idaho. A typical man. They don't exist, and yet there he was, looking like someone who would get caught in a loop on the lonely, lonely roads that stretch into infinity in the American Midwest. Pediatrician, he said, in Manhattan, though now he was working for Doctors Without Borders. I could see my surprised expression in his gleaming black eyes. He had come here for an international conference on noma infection that was taking place in the town this week.

"Noma infection?"

"You don't want to know."

"Yes, I do."

"No, you don't. Believe me." Noma was God's punishment for mankind, especially children. He pronounced the disease with a capital letter and God with a small letter. Perhaps you reach that point when you have witnessed enough suffering. We talked about the fires instead.

Trust or alcohol, something made me start talking. He didn't drink himself, refused when I offered him a glass. Normally I don't trust men who don't drink, especially if they're sitting alone in a bar. But from time to time exceptions have to be made. The fact of the matter was that he was far too good-looking for me to leave.

"I'm a doctor, I know what that stuff does to your brain." I knew as well, but that didn't stop me.

"I would like to live sober and die drunk." So would I, but how can you know when it's time? . . . I want to be prepared.

"Aren't you a bit too young to be taking death so seriously?" he asked, lighting a cigarette.

"Aren't you a bit too old to be concerned about your future brain capacity?" I asked. He was handsome, but certainly over fifty.

"You little rascal," he exclaimed, amazed. I'm not usually good with older men. I never know how to deal with them. They are so sensitive, and I am always hurting their feelings. But I was enjoying this.

"You black marauder," I retorted. Heard him draw breath. It was in the balance.

If he could call me a little rascal, I could call him a black marauder. As he was a pediatrician he must be accustomed to charming insults, and anyway he knew exactly how handsome he was. He was no doubt always gathering nurses like ripened grapes, and could do with a bit of opposition, someone who didn't just fall into his hands.

"What do you want?" It seemed he hadn't made up his mind to leave, but was giving it serious consideration. I wasn't in the habit of being quite so blunt, but because he asked me, I didn't beat around the bush.

"Okay," he said, "but we can talk first." Talk? Of course . . . I have nothing against talking. I wasn't the one who had to get up early for a conference. He ordered a cup of green tea for himself, and I ordered a glass of slivovitz.

"You'll have to pay for that yourself. I never buy women alcohol." And innocence made him melancholy? He was full of contradictions. I paid for mine and we talked about the fires. I told him what I had heard as a child, how long a fire can continue to burn underground, the smoldering roots giving no outward sign of the catastrophic damage being caused.

UNFAMILIAR FORESTS

I've been warned about unfamiliar forests, full of hidden dangers, the importance of staying close to home where the situation is known. I've never followed that advice. As soon as a place begins to resemble a home, I move on. Objects are so alien. People too, the more one gets to know them. The view over a strange town from a room rented for the night gives me a sense of calm. I feel most at home when I'm somewhere else. Away from my belongings, away from those I love. Could be in any town at all and feel the same loneliness. Yearn for a place that doesn't exist. Home is where each person's own smell merges into the smells of the others. There is no such place for me.

I travel without an aim, but I've read somewhere that all journeys have secret destinations of which the traveler is not aware. In April, the cruelest of months, there are no sunglasses dark enough for the spring light on the streets of Kazimierz. I look straight into the sun and don't care if someone is sucked into my eye and burned to ash.

There are as many dogs roaming loose here as there are domestic ones. The tame ones prowl around with their tails rigid, constantly on their guard. The wild ones are placid, taking no notice of humans. The dogs doze in the afternoon sun. It's a beautiful day. Time is running out, somebody or something is approaching, a breeze stirs along the ground, the dogs' eyes roll in their sleep. The stray mongrels are just one incidental piece of the street scene. They could rise to their feet at any time and move somewhere else, quick to react to impulses of need and flight.

Fall asleep forgetting who I am, wake up as someone else, with another face—go out to buy a new pair of boots and throw away the old ones—I do this on the third day. Dark red with brightly colored flowers embroidered on the leg. A tingling in the tip of my tongue, like a secret message. A good day. I can feel it. A good day, a good spring.

With every step I am reminded of my new footwear. The hard leather is gripping my calves tightly, but it's not uncomfortable. Sense a new level of awareness, unnerving and at the same time arousing, as I follow the river downstream, the morning still young.

The faces of the women in this town have so many aspects. Most beautiful of all are their early morning faces, closed and serene like sleeping birds, walking along the river, ready for the drones who have to fix new boundaries between themselves every day. Traces of the night's love encounters are on their bare necks, oval blue blotches that can't be washed away but have to be covered with makeup before they can climb aboard the trolley buses and the trams on their way to work. I wanted to be one of them and now I am. Learn to keep pace with the gentle flow of the water, adjust to the women's ways and movements, blend in. The only thing distinguishing us is language, but during the silent morning walks along the riverbank, nobody notices. I can feel the change in me this town is causing, the light, the men, the women.

Sit for a while by the river and rest my feet, aching from the new boots. See a man at the edge of the water doling out food from a plastic bag to some of the stray dogs. A performance, how he tries to direct the group to prevent the pushy ones from taking everything and leaving nothing for the lowest ranks. He shouts something to me and smiles. I smile back and indicate that I don't understand, and that just makes him repeat the sentence, louder, as if that would help me. Then he tries to drive away his four-legged friends and approaches me with half the troop still circling around his legs.

I stand up. There are a lot of them and they appear more wild than tame.

"*Nie mówie po polsku,*" I say.

"That was perfect Polish," he says. Of course, but *I don't speak Polish* is the only thing in Polish I can say.

"English is okay." He smiles. "And I really like your boots."

The psychopath is often charming, generally has success with the opposite sex. I cast around in my memory. Dogs . . . do they like dogs? Do they like to feed abandoned animals? To give them a feeling of power . . . No, I don't remember. He comes nearer, walking as if he owns the diminishing distance between us. When he extends his hand and notices that I hesitate, he wipes off bits of the dogs' food on his trouser leg and offers it again. *The psychopath often has children with several women. The psychopath seldom takes his own life, because he does not have strong feelings of regret or failure.* Why must the psychopath always be a man? And why must he always come up to me? What is it about me and maniacs? Where is the power of my attraction in their eyes? I want to know . . . so that I can do something about it. Is it the color of my lipstick, or my habit of watching people too unashamedly, averting my gaze a fatal second too late? "I'm Jiri," he says, shooing away the dogs.

"Lo."

"What does that mean?"

"Wildcat," I reply.

"Wildcat . . . In what language?"

"Mine."

"Ah, in *your* language. You've got your own language? Wildcat language?"

He himself looks rather wolflike. Predatory teeth, amber eyes, gray suit. The suit, is it ironic? It must be. He is wearing it with sneakers. Perhaps he belongs to the category of intelligent lunatics, attractive psychopaths, treacherous high-risk projects.

"You're popular," I say, nodding toward the dogs strutting around his feet.

"Yes, I've spoiled them, or rather . . . bought their love. I bet yours can't be bought, eh?" he says and shakes out a cigarette.

Indiscretion is the order of the evening. Too much vodka in a dingy bar by the river. Too much darkness, too much river, too many of Jiri's friends, too many strangers, too many men. Too many languages—English, German, Russian—which in drunkenness merge into Polish, Swedish, Slovak. In the end people can't even speak their own language. We just laugh, and in so doing we understand each other for the first time that night.

When I try to slow the pace he smiles at me. He says his name is Jiri, but his friends call him something else. You can always drink three glasses, he says, three before, three during, three after. I can trust him because he has a hell of a long list of academic qualifications.

"Before, during, and after what?"

"No idea, it's just a saying." He laughs. I've heard that in these parts they use vodka as a contraceptive . . . not before, during, or after, but instead. He doesn't laugh at that. Alcohol can be the subject of jokes almost all over, but not religion and not sex, and definitely not at the same time. Why do I never learn? I know his type, who take themselves very seriously under the thin mask of intelligent irony. I have a certain weakness for them and that irritates me. A sophisticated layabout, sexy but graced with ironic taste in clothes and a soft spot for hungry abandoned dogs. What promise does that hold? For all I know, we may well sleep together before the night is over, but one thing is certain—we won't joke about it.

I begin to think that we'll never shake off his friends, but suddenly they're gone. Jiri makes sure that we're alone, stops a clapped-out car on the street, and pays a young man to take us to his place on the other side of town. We are too drunk, sleep first and have sex later, making us feel less like strangers, as if we had been together before. But no, I would have remembered him. He moves in time with the breeze, the most sensual rhythm.

No one has to have everything, but everyone has to have something. It might only be a fragrance one has never smelled before. Beautiful Slavic features. Handsome neck. Worn-out shoes that look as though they have walked far. Dark humor. A face exceptionally open. Exceptionally shut. A photo of children next to his heart. A story to tell. A weak point. A flaw. I don't know if any of this is really him, but the fact that I can't put my finger on what I find tempting about him—this is the tempting thing.

"You fire into the blind spot between the eyes," he says and marks the spot with two fingers against my forehead, as if he wants to anoint me or execute me or both at the same time. "The heavy body falls," he mumbles, "it's slack." I'm not sure what he is talking about. Although his English is good I don't understand what he means. The walls of the badly lit one-room apartment are dripping with damp, like the inside of a glass jar. It is meager accommodation for someone who works at the university, as he claims to do, devoid of books too. Salt mines, steelworks, I think when I see his hands. He is better looking without the suit, before a world opens up of . . . I wish I knew what it was called in his language: pleasure. I run my hand over the network of small hard muscles in his back. Dung-clearing muscles, he says. He has to go home to work on his parents' farm as soon as he has some time off, as his father is getting old and has been blessed with only one son. Five daughters and only one son, and, what's more, he doesn't want to take over the farm. A minor catastrophe.

"I could help them financially instead of going home to toil away in their muddy fields. But it's not a question of money. Do you understand?" I understand precisely. He rolls onto his back and pulls me down on top of him, alleges that I was murmuring a name in my sleep, could I be married? Without waiting for an answer, as if it is not very important, at least not more important than hunger, he gets up, restless, and disappears into the hallway. Returns from the floor's communal kitchen with his hands full of bread, lard, pickles, and beer.

Most people play their best cards first, so why not part then with the illusion intact? An illusion is not exactly a lie, it is its own truth, a short interval while the oxygen lasts in the floating bubble. A man who is pleasant one evening is indeed pleasant in that place and at that time, even if in his normal life he's despicable, before and after that evening, always has been and always will be despicable. He shows his best side—offers it to me—before the smell of sweat penetrates the smell of aftershave. And now and then I may prefer it that way.

Sex is sometimes the price you have to pay for the delight of seducing a man. Sometimes more, sometimes less. Make him fall, preferably slowly enough to see it happen. Was Venus ever afraid when she lured men? But she wasn't a normal woman, wasn't subject to normal laws. She enticed men up onto her mountain and seduced them. Mound of Venus: the raised, hair-covered part above the pubic bone in a woman. In this perilous place all her men fell victim.

As soon as Jiri is sleeping soundly I creep away, back to my hotel room.

The last thing I notice before I drop into bed is a growing dark cloud outside the window, as if an enormous sack of thousands of bats is emptied over the hotel's pointed roof. Then everything is black. Not a darkness that eyes become accustomed to, no, pitch black like closed-down factories at night, like the lake back home, at its deepest point.

AX

"You've slept with every one of the men, haven't you?" Mama says and lifts the ax.

"Yes," I reply, "but only once." She lowers the tool and shades her eyes with her hand. They're almost white in the bright light. "Apart from with the great love of my life," I add. She weighs the heavy ax in her right hand, wary.

"How many times did you sleep with him, then?" She raises the deadly instrument again and swings it over her head with such dexterity that with the first blow the birch log whimpers and splits and leaps away, hitting the wall of the woodshed with a dull thud. My mama with an ax, a scene that always scared me as a child. She was terrifying even without an ax.

"Don't come back saying I didn't warn you," she mutters. I instinctively flinch as she lifts the hefty ax once more. I wish I could blame her, I really do, but the truth is for the whole of my life she has warned me about love.

She looks as though she'd like to laugh but has forgotten how. Instead she takes aim again, stretches, and applies her now failing strength. She's still just as skillful, her technique does not let her down, but she lacks the weight and speed required for the ax to do its job effectively.

She was chopping wood when her water broke and when Papa left. Chopping. Every time. When someone died, when someone deceived her, when I moved, when she caught Lukas and me in the act, when she and Papa's father had argued. When she was sad she took the ax and went out. I was used to it. The noise from the woodpile was the beat that accompanied all disasters, large and small, as I was growing up. I knew what a catastrophe sounded like. Heavy, slow, ominous. When I left the village the sound of the ax accompanied me.

She is in her element cutting wood, the steel that cleaves the air that cleaves the tree that cleaves the silence. I have always liked watching her while she chops. There's something alarming in the sight and at the same time awe-inspiring. If something were to happen, an outward threat of any kind, it would still be she who would protect me, not the other way around. With every stroke I am convinced of this. A mother-goddess in a struggle with her demons, spider woman in her most terrifying form. Mama would like to weave the web of my fate—like the cosmic spider drawing all humans together with umbilical-cord thread, entwining them into the huge pattern.

"To belong to everyone is to belong to no one," she reminds me.

"I know."

"Do you?"

"Yes. But that's how I want it." Now she lays down the ax and rubs into her aching hands the same mink fat she uses for her woodcutting boots. It's universal, like everything else in her life; it wouldn't surprise me if she fried herring in it too. She doesn't ask who he is, the love of my life, the one who dazzled me so completely. Perhaps she thinks she already knows, in the way that mothers believe they know because we once shared the same bloodstream—they never let us forget.

"I can't understand how you manage it. Honestly, girl, what sort of stuff are you made of?"

"Some kind of hard timber from the north, I imagine."

"Silver birch? With titanium screws in that case," she says sourly.

Her eyes: twinkling blue. I try to be truthful with her, even though I know that she doesn't like it and she doesn't want to understand.

"What do you actually want from them? All they'll bring you is emptiness, that's what I think. What one gives you, another will take away." I'm determined not to be provoked, but it's already too late. "You were given too much love when you were little," she adds and shoots an impenetrable look in my direction through the yellow lenses of her dark glasses. They look ridiculous. Hope she takes them off if anyone comes, whoever that might be . . . "Too much love. That's the reason," she repeats.

"The reason for what?"

"The men."

Yes, I do sleep with every man, but not with just anybody, only with the ones I have selected, and they are a tiny percentage of all the men who cross my path, and then . . . well, then I leave them before they have a chance to display their less attractive side, which often means right away. What do I want of them? Not faithfulness under a cloud of creamy white tulle, at any rate. Not the Hiroshima four-poster bed, not the padded Alcatraz cell.

And what do they want of me? "Fascinating," "special," I hear more often than not—that means I'm not pretty. I'm not one of the most beautiful of women, and that gives me a broad spectrum of potential men to choose from. Stunningly attractive women often seem so alone; it's only when they're tipsy that men dare to approach them. Or when the men themselves are tipsy and looking to offend them in some way.

Whatever Mama believes, I select them with great care. Of course I have made mistakes, but that can happen in choosing one only—a misjudgment or bad luck can lead to a lifetime of regret. I once met a man who despised all the women he couldn't have, almost as much as he despised those he could have. But I can't make all men scapegoats for that.

"Be careful," Mama warns in her icy dialect. If she can no longer be my guardian angel, she wants to be my bird of foreboding. "Life's not a carnival, Lo." I know. But maybe it can be. A man who smells of Jicky cannot be utterly without hope. Or Eau Sauvage, Équipage, Hypnôse. Ozone perfumes are the ones I rely on most, the brackish, sweet and salty unisex fragrances, water scents. The animal, glandular smells like musk and civet make me more cautious. It has to be very late and only certain sorts of nights.

"Someday your past's going to come back to haunt you. Somebody who took it harder than you thought. Men are . . ."

"Dangerous?"

"Romantics," Mama says and fixes me with her eye through the yellow glasses. It has grown cold and we've moved into the kitchen, where she fills the pan with water and fumbles for the coffee can in the cool cupboard. "Romantics, Lo. You ought to know that. And yes, that sometimes makes them dangerous." I know that her loyalty to me is great, but it can't be sought. Now she suddenly looks hard, turns on the gas, strikes a match. I always hold my breath when she lights the gas stove. She refuses to replace it. If she's going to die, she'll go up in flames, not fade away. *I have only daughters, God, my God, why have you forsaken me?* laments a woman on the radio. Mama is listening.

"Daughters," she mutters to herself, "greater happiness and greater sorrow." That was what her mother always said.

You can't just toy with them and quit when you tire yourself, or one day it will turn out badly. Pouched animals . . . that's what Mama calls them. But she's a marsupial herself—she carried me. I may have clambered out of her pouch early and taken off, but sometimes I long to be back in her protective presence again.

THE RED ZONE

I met him on the streetcar between Buda and Pest that spring when the catalpa trees flowered too early and the month of April was so warm that by summer it would be unbearable to stay in town. He was the last one to squeeze on when it had already started to move. My eye caught the paisley pattern on his shirt. Only madmen go barefoot on a tram, I was thinking when I saw him hanging on, his hip against the chrome post, drinking from a bottle and smiling. What was he smiling at? Nothing in particular . . . just a smile? He lit an imaginary cigarette and suddenly I had a sneaking suspicion that I had provoked the smile. Discreetly I wiped my lips; perhaps a little of the paprika filling had ended up outside my mouth as I ran across the street from the market hall to the streetcar stop with my warm Hungarian bread.

Nothing is quite like the light in April, not in this town. Budapest at this time is like a mirror, the kind that lies and tells you that you look better than you do. We were traveling right into the shining brilliance over the water of the Danube. The last thing I saw before my vision was flooded with white was a drop of soda trickling down his smooth suntanned chin. I wanted to catch it with my tongue while he was dazzled, but we were already through to the other side.

The first thing I could distinguish when the brightness dimmed was his hand. An animal, presumably a dog, had disfigured it. Small stumps remained in the place where his fingers should be, but the hand was so deformed it could scarcely be called one. He dragged it nonchalantly through his hair, and I couldn't help watching, wondering how it would feel to be caressed by a hand like that, if it had any sensation left in it, feeling. Perhaps his hand had not forgotten—life before the accident—what it was like to experience the tiniest details in your fingertips.

I searched for something else I could let my gaze rest on. Around his neck he wore a loosely knotted tie with the Taj Mahal embossed in the fabric. I'd never seen such a handsome man with such awful taste in clothes. Perhaps I was wrong, but it seemed as though something burned within him, from his hand right up to the intense look in his eye.

We rode in a wide arc through the town. Lukas's town. I tried to imagine him standing on a street corner, but I couldn't picture him. He didn't fit in here. Then we traveled back over the river, and by the time we stepped off at the last stop it had turned to autumn, or it felt like it, cool, with a hint of rain in the air. The two of us and a whole crowd of youngsters of different sizes on their way to school in newly pressed uniforms. The children went in one direction; he went in the other. I went the same way.

The smell of lilac at the wrong time of year disturbed and confused me, until I saw the soap factory. He walked slowly, as if wanting me to keep up, past the factory toward the apartment blocks in its shadow. We cut across the empty gardens of the subdivision, and when we emerged at the other side the buildings came to an abrupt end. Flat fields covered in weeds quite unlike the ones at home stretched out toward the highway in the distance.

Where was he going? The gauge was registering in the red zone. Never go with any man who obviously wants you to go with him. But I hadn't yet developed a fear of strangers. The rain was so light it was hardly noticeable, just a film of moisture on the forehead and cheeks. He raised his shoulders in the thin shirt, increased his pace, and by a field that appeared to be lying fallow, overgrown with thistles, he stopped without warning and turned around.

"What do you want?"

I didn't want to look at his disfigured hand, but it was impossible not to, as if it were whispering, "*Hey, you . . . yes, you . . . Look at me. Don't be afraid.*"

It should be possible to spend a day or preferably a whole week in a new town without going to bed with someone. On a purely theoretical level I know it's feasible, but single men in the transit hall, freshly showered men in the breakfast room, the backs of beautiful heads at the check-in desk, someone's profile in the elevator mirror, a smell along the sidewalk or on the tram, that's all it takes.

Men with grandiose dreams. Men with dogs. Young men who drink too quickly, older men with eyes like desert islands. The ones who shoot from the hip. Softhearted killers. Men in exceptional circumstances. Men with style. Men without. Men who don't know what they want or why. Or men who know exactly. It's not that they are all walking around waiting to be seduced, but if the opportunity presents itself, I don't see what would stand in their way.

"You're peaceful when you make love and violent when you sleep," someone said.

"Your laugh's like a wave machine—it makes me seasick," said another.

"Come," said the black marauder. And I did.

The rest of the weekend we spent in his summer cottage just outside Pest. Roasted last year's remaining chestnuts in sooty cans on the woodstove and ate them piping hot out of their skins with salt, drank moonshine strong enough to put a wild boar to sleep. It wasn't a dog that was responsible for Miklós's ragged hand, but a machine at the soap factory. When he touched me I felt calm. His hand didn't feel repellent, just different, softer than a child's.

There was something soft about his mouth too, like biting into a plum overflowing with pungent dark red juice from his generous lips as they grew more and more red. His mouth breathed, "Bite!" And I bit. Fleeting shadows moved across the cottage wallpaper and the clouds rolled by.

"You know Eskimos," he said suddenly, when we were back in bed after eating all the chestnuts, even the charred ones, to quell our evening hunger. We didn't lack food, but a feeling of being full. "To increase the strength and endurance of the sleigh dogs, they used to leave a bitch tied up for the wolves to mate with," he said. On top of him, I was quiet. Outside the French window darkness had fallen over the garden, so all that could be seen were the out-lines of handprints on the inside of the dirty windowpane. Lots of handprints, as if someone had tried to get out. "And they let the cold take the girls," he continued. "They laid them in the entrance to the igloo where they soon froze to death. Two out of three newly born. But only in times of necessity. In the summer they built a little stone grave by the tent and put the girl in there to die. If it was spring or autumn they suffocated her with a sealskin. Some lives had to be sacrificed so that the others could survive—always the girls, because they could never be hunters."

His eyes were still as soft, his eyes and voice as well, but some-thing else had been altered. Something within me.

Fear is like an animal. In fear we are changed into a creature with four legs, feeling the chill beneath our paws. *Come,* he whispered. *Go,* I said to myself. *Trust your fear. Go now. Go.*

The smell in the room had changed from pleasure to discomfort. I recalled it from somewhere—childhood, frogs rotting in the rain, sweet like urine.

"Be quick," he said, when I spluttered that I had to go out. Fuck-ing unnecessary right in the middle of it, seemed to be his opinion.

The lie was fairly transparent, but there was no time to consider. He had said that the old water closet inside the house was broken, that you had to go out between the gable end of the house and the empty dovecote. "Hurry up," he said, in spite of the fact that hurrying was the only thing I could think about, anxious that he would sense how cold my body had become, how white, how bloodless, how rigid with fear.

And then, as if he had suddenly changed his mind, he held on to me. Not with the soft, damaged hand that I liked, but with the other, less sensitive one.

"Your bladder must be as small as a bird's . . . What did you say your name was?" His fingers were tight around my wrist, so he must have felt that it was frozen to the bone. I tried cautiously to wriggle free and said my name again. It wasn't difficult. Two letters. I didn't understand why he couldn't grasp it. He had already asked me several times, as if dissatisfied with my answer.

We had laughed and toasted each other and I had lost count of how many glasses I had consumed of his aromatic home distillation as it went down to the quarter-cup line on a plastic jerry can without a label. Now for the first time I could taste it, sharp like a cut in the throat. What had he given me—liquid insecticide, weed killer, diluted rat poison? Any of those toxic substances was readily available in a house in the country.

"You're cold," he said, "freezing cold. What is it?"

"I need to . . ." I searched for the word in German, but it was gone "Let go!" As soon as my hands were free I pulled away and dragged on what I thought was my dress. It turned out to be his shirt, but there was no time to change. I just stumbled away through the darkness without looking to see if he was following. I tried to find my bearings by the light, but it was black everywhere. As I groped my way along the walls I found only locked doors.

I had swallowed his trash, laughed my most childish laugh,

seduced and allowed myself to be seduced as if life had taught me nothing. His tongue in my mouth, my hand in his shorts, more spirits in the glass, falling on my back with him on top of me, just as drunk . . . or only pretending to be. Maybe he was stone cold sober the whole time? Alert and focused, right behind me now, just wanting to give me a head start to increase the thrill?

I banged my hip on something hard without feeling any pain, fumbled farther along. Thought I heard him say my name, but it might have been the wind rising. The gaps in the walls of the wooden house made it sound like a broken instrument the wind blew through. Finally, at the end of the kitchen, I found a back door with a key in the lock. The night air hit me and I breathed it in with the vigor of having just surfaced, then kept on out into the overgrown garden, where briars ripped thin material off the shirt. I wandered around in circles until I knocked against the metal railing at the boundary of the plot, climbed over, and hastened farther into the unknown darkness.

I have no stamina when it comes to fear—it drained away from me as I was running. Like a quarry who stops in the midst of the hunt and wonders why she is fleeing—empty, disoriented, slightly stupid—I came to a standstill in the middle of the desolate field. The wind was cold and my mouth tasted of sooty chestnuts and smoke from his mouth, a trace of blood. I crouched down to catch my breath. No longer sufficiently agitated for fear to outweigh tiredness, I longed for a bed, any bed, my warm hotel bed or his lumpy mattress—just to give in to exhaustion, shut my eyes, and fall asleep. In my imagination as I ran, the highway in the distance with its sporadic night traffic had been my salvation. Now that I was standing close I didn't feel so sure. I might get into the wrong car—anyone at all could pick me up. There was nothing to suggest I was safer out here than in the house with him.

Of all evil things he's not the worst, I thought. From a distance the summer cottage looked like a sleeping hare alone under the night sky. Blue smoke indicated that the stove in which we had roasted the chestnuts was still burning, a rustic idyll shrouded in the peaceful darkness of spring. Somewhere far away the sound of a nightjar. From a distance everything beautiful, simple.

I turned back.

When I reached the fence I saw him standing by the French window in the bedroom, waiting, naked with a towel around his hips, and even when he pushed open the door and stepped out into the garden, he did not appear to see me. For a long time he stood listening, instead of calling for me. Was it in these parts that there were bears who went right up to the houses and ate out of the trash cans at night? I had heard about it, thought that must be what stopped him shouting for me. Or perhaps the knowledge that there were those giant bloodsucking bats that . . . no, surely it was not here, but farther east in Transylvania? Probably he had just forgotten my name again. That was why he was standing in the dark, waiting. I could make him out clearly in the faint glimmer of light from the bedroom, and despite the distance I could see how the wind took hold of the towel he had twisted around his hips, lifted it up and exposed him before he had time to cover himself. As if he sensed that someone in the surrounding darkness could see him.

Upright between the tall trees, half naked, calm, he seemed so much less than the man in my head as I ran away. The alarming disquiet in bed, the sudden uneasiness under my skin: what had triggered the reflex of fear? I was there of my own free will and enjoyed being with him. It wasn't the place, not the situation, not him. He was a careless lover, but I liked him. And his spider hand had enticed me, caused me to notice him and want to know who he was. How it would feel to be caressed by it. But he had two faces, as different as his hands.

In every culture throughout every age the same ritual: a feared animal is worshipped in order for it to be appeased. The more one
fears man, wolf, bat, spider, the more one idolizes them. I once had
a phobia for spiders, especially the large, hairy variety. Made up my
mind that their bite was deadly, but that was just as superstitious as
the belief that the bite could be cured by an exhausting dance, the
trancelike tarantella. The venom was quite harmless and most spiders' jaws were too weak to penetrate human skin. But what good
did knowing that do? Not even when I read that spiders have a
heart did my fear of them diminish. Fear is fear, irrational and persistent. Intense, manipulative. Fast-working. From one second to
the next you lose your balance. You have control for as long as you
can keep it, then it's gone, sliding through your hands like a slippery piece of soap, and when you've lost control, the only thing
that remains is fear.

My fear of spiders may have caused the problem in bed. Desire and
fear—sometimes they run into each other, mixed, confused, impossible to separate. The Eskimo girls were certainly responsible, stories
I'd heard when I was a child, pestered to be allowed to hear them . . .
until I found out how many sleepless nights they would give me.
That in the past in times of necessity they suffocated their newborn
daughters—that your own family could do this—turned my whole
world as a girl upside down. I couldn't stop thinking about those
little girls, how their tiny round legs jerked until they fell to the
sides, loose, under the sealskin closed so tightly over their mouths.

When we arrived at his isolated retreat in daylight, I hadn't noticed
any other inhabited houses nearby, only a few derelict buildings.
We'd taken a bus and then walked a long way through the countryside, peaceful and deserted, to reach his remote summer residence.

"What are you thinking?" he asked after a long silence. I scarcely knew where I was anymore, or if I would have any chance of finding my way back to town by myself. He sounded wary, perhaps supposing that I disliked this neglected area that made the prosperity of Budapest seem very far away. But in my eyes this scene was grudgingly beautiful, a childhood landscape I hadn't encountered for a long time.

He walked down the middle of the gravel track. No car passed, no person. We were alone with each other and a hawk soaring over the field, the mangled hand between us a reminder of everything I didn't yet know about him.

He regretted his decision. It was obvious in the way he didn't look at me. He could have tried to hide it, but he didn't. From the moment we got off the bus he had been silent, maybe thinking how foolishly impulsive it was for the two of us to come out here to his summer cottage together, as if we had both forgotten where we were supposed to be going that day. We knew nothing about each other and could only communicate after a fashion. Not that language was a problem—he had worked on construction sites in Berlin and Nuremberg, so his German was better than mine and English filled in the gaps for us both. But we had no idea at all what we should talk to each other about.

He hadn't asked a single question about who I was, wanted to know nothing about me other than my name. And what did I really want to know about him, besides how his deformed hand would feel on my skin?

His cheekbone reminded me of Lukas's: a face that could instantly change from hard to tender. I loved the way the light affected Lukas's face, but he wouldn't have liked to hear me say that. Compliments were always an exaggeration, and exaggeration made him embarrassed.

"You're pretty," he said.

I remember it, because he said it only once.

After leaving the bus a long way out of town, I hadn't heard so much as a dog barking, not even from afar, no sign of life anywhere. As if this area had been evacuated and left to the birds of prey. Just as I was growing accustomed to the impenetrable silence between us, it was shattered by his question. What was I thinking about? Women with faces translucent with age, how my throat was sticky with dust from the road, that somewhere around here Lukas had been born, that there was a strong smell of wild rosemary along these roads, his injured hand, smooth with a new layer of skin, right next to my hand as we walked. But mostly I was thinking about snakes—that we were walking through typical snake terrain, that I've never liked snakes, neither before nor after I was bitten as a child, that they are the only thing I cannot disguise my fear of.

My limited German was not adequate to explain all of that, so instead I asked him what he was thinking.

"That I've forgotten your name," he said, without looking at me. I followed his gaze and caught sight of the hawk again. It was gliding nearer. Characteristic buzzard movements, slowly circling high up, the very behavior that usually indicates the presence of snakes. The hawk might mean that the place was teeming with suitable food, or that the situation was under control, that somebody was doing his best to hold the reptile population in check. But my fear needed no proof, just one buzzard circling over fields in this way, the summerlike April warmth bringing them out of the holes where they've kept themselves alive all winter with the heat of one another. I often saw them down by the lake when I was a child, black adders, where did they go? When I was a teenager they had disappeared. Or had I lost my eye for snakes?

Lukas maintained that they gave birth to their young. I could visualize it: a nightmare of unrestrained adders reproducing fully formed new adders. It was some hybrid thing, according to Lukas, producing eggs that they hatched inside their own bodies. Most of all I was frightened of snakes underwater. Both adders and grass snakes were excellent swimmers and often went out into the lake to catch small fish. You had to be faster than your own shadow to avert that threat. You needed the right amount of fear to be as fast as that. I was paralyzed.

"Are we there yet?" I let my eye sweep along the gravel track to discern any suspicious twisting and slithering movements, aware of a sudden cold wind blowing in toward town.

"There," Miklós said. I gave a start, but it wasn't a snake. It was the house. A peeling turquoise summer cottage with shutters closed, partly hidden by shrubs and soapwort growing wild all over the yard. "Come on," he said and vaulted over the rusty gate. I hurried after him, relieved to be close to safety.

At the bottom of the steps he stopped. In the sharp midday light a snake was lying on the top step, warmed by the sun. A type I did not recognize, but evidently he did, because his bearing changed in an instant. He was moving so slowly that he appeared to be standing still. The snake lay coiled up, amassing heat, waiting. He took hold of a fallen branch—had clearly done this before. With the skill of an expert he caught the creature and flung it at lightning speed in a high arc into the thorny bushes by the gable, then unlocked the door and showed me in.

There had been nothing sensational about his face when I first caught sight of him on the tram. Discreet and ordinary. I've always had a weakness for ordinary faces. It wasn't his hand that caused me to notice him, but his smile, unnerving like everything else that breaks the pattern when you are confined with strangers. First the smile, then the hand. I recoiled, unable to conceal my instinct for detecting trouble. It was obvious that he could see how my pupils dilated and how involuntary distaste made me press my back into the plastic seat and in my embarrassment bite off too large a piece of bread. No doubt he was used to all possible insensitive reactions, but can one ever get used to arousing unprovoked repugnance in others? My eye was drawn back to his hand, the fleshy pink tarantula that he pushed through his hair in an attempt to straighten his windblown locks. With a hand like that perhaps you are extra scrupulous about other details.

When I was a child I saw many men who had lost one or more fingers when they got in the way of an ax, the blade of a saw, a roller, chain, or bad-tempered sow, not to mention gangrene and frostbite. But this hand is not slightly maimed—it is mutilated beyond recognition. And yet . . . where there is aversion there is also desire. His hand appealed to something within me that hadn't been stirred before.

When I creep back into the house he is asleep. Or perhaps pretends to be sleeping and wakes up, turns over, and calls me to him. Once distaste has merged with desire and mingled together, it is difficult to separate them. I ought to go, leave this place, I'm thinking as I walk toward his bed, and as I crawl between the sheets with him, willing and yet unwilling, and even more as he lays his hand between my shoulder blades. I don't want him to feel the bulge there, the raised back of the reptile that is fear.

Suspicious, he asks me where I have been . . . gone so long. Must have gotten lost, I answer. Impossible to get lost in a yard this size, fenced in as well. Bad sense of direction, I say vaguely, hear how idiotic it sounds and add something about vision being impaired in the dark. Then he feels my muddy feet under the cover.

"There's no mud in my garden. You were out in the fields running away, weren't you?" I shake my head, but he can feel the holes in his shirt from the blackthorn bushes and asks if I was trying to run off. I say I wasn't. "You're lying." I don't deny it. The scratches hurt when he pulls me toward him. On the wall above his head a quotation has been pinned up: *I never forget a face, but in your case I'll be glad to make an exception.* Groucho Marx, I think as he enters me.

Dawn is beginning to break, and a cold mildew-blue light is spreading over the walls of the cottage. He holds my face between his hands, the whole one and the impaired one, bites my neck. His hands have a smell that makes me recoil before I realize what it is, that it is myself I smell the scent of. The smell of me on his hands, from before when we made love.

We're always someone else when we make love. Whenever I meet somebody like him, I have the urge to confront the other in him, andros, the man. The one he becomes when he makes love.

NEITHER NEITHER NOR NOR

I liked sleeping with Lukas, our secret sleep. In the middle of the day in the pearl fisher's house we let the hours slip past, float away until darkness fell. We drifted, surrendering, along the verge of wakefulness, half-sleep, sleep, dreams, unconsciousness. He lay on my arm or I lay on his, and I tried to imagine that he'd had that look long before he met me. That actually it had nothing to do with me, that it wasn't my fault he had such a look in his eyes—as though something were missing every time he saw me.

Bodies. Physical contact. In the end it all revolves around this, when you have spent so much time in each other's company that there is nothing left to say. Lukas's nakedness didn't excite me, nor did it bother me. I was as familiar with it as I was with my own. Just a body, no surprises from one day to the next. Some variations according to the season: a little bit more fat beneath the skin in winter and a little thinner and more languid in summer. And then that other change, not cyclical or connected to the time of year but irreversible. From child to teenager through a long-drawn-out adolescence, and for Lukas the change to an adult body. So slowly that you didn't see it until it had already happened.

As long as I remained in the body of a child we could continue to be friends, but when I let it go? It had to happen one day. It was as if Lukas were waiting for that. He looked at my slender hips.

"Haven't you thought about starting to grow yet?" What? Did I need to hurry? I took his hands away.

"You must be the smallest in the class." I wasn't. There were even some boys who were smaller than I was. Compared with them, Lukas was a skinny giant with hands like horse chestnut leaves and a pack of heaving muscles under his skin. He lifted me up in the water and flung me out of my depth so that I would learn to swim.

Sun, sleep, play. Summer existed just for us, and we existed just for summer. Grasshoppers dipped in wild honey, leftover food smuggled out of the house. Drink out of the rainwater tank, shower in a downpour of rain. Sleep. More than anything else, we slept our secret sleep. Lukas could never sleep enough. I had to learn to like it also, or at least to be patient with him. Lie beside him and study the rhythm of his slow breathing, the sleeping presence of his warm, outstretched body. As time passed I thought he became less and less like a hunted dog. We thought we were safe when we went around, unsuspecting and spontaneous, near to the line without overstepping it. We just pushed it ahead of us, neither neither nor nor.

"What's happening? Where do you get to when you suddenly disappear? What on earth are you doing?" Mama said, in the big sunglasses that made her look like a deadly hornet, especially in that striped top, so baggy at the neck that you could see down between her breasts.

"All sorts. Playing."

"Just think, the *Communist Manifesto* and *Alice in Wonderland* were written at about the same time," said Papa's father, who was sitting in front of Mama's bookcase, carefully passing his finger over the spines.

"All sorts. Playing," she mimicked. "You're not meeting that Lukas, are you?" Her pupils contracted. I avoided her eye.

"That Lukas, is his father's surname really Puskás?" Grandfather's voice sounded almost respectful when he pronounced the name. "What?" Mama asked unkindly. Puskás . . . one of the world's finest soccer players of all time, in the fifties when the Hungarians were the best, the Magnificent Magyars . . . had she never heard about them? Mama shook her head. She didn't like anyone touching her books, and she definitely didn't like talking about Lukas. Her pupils were as tiny and piercing as pinpricks—like Lukas's when he was messing around with whippets—though if anything Mama was about to go up a gear rather than down.

"And what does that have to with anything at all?" she asked maliciously.

"I just thought they might be related."

"As if that would help," Mama said.

Mama was the only one in the house to have a bookcase, even though the books filled just one shelf. Grandfather had some books in a wooden box under his bed, as if a proper shelf were something alien to him. In the pearl fisher's house Lukas and I found twenty identical moldy black leather volumes, arranged alphabetically. A pattern. The way Lukas's brain worked, every pattern bore a deeper meaning. It *had* to form a whole, the threads of an invisible spiderweb that held the chaos of existence together. He wanted to try to piece together the world around us, to make up a picture that at least made some sort of sense. A picture of what? I asked, but he didn't know yet. My job was to decipher my way through the text, while Lukas explained to me what I'd just read. He was bad at reading, but he knew a lot, mostly what he'd picked up from the television.

Coral, bats, fire, spiders—by the end of the summer he was talking more and more about the spider. At the center of its web it was biding its time. Fate. The great cosmic mother in her most terrifying form. I don't know if it was his own mother he was thinking of. No, hardly, he didn't have one.

Large trees of coral, salt-white, like porcelain, meticulously adorned by nature, stood in the windows of the pearl fisher's house, probably smuggled back from his many journeys to Japan. The skeleton of the coral, I read, was attached on the outside, like a protective coating. That is what Lukas should have had. When I stood waiting for him, I heard them arguing, him and his father, each one in his own language. I never understood what it was about, only that it had become worse as Lukas grew older. Before, he never answered back, but now he made cautious attempts not to flee, to stay and take what was coming. Or not take it.

The bruises disappeared and were replaced with new ones. However much love my own family tried to smother me in, what help was it when Lukas's existence was endless prowling around, watching and waiting? Sometimes he stayed the night in our hiding place, waiting for the lights to go out at home. I was setting myself free from the ones I had always belonged to and swimming out to him. What went on between us never ended—it was just sucked down into a new hole, and then another, and on it went.

No matter how long the pearl fisher's house had been left abandoned, we were in point of fact intruders. But no one could call us vandals. Lukas was very particular that we should keep it neat and tidy. He seemed to think that the pearl fisher *would* come back, though he must have been buried long ago. The dust over everything was undeniably fifty years thick. Simple math.

One blustery evening in winter Lukas stopped in the middle of the lifeless forest, listening out over the lake. I heard it as well. The pulse. There is a pulse in everything that lives. As we stood still and just listened, we no longer felt the cold, having become part of it.

The waves pounded under the ice, rhythmically, like blood between the atrium and the ventricle.

Later that evening I felt it in him too, how he pulsed. We had crept close together in bed to try to keep warm, barely keep warm, because it was hellishly cold. Lukas was fighting against sleep, unusual for him. It was as if he didn't want to disappear into it. Sleep was sad. It meant that you had to part.

"People say 'sleep together,' but that's wrong. You're alone when you sleep," he said and exhaled the smoke slowly through his lips like Jean-Paul Belmondo. I had learned how to sleep so lightly that I was still aware of his presence.

Lukas's winter belly was the same color as the soft foam on the water at the power station, his skin as smooth as catkins, flushed cheeks, hands, lips. I felt his heart . . . how it beat resentfully, as if something trapped inside was trying to force its way out. The whole time it crashed against the bars of his rib cage. It will have to give up in the end, sometime.

When I was small I had once made a hole in the ice with a shovel, so that the migrant birds could come out. Mama's mother had told me that they spent the winter at the bottom of the lake, waiting for spring, and I was quite sure that they wanted to come out. But it was just a fairy tale, I knew that. Lukas listened and then shook his head.

"No, Lo," he said, "there's no such thing as fairy tales."

I could float. That was my first achievement. Nothing could drag me down, my childhood was happy, and if it wasn't, I didn't realize. I could soon swim almost as well outside my mother's womb as I had inside. She could never really accept that. "We're all born wild," she said, "especially you, Lo." I grew quite tame later, but it was a superficial change.

Surrounded as I was by thirteen adults, I had no need to share their attention with anyone. I had a tough time trying to avoid it. Twenty-six eyes looked around every bend, into every blind spot, through every wall, saw dangers before I detected them myself. After my aunt Katja was injured by a metal splinter from the circular saw, there were still twenty-five eyes keeping track of me.

If I was to be anyone's accomplice, I would be his. When Lukas was shoplifting he just pulled his stomach in and slipped whatever he wanted into the waistband of his skater jeans, huge and khaki-colored, with drawstrings around the ankles. They accommodated however much we needed: food if we were hungry, drink if we were thirsty. I stood behind the shop waiting for him to come out and empty his haul into a backpack that we took back to our hideout.

He experimented with everything he could, cigarettes that he emptied of tobacco and mixed with something; he didn't tell me where it came from. On some occasions he tried canisters of laughing gas while he was smoking, to heighten the effect. Sometimes I took him mixed leftovers from cans and bottles, because his own father didn't drink. Once he got hold of ketamine, an anesthetic for horses he had bought at some less than scrupulous farm nearby. He'd heard that it gave you a high. It left him utterly beyond reach: he lay on the floor next to the bed and was gone. Like being sucked down into a black hole, he explained afterward. A well of deliverance that you wanted to return to. I was terrified he would never come back.

Most of it was innocent, but it soon became second nature to associate pleasure with danger. Once when we were talking about the fire along the railway line, he said that he'd started it. I didn't know what to think. Why? Because otherwise we would never have met?

There was so much we had to fit in that there was no time to go to school, or at least not stay there the whole day. We ran. We passed through our childhood running. Lukas tucked elaborate secrets into me.

His words touched on everything: secrets, promises, devilry. Apart from the shadow of his father, adults scarcely figured in our world, nor did the other children at school, or the factories, freight trains, cold, hunger, tiredness, mealtimes, bedtimes, seasons. We were fast and determined, as if we had a sixth sense that the future was against us.

Of all the secrets that bound us together, the hardest one to keep was the one about the rats. It was Lukas's job to empty the traps his father set. The fat river rats would gnaw at the roof beams if you didn't keep a check on them and would go down into the kitchen at night. His father, Gábriel, took great care to keep things clean and filled the attic with the worst sort of traps. Then he showed his son how they should be emptied and gave him to understand that from then on it was his job.

When Gábriel wasn't looking, it was I who brought them down from the attic and stuffed them into the zinc tub behind the house until the cages stopped shaking, while Lukas stood, pressed up against the wall in shame, shame that he'd left the worst to me. He looked as though he was the one about to be drowned. He would rather not have been anywhere in the vicinity, but he was forced to keep watch, so that his father didn't see that it was I who saw to the demise of those rats.

The old metal cages were heavy, especially when the rats had been in the water awhile, and the next step was to empty their lifeless contents into the barrel in which Gábriel used to burn leaves. Not into the compost, because that would just attract more rats. Lukas never got used to it, and he could hardly bear the thought that I did it. They had intelligent eyes, he said. He had tried to do it himself, but in the end he just let them go, which made his father furious, as the rats ran through the high grass and shrieked like rubber ducks someone has stepped on. They shrieked when they were drowning as well, a screech like red-hot barbed wire. Despite our attempts to keep the secret, his father found us out. I'd never seen him so enraged, never seen Lukas get such a beating, though he was always getting them for nothing.

IF EVER

The penultimate summer of my childhood, our days in the pearl fisher's house changed. Lukas had dropped out of school to work at the leather factory with his father. A sabbatical, he called it, but no one believed that. Sometimes I cycled up to the factory and waited for him to finish his shift. People poured out of the building, but Lukas was easy to spot in the crowd, always first out.

They tanned a hundred tons a week, and it showed on him—as if he tanned them all himself. The youngest invariably looked the most tired, worn out by the unfamiliar. Nonetheless, he never refused to come with me to the pearl fisher's house. He just had to go home first to shower away the smell, even though he had showered once at the factory.

We sat in the blazing hot sun against the wall of the house, dozing off and listening to music. When our skin started to blister, we undressed and went out into the water. I don't remember if summer was ahead of us or behind us, as we were in an everlasting season of warmth and an intermingling of identical days. I just remember how Lukas lifted me up in the water and hurled me like a grenade that exploded on contact with the quicksilver surface. I quickly swam back to land, though I knew that as soon as I came within reach he would catch me again, throw me far out once more, fling me into my place, make me feel how light I was compared with him.

I wriggled away, dived down and grabbed hold of his slippery penis, and pulled as hard as I could. That was the only weapon

I had. Under the water his yell sounded like a muffled gurgling. I could feel him catch me and hold me down under the surface, so that I would panic and let go. I did in the end, but as soon as I felt his grip on my head loosen I swam between his legs, where he was standing with his feet apart in the water to keep his balance. I shot up behind him, twisted as I passed from water to air, threw myself onto his back, and then we whirled around again under the surface. His lungs could hold twice as much air as mine, so I was always the one who had to give in and go up for oxygen first. We kept on like this until we were blue with cold.

It was an entirely normal evening, but in the dusty greenery by the lake disaster lay in wait. I didn't notice my father's brother until it was too late, when he had already seen everything he believed he had seen. I had no time to warn Lukas. Rikard was quick. After a couple of strides out into the water, he tore me out of Lukas's arms and pushed me up onto land, ordering me to get dressed. Without waiting for explanation, he hit Lukas. Hadn't reckoned that he would stay on his feet, that he would have to hit him again. And that Lukas would remain standing. As if the blow were simply an unusually strong gust of wind between the trees. Rikard probably hadn't had a chance to think anything at all. He'd stop thinking the second he lost his temper, and because he lost the power of speech too, he gave the impression that he was stupid.

Certain things about Lukas were difficult to get used to—how swiftly he switched between bravado and subservience, a dangerous mix of extremes. An unpredictability that would have seemed alarming if I hadn't grown up with it. But he was like an untrustworthy dog you had known since he was a puppy, and it didn't frighten me, which was not the same thing as my relying on him.

He didn't dare hit back, but at least he should have defended himself instead of just standing there, uncomfortably resistant to the impact. I screamed at Rikard until my voice shattered his concentration. Only then did the nightmare end and Lukas staggered backward and sat down on the grass, his face covered in blood. I flew at Rikard, but bounced away like an insect, flew at him again, bounced away. Bent over Lukas at a menacing angle, Rikard hissed:

"This is just a little warning. Next time I won't be as careful. I don't know . . . how old you are . . . but my niece here is *eleven*."

When Rikard marched off with me I could see over his shoulder that Lukas was trying to stand up but fell down in the grass again. It had never taken much to make him throw up, and now the concussion produced a cascade over the grass. At that moment he didn't seem to care where I'd gone. Behind me I heard a long string of words in Gábriel's language. It happened sometimes, words Lukas didn't even know the meaning of, tirades he had grown up with.

You feel no pain, Mama used to say. It wasn't true. Seeing Lukas there was unspeakably painful. Rikard carried me to make sure that he got me home, and the whole way he blamed Papa for everything: since David went this and since David went that . . . I had become unmanageable, they couldn't let me out of their sight for a second . . . Papa could be held responsible for all the things that had gone wrong since he disappeared.

We were hardly through the door before Rikard reported Lukas and me to the security police in the house. It always happened this way at home—no private life, no integrity or honor.

"I understand why Papa ran off," I stood in the corner of the kitchen and howled, "and I intend to report you for assault, Rikard, just so you know!" No one took any notice of me. Rikard and Mama wound each other up; they were the most indignant people in the kitchen, on a sliding scale down to Papa's father, who was sitting at his place by the table looking moderately shaken.

"Lukas isn't a child anymore, he's an adult now," Mama said, in a voice that indicated that this was bad news, and a glance at Grand-father that meant he needed to do something about it.

"You're not going to report anything," was all Grandfather said to me gently. "If anybody needs to be concerned, it's that lad and his family."

"He has no family," I spat out. "No one, no one!"

Rikard stopped me when I tried to slip out of the kitchen. "Yes, but he has a father, and that's the person we're going to speak to."

"You said yourselves that he's an adult, so don't talk to his fa-ther . . . he beats him all the time."

Mama stopped, midstep. "You've never said that before." As if she didn't believe me. As if it were just a means of diverting atten-tion away from Lukas's crime.

"Well, that is *not* what all this is about right now," Rikard ob-jected, his voice cold.

When Mama went off to speak to Gábriel, to get him to under-stand that the family's patience with his son had run out, Grandfa-ther accompanied her. Not because she asked him to, but perhaps to offer some protection—to her or to Lukas's father wasn't clear.

It didn't reflect on me. I was just a child, they said. A name and a reputation—if nothing else, at least we have that. That applied to Lukas and his father too, and they ought to bear it in mind. That was Papa's mother's opinion.

That night I sneaked out after they had all gone to sleep, down to Lukas's house. He was sleeping in the room behind the kitchen, woke up and let me in through the window. When he switched on the light I got a shock. Which of the injuries were caused by Ri-kard's outburst by the lake and which were caused by Gábriel, I didn't know, but the sight of him . . .

"What does he think I've done with you? That Rikard," Lukas mumbled. "I've never . . . I've just . . ." I laid my hand on his split lips, frightened that Gábriel would wake up. Explained that Rikard believed that he had to play the part of my papa now, and obviously thought that this was the sort of thing fathers did.

"It's not your fault," Lukas said, but what he was thinking in reality I don't know. His dark eyes were ashen. "Has he hit you too?" I shook my head, no, no, Rikard would never do that, he just told me off, made threats, imposed restrictions, involved the whole family, raised hell, and said that if Lukas and I ever . . .

I had collected some toads after the rain. Heavy and still from the warmth of the night, they had been lying on the gravel track between our houses and let me pick them up. When I was banned from going out they starved to death in the buckets in the pearl fisher's house. A peaceful death, Lukas consoled me, but they didn't look peaceful where they'd been trying to escape by scrambling over one another and died in a sinking tower of toad flesh. In the place where he buried them the grass stopped growing.

We continued to meet, but took more safety measures. As if nothing had happened and as if no harm could come to us again. But it had, of course, and it could happen again. Something had changed, and I didn't want to see him through the same eyes my family had, but it was hard to stop myself.

"Sex is the only thing grown-ups think about," I said, testing.

Lukas tensed.

"They can't stop us from seeing each other," I added.

"I think they can."

"No."

He looked doubtful. "Anyway, we have to make them think that they can," he said.

ILLUSION

If only I'd just had an inkling of what would happen, a hint of a threat brewing, a shift on the horizon, something. Not this: cloudless sky and then lightning that suddenly struck and without a sound set fire to everything. Papa had been standing in the yard one morning in late winter, his bags packed, his brother Jon behind the wheel of the Volvo to drive him somewhere. Where? The world's end? Mama's mother was crying, at any rate. Not Papa's mother, she wasn't the crying type, nor Mama; she just stood by the open front door with a face I didn't recognize. Rikard, newly awakened, came down from upstairs, Papa's father was nowhere to be seen—at least afterward I couldn't remember him. The rest of the family was scattered here and there in the yard, as if something had flung them apart, a shock wave or simply a feeling of bewilderment. The consternation was still palpable. I was sitting on Papa's hip, clinging on with all my strength as his hands were full.

"Where are you going? When are you coming home? I want to come too." Not that I wanted to. I had never traveled anywhere and would rather stay at home. But he looked lonely. No one in the family had gone away alone before. That was not the way we did things.

Around Mama was an impenetrable air of "leave me alone." The others in the family took turns keeping me occupied so that I would leave her be. No one explained what had happened or why.

If only I could remember a single time that Mama and Papa had argued. Had I forgotten? Or had they lived a secret life that I had not even seen? It's true that they didn't sleep together, but it had been like that for as long as I could remember. Papa slept in the narrow passage above the stairs, Mama in the north room with his sister Marina.

That very night previous, I had been woken by something, a noise or a dream, sneaked out of bed, discovered that Mama was not in fact lying in the double bed back to back with Marina as usual. In my drowsy state I thought that maybe she had gone to sleep with Papa after all. I crept in next to Marina feeling muddled but contented, and fell asleep as soon as I felt her warm back against mine. In the morning I awoke to full-blown disaster.

After Papa disappeared, Mama didn't want to keep any happy pictures of him. She took them out of the albums. I rescued them from the trash can and hid them among the other forbidden things in the dust under her wardrobe. She never gave away their secret, not even in revenge for Papa leaving. No revelation, apart from what I heard her say to his father—to destroy a man is not difficult, the difficult thing is to get along with him. The words etched themselves as a permanent enigma.

A cloud perhaps, if I thought hard about it. They were chopping wood in a race against each other once. An unreal atmosphere in the yard with their rhythmic breathing, more and more vehement. Mama won by a mile. Papa's talent wasn't for chopping firewood. I don't know what it was, but not chopping wood, at any rate. He was weak, his father maintained, and I thought that perhaps that was why he could walk on water, or at least on ice, something no one else in our family could do . . . because he weighed nothing. But he wasn't weak. Though I didn't tell Grandfather this, once a long time ago I saw him hit Mama in the scullery. It was only the one time, and she hit back, and by dinnertime they were pretending nothing had happened. And perhaps Grandfather was right in one way. Perhaps it was just because he was weak that he lashed out.

"Don't think about him," Rikard said when he came with me down to the lake to bathe, "and if you don't think about him, he might come back." Rikard's back was warm from the sun when I laid my wet stomach against him and said, "Can't you marry Mama . . . ?" Papa had been away for several weeks by that point and I'd realized he wasn't going to return. Rikard stiffened and then he began to laugh.

"You mean one of those brother-in-law marriages? So that the property won't leave the family?" He rolled me off into the grass. I didn't know what "brother-in-law marriage" or "property" meant. But I assumed that I was "property"—and I most definitely did not want to leave the family. "If your mother had wanted me I would have married her long ago. Well, supposing I didn't regard her as my big sister, that is. David should have done the same, for that matter. Not messed it up like this." My mouth tasted of water lily. I wrapped myself up in the towel, shivering, and waited for him to continue. Because it felt as though he ought to say something more, something about . . . supposing my parents had not messed it up, I wouldn't have existed. But he said nothing.

When Rikard lifted me up I was weightless. He walked out into the water and flung me out over the surface, light as a fishing net, just the way he knew I loved. How could he leave her, I thought as I sank to the bottom, how could he? For that was what he'd done, though no one said so, wounds just left to heal themselves. Conflicts were settled between those affected; you left other people's lives in peace. That was how we did things more often than not.

I let myself sink so that I could be rescued, but Rikard would have to hurry now. What was he doing? The cold water from the bottom of the lake shimmered toward me as I sank deeper and deeper. He didn't come to save me, not this time. I had to fight my way up with sludge water in my mouth, blue-lipped. He was sitting in a patch of sun on the grass looking at me.

"When do you intend to learn to swim, Lo?" I could swim, only I dared not show I could as it was Lukas who had taught me. "When are you going to grow up?" I realized that it was time. I was nearly nine and to all intents and purposes fatherless now. No one was going to rescue me.

Mealtimes were a wordless torture. May I have the butter; pass the salt. Mama didn't even say that. Quietest of all. Go out and play, I saw in her eyes as soon as I happened to fall within her field of vision.

I tried to wear down their patience with questions, but it led no-where. Papa's father had the shortest temper in the family, so I started to work on him carefully. At first he paid no attention to my nagging, then he got annoyed. Finally he gave in. Late one evening he came into my room and gave me a picture of an oil rig, high as a skyscraper out in the middle of a blue-black sea with no land in sight. This was where my papa was, on this great steel monster that was drilling oil from the seabed far out in the North Sea.

"Stop going on about it now," Grandfather demanded in return. As if Papa's reappearance were a kitten I was never going to get. I cried myself to sleep that night. Not because he was there—I knew he wasn't, knew he had such bad vertigo that he couldn't even go up into the attic with both Mama and Grandfather holding the steps. I cried because they had lied to me. One lie turns everything into a lie.

The picture of the oil rig where Grandfather alleged Papa was working hung like a fixture over my bed, even though I was sure he was not there. It's true he could walk on water, but only when it was frozen, and I found it impossible to imagine my father in the dark with his vertigo drilling oil from the bottom of the sea with storms and albatrosses howling around his ears. Alone among men, according to Grandfather. It was only men who worked out there, real men.

I thought that it might have something to do with her—the one who disappeared under the ice—but it was so long ago now and I wasn't sure what the connection could be. The picture nailed to the wall as a reminder. That adults are not to be trusted. In my dreams the steel monstrosity moved like a giant spider through a desolate sea in a heavy storm. In contrast to me, Lukas was impressed. He didn't really care that it was a lie. A lie was at least an answer, but he didn't even have a lie as explanation for what had happened to his mother.

After Papa went off I began to see adults as merely shadows who carried their secrets and lies and lunchboxes and their tension head-aches, their hideous hairstyles and tennis elbows, through a town that didn't even have a tennis court. The elbows they had acquired at the factory. The hairstyles at the Greek's. They carried them be-tween work and the shop, home and the public baths and the lake. Carried their plastic bags and secrets, their tiredness, their hopes, their exaggerated optimism for the future and private despair, and everything in terry toweling, gabardine, denim, corduroy, and rib knits, and the jerry cans, shotguns, snow cannons, bicycle chains, cod for the soup, gossip, holiday plans. Much of it came to nothing. Some things succeeded, but most did not. The adults carried every-thing around apart from their children, for there was a do-not-indulge mentality that they all made their common cause. All except those who carried me. Long after I could walk they took turns carrying me, competed for it. I was big when I discovered by mistake that I could in fact walk by myself. They would rather I had never discovered it, that I had never noticed the smell of those secrets.

Don't indulge. Don't disgrace yourself. It was the unspoken rule that applied to all other children, it was part of the community, but we didn't belong to it, so we could just as well behave as we liked.

VERTIGO

It was Papa's father who'd given him permission to go out. He who said that the ice was safe. Perfect ice to hammer a hole for burbot fishing. It had been an ordinary day at the beginning of winter. Mama's sister, who was only eight, had gone with him, the thirteen-year-old. He couldn't save her. The red jacket had slipped from her, just as a petal drops from a rose, without a sound. The red material floated in the hole in the ice long after she had been sucked under and disappeared into the center of the lake.

The ice hole where she drowned recurred constantly in Papa's dreams. The silence. He dreamed of silence—that the disaster was so silent and quick and calm was the most frightening thing of all. It was too late to do anything. To make a sound or even try to save her. He just stood there in the middle of the lake, alone.

There then followed a winter that would never end. They knew that she was there somewhere beneath the ice, her body drifting along the bottom, or perhaps it had stuck fast in the ice during the coldest nights. Only when the ice thawed, which happened unusually late that spring, did they find her. Preserved by the cold, naked except for her baptism cross. Identification was a formality but a nightmare nevertheless. Papa's parents went in place of Mama's, and Papa went too because his father thought he should. He stood a little apart and was upset that they showed her naked in the cold light of the room at the mortuary. To see her again . . . after all those months. Dead, answered Papa when I hesitantly asked what she looked like. And yet not dead. He was quite sure that he saw a movement in her pale eyelashes, but perhaps it was just something thawing—not enough to bring her back to life, but enough to cause a movement. It was his fault. No one needed to say it.

I was afraid of the wind openings—large open holes where the wind kept the water open, invisible to the eye, the most sinister traps in the ice. Sinkholes, gas holes, erosion holes. Warm currents that made the ice so fragile that it wouldn't even bear the weight of a tiny lynx out hunting. In late winter the sun could be so high that it penetrated the ice and melted the frozen water from below. The ice was a dangerous world that you needed to understand. As a child Papa had been forced to learn to read it—risks, bearing capacity, signs—but there were never any guarantees. Once-only ice could only stand one person walking over it—the next person tumbled through. That was how Mama's youngest sister had drowned. Papa had turned around and watched it happen without being able to do anything. The ice that a moment ago had supported him didn't support her, even though she was much lighter.

I followed close behind Papa's back. The mist drifted over the frozen water. We were father and daughter out hunting, right out toward the sun. Every so often I stopped behind him, took aim, and shot. When we heard the ice lowing we were well out on the lake. Appalled, I saw the fracture open up between his legs and mine, convinced that it would widen, separate us, swallow us up. But a glance at Papa's face told me that the ice would hold. The shots that went off beneath us just meant that the day was exceptionally cold and the ice thicker than usual and it was cracking because of temperature stresses. The warning noise of the thaw was quite different; you had to learn to hear the distinction.

There seemed to have been something special about Mama's sister even before she drowned, perhaps just that she was the youngest.

"As small as you, Lo, and yet she still fell through the ice I'd walked on a moment earlier. If she'd gone first she'd have been fine and I'd have drowned," Papa said as we were standing right out in the deepest part. Once-only ice, nightmare ice. To be the death of someone else in that way, to want to protect but instead to weaken the ice so that it broke the minute the next person put her foot on it.

Salt ice, sweet ice, blue ice, glass ice, wreck ice, floe ice, diabase ice. Ice that looked like frozen carbon dioxide. Walking along I almost dozed off to his soothing voice, as he explained to me how the water was arranged in different layers, coldest uppermost in winter, warmest uppermost in summer. Papa knew just as much about the ice as Mama knew about the art of handling an ax. The drowning accident didn't make him afraid of ice. It was the depth that frightened him, the vertigo, the feeling of great height, a fear of falling that could strike at any time. But he still went out onto the ice as soon as it froze, set pike traps though there were hardly any fish here. He never asked me to come with him. Nor did he stop me when I put on my ski boots and followed.

It was mostly for the stories that I went with him. The stories belonged to the ice. About the dogs that were let loose during the polar bear hunt, still leashed together in pairs, and two by two they surrounded the quarry, which instinctively reared up in defense. Upright on its back legs the bear became an easy target for the hunters. When Papa described this to me I thought of his father, who in an upright position was as large as the animal from which he took his name. He and Papa didn't see eye to eye. It was something you just knew—that they were like dog and bear together.

"Were you really all born out of the ice?" I had gone around shaping this question until it had gotten soft and sweaty—that was the picture I had before me when Papa's mother said that she and

Mama's mother gave birth to one child every winter. I imagined that they went out and pulled them up from a hole in the ice. But all at once Papa's desire to tell me things vanished into thin air.

"When we get home, tell your mother to explain how children are made. She can give you all the details."

And she did. About the bakehouse that was next door to the house they lived in, and in the bakehouse there was a warm wall, and by the warm wall they had made a bunk bed, and to this bunk bed you could go if you wanted some time to yourself. This is where they had been made, one after the other. In the heat lost from the oven that was often newly lit, in the familiar smell of birchwood and barley flour. If you took a tub of butter with you, you could eat some of the leftover bits of bread if you were hungry afterward. And you were.

What about me, though? Where was I made? By the warm wall as well? Mama looked at me as she sat on the chopping block with the ax and the sharpener and answered that no, the bakehouse belonged to a different time and a different place.

The story of the day I was born had been related to me many times, but never how I was in fact made. Why them? The most ill-matched pair. Papa was a perfectly normal father, but Mama . . .

"Not by the warm wall, Lo. You were made under the sloping ceiling."

Under the sloping ceiling? Was that the only answer she could think of? That explained nothing. There wasn't even a sloping ceiling in our house.

Certain memories are so clear that everything surrounding them seems blurred. It was late one evening several months after Papa had gone, with the hollow sound of the bittern's cry from down at the lake, a sound like blowing into an empty bottle. An invisible and sinister bird, I had only glimpsed it once, how it flew, heavy at the front, like a bird of prey over the quicksilver water.

I turned on the television to block out the eerie noise. Lying in Rikard's room on a bean bag on the floor and bored. The news. Blah, blah, blah. Lay so that I could watch the screen upside down to make it less boring.

Reporter struggling against the wind, raging storm with gusts of hurricane strength, camera lens so spotted with rain it was almost impossible to see anything, but I saw anyway . . . there in the background . . . I stared, lying upside down until all the blood collected in my head and burst. The ominous words *Alexander Kielland* suspended over everything, the whole disaster. The sea in complete tumult, huge waves. The legs had broken, the platform capsized, tipped over, turned upside down. And sank.

Everything had happened very fast. Most of the crew had fallen in and those who didn't fall threw themselves into the ice-cold sea. Why? Because everyone else did? Because there was a risk that the oil would begin to burn? But was the water not also full of leaking oil? Were they not going to drown in the thick black sticky soup like helpless seabirds? Without survival gear they wouldn't last many minutes in the cold, the reporter said, and anyway, what would that matter? When the sea began to burn. A burning sea. I crept nearer to the screen, tried to imagine a burning sea.

They didn't yet know how many had been killed. Their relatives would be informed before the names of the dead were released. I flung myself forward and switched off in the middle of the broadcast, strained to hear if there was a noise from downstairs, but the television was not on down there. There was only me who had heard what had happened. The appalling event. The oil rig disaster. Horrific words. And all of a sudden I was no longer in any doubt that Papa was there. I knew he was. If anyone was to have bad luck it was him. I ran. Down into the kitchen where Papa's mother and Mama were standing by the sink, scaling herrings. Buried my face in Grandmother's fishy apron, refused to tell them what had happened.

The next few days I wandered around in a shocked trance, a bittern in my head, its boom foreboding and echoing, day and night. No one said anything. As if the accident hadn't happened. As if none of them had heard about it, or they tried to keep me in the dark—how could they act so well? Eat and sleep and work as usual. Laugh as usual.

"If he was one of the ones who drowned, they would've told you," Lukas assured me. If he had been one of the few who survived, they would also have told me. Silence could only mean the worst.

Days of disquieting normalcy ensued. The kitchen in cold sunlight, Mama chopping wood, Rikard and Katja stacking the wood, Erik and Marina washing the cars, Helena lying on the television sofa with her boyfriend, Jon arguing with his girlfriend on the phone, boyfriends and girlfriends coming and going—they never lasted long in this house. And there was Papa's mother putting the dishes in to soak, while his father had retired to the arboretum. Mama's mother was wiping down all the surfaces, touching things with light hands. In the evenings I crept down between Mama and Marina again, as I had when I was small, lay there with eyes wide open, while they appeared to sleep, a sleep as peaceful and deep as ever.

"Girl, you're going around and around like a dog about to have puppies. What is it?" Mama murmured in the darkness. I tried to say something about Papa, but I couldn't get the words out. "Think about something nice. Your birthday. Think about what you'd like. Shall we ask David to come?"

I twisted my head into the pillow. "Stop it! I know he's dead!"

Mama sat straight up in bed. "Pull yourself together. That wasn't funny."

I buried my face deeper into the foam-rubber pillow. "Ask Grandfather!" I howled.

She grabbed me firmly by the hand and dragged me along the hallway in the cold of the night, down the black staircase to Papa's parents' room. Went in and fetched out a sleepy Grandfather for interrogation in the kitchen.

"Are you out of your mind? Have you told her that her father's dead? Have you no heart, no shame, are you mad?" she screamed at him. Grandfather looked as though he thought he was still dreaming, pressed up against the sink by the sheer force of Mama's voice. I slipped away to get the picture of the oil rig, the one that was no longer standing out there at sea but lying on the bottom, collapsed like a house of cards with 123 dead men. That was the final death toll Lukas had heard on the television and passed on to me. More had died than had survived, and Papa was like Lukas: if anyone was unlucky, it was him.

Before I entered the kitchen I heard Grandfather's voice. "What the hell should I have said, then? The child was asking and asking. Should I have told her that her father lives so close and still never comes to visit her because of—" Because of us, I thought he said, but just then he caught sight of me and swallowed the last bit.

The smell of his night sweat, salty like nettles. He lay on his back with his arms under his head, opened his eyes right next to my face. He had just fallen asleep, but not so deeply that he didn't hear my question. His eyes very dark blue with a circle of rust around the pupils.

"Do you love Mama?"

He looked at me, as if my words reached him very slowly.

"I have never loved anyone else."

It wasn't an answer to my question. It didn't reveal whether he still loved her. Not even if he had ever loved her.

Just a few weeks later he packed his bags and left, and I was overwhelmed with the sense that I shouldn't have asked.

"Do you love Papa?" Mama was filling the laundry room with white sheets and underclothes. She answered as naturally as if I had asked if the night was dark and the mountain of washing endless. But she never showed it. I tried to remember if I had ever seen her put her arms around him, or he her. I couldn't recall a single instance.

I'd been born into the best of worlds, but I no longer lived there. When I was growing up the picture was complete, everyone was there and no one was going to disappear. Dangers were only things adults spoke about when they thought I had fallen asleep on the television sofa. Oil crisis and Falklands War and embassy bombings, inadequate safety at the factory, the risk of rain during the holiday.

Papa was the first. When he disappeared the balance was disturbed, and then things settled down and we thought that nothing else would happen. Mama's and Papa's brothers and sisters had all the patience Mama was lacking, shared the burden of me between themselves. I had taken for granted that they existed just for me, felt hurt if I could not join in, if a door was closed, took it as a personal insult that they had to go to work sometimes, without me. To belong to everyone is to belong to no one. It was only after the family started to scatter in the wind that I belonged to Mama.

The chain reaction had started, it was work and love and homesickness and a fish-gutting factory in Iceland that lured. Quick money—you could earn gold at the conveyor belt, if you could just stand the cold and smell and didn't need any sleep and could live on a shoestring for a while. The house became more and more empty. The fish-gutting factory, homesickness, and finally death. Mama's father died of chemical pneumonia. He had inhaled a corrosive substance at the factory and his lungs began to burn. He left his shift at the paper mill an hour early on the Friday afternoon and by Monday he was dead.

His boots stood in the hall the whole winter, waiting for his broad feet, were shoved back and forth among the others. Who was going to take them away? There were many of us who could have done it—but no one who wanted to. I took care of the broken pieces that Grandmother produced in a steady stream in the kitchen when things inexplicably slipped out of her hands. Grandfather's coffee cup, schnapps glass, soured-milk bowl—buried at the edge of the field behind the house, they came up every year when they were plowing, like a memorial.

Mama's mother died among the currant bushes. She'd half filled her plastic tub when her heart gave a double beat in a warning that was altogether too late, and stopped. She'd been a little confused for a long time, and since Grandfather's death she had been comfort-eating to the extent that her wedding ring disappeared into white flesh, in the end her body so unwieldy that she could no longer climb the stairs in the house. Why she needed to be out in the currant patch on the hottest day of summer with her weak heart, no one could understand. Least of all her doctor. Her death could have been avoided, he said.

But it cannot be.

The currants flew through the air like a bloodstain onto the layer of manure she'd just put under the bushes that morning. Grandmother in her frumpy white dress smeared with berries and blood and earth.

She had told Papa's mother that she wanted to be buried at home, and this wasn't home. It cost a fortune to get her there, so much more than if she had been alive. Papa's parents' last savings.

"A little while ago I was young, wasn't I?" Mama's face in the bedroom mirror was changed. It was still her face, but it was as if an older face had been pulled over it. I wanted her to take off the pale, lifeless mask that was not her. Grandmother stroked her hair, but didn't contradict her—she *did* look old, overnight. I didn't realize that such a thing could truly happen. When Grandmother didn't reply, Mama turned to me instead, as if I would be able to explain what had happened—where the stranger's face in the mirror came from.

Losing both her parents had happened so fast. As long as one of your parents is still alive your childhood carries on, I heard Grandmother say. When you're no longer anyone's child—that is when you realize what you've lost.

Then Grandmother herself became ill, almost without our noticing. Unlike Mama's parents, she died slowly. No visible decline. It was more as if she was dying from the inside out, her vital organs succumbing one after the other. In the end there was nothing left of her, the cancer had eaten everything, though she looked normal from the outside. The doctor had gauged how much time she had, and it turned out to be correct to within a few days.

When Rikard, the last of the brothers and sisters, moved to a hotel job in Stockholm that Marina had fixed up for him, it was almost worse than when Papa left. Now there was just Papa's father, Mama, and me. Rumors started to circulate in the village, but Mama had forbidden me to listen to them. It was something about Mama and Grandfather, a little domestic war going on, the causes of which only they knew. Love, hate, either-or, or both-and—just like turning on old taps and the water coming out ice cold and scalding hot by turns.

"I ought to move out for Lo's sake," I heard Grandfather say from inside the woodshed.

"If you move, then I'll move."

"But that solves nothing, Karenina."

"Don't call me Karenina!" I couldn't catch any more through the thick partition wall before Mama strode away. Soon noises could be heard from the arboretum, Grandfather's black poplar, how she axed it down in a frenzied rage, with the strength and fury of a pig. Smashed it to smithereens, which she crammed into the stove that evening, piece by piece. A few days later she bought electric heaters for all the rooms, despite Grandfather's protests. One thing was certain: she had felt cold for the last time. This is still my house, I'm not dead yet, warned Grandfather. Mama turned in the cold light of late winter and stared at him. There are some people who must not die. He was one of them.

"Dead?" she said, unable to grasp this, as if it had never even crossed her mind that he also . . .

"No, not *yet*," Grandfather said. "It is still me who makes the decisions around here." It never had been him, of course—but it's true that it was still his house, and when that was no longer the case, then I would inherit, he said, something he had suddenly just decided. "You brothers and sisters can hardly divide it into nine parts, Katarina. There'd only be a window each."

There was a time when we didn't know how there would be enough room for all the beds, crisscrossed throughout the house, but now the problem was filling the rooms, stopping the echoes. And then Grandfather started to talk about leaving as well, and that I had to stay behind so that Mama wouldn't be totally alone.

"Your grandfather," Mama said coldly, "talks so much. Haven't you noticed? He claims that he's going to die too." The word "die" flew from her mouth with the speed of spit. Grandfather wasn't even ill yet, but all the others had gone, so how could we be sure that he would stay?

However much I missed the rest of the family, what I missed most was Mama the way she was before the others disappeared. Now she, Grandfather, and I were the only ones left. I would soon be fifteen and no one could be bothered any longer about what I did.

ADOLESCENCE

Childhood trickled away and was gone, leaving only a few sun-bleached fragments of regret. Suddenly I was at an age when I read *Bonjour Tristesse,* read whatever I happened to find in Mama's bookcase. She must have lost her faith in books at some point in her youth, because all she had in her bookcase were from that time. In the absence of any revealing diaries that I could read surreptitiously, the novels were the only way I could sneak a look into that period of her life. A glimpse of the outlook she must have had then. There was the scent of pine trees, American suburbs, and deserted French cafés when I opened them and let myself be transported away. Lukas was jealous. Books made me unreachable even when I was lying right next to him in bed. He watched me disappear, but didn't understand where—still less why. Novels? There was nothing wrong with this world, where *he* existed, where *he* was waiting. He waited for me to finish, whether I wanted him to or not, lit a new cigarette whenever I turned a page, blew the smoke out over the book, looked at me.

I read everything I could lay my hands on. Books made time stand still, while the world was expanding. Everything is beautiful from a distance, like the river delta seen from above, free from the stench of rotting sediment and silt. Made clear and enticing like illustrated maps of inaccessible places no man can live on.

I read about the Chinese method of describing the passage of time, with what logical beauty it elapsed in their eyes. Instead of four clumsily measured seasons they talked about the slight cold, great cold, beginning of spring, rainwater, waking of insects, pure brightness, grain rain, beginning of summer, grain fills, grain in ear. Then the summer solstice that led to the slight heat, great heat, beginning of autumn, limit of heat, white dew. And then the autumnal equinox followed by cold dew, the first frosty night when the migrant birds leave Peking and the chrysanthemums are at their most beautiful. And then the descent of frost, beginning of winter, slight snow, great snow, until light's turning point is reached again.

September arrived with its long shadows, migrant birds, autumn moon. Virgo's month, my month, virgin, sapphire. We had never been so close together before as we would be when I turned fifteen. When I was a child he was a teenager, and when I was a teenager he was an adult. Soon for the first time we would both be on the same side of the crucial line. It would no longer be a case of exploitation of a child, Lukas said as we went down for what was to be the last dip in the lake that year—if something happened. "Happened?" Between us, he said.

There was something in the air, I had felt it for a long time, perhaps just a faint tension, a hint of unrest and change when one season crosses over into the next. Lukas had commented on my fifteenth birthday many times, that it was a dividing line, but between what? I had already been a teenager for two years.

"But at fifteen, Lo, no one's really a child any longer." The imaginary threshold between the possible and the impossible, as if the borderline itself would make something possible that had not been possible before. He seemed to be imagining this. He had built up a sense of anticipation that made me also believe that in a purely physical way I would feel I had passed a certain point.

It was as if a sun had been scorching him from the inside the whole summer, plaguing him, parched and surly. To live is to wait. At least for Lukas, waiting for the snake to show its real face. It was the year of the snake the year I turned fifteen, which according to the Chinese calendar in Mama's bookcase meant duplicity and betrayal: sign no contracts, don't change the bedclothes, take care with fire, don't participate in legal proceedings, don't sell your soul to the devil, avoid open water and washing your hair, eat no peaches, only pay debts if absolutely necessary, avoid distress and family gatherings, inauspicious time to make new friendships, refrain from disruptive disputes and long journeys.

As the day approached it appeared that Lukas had forgotten all about it. No special plans and no questions about how I wanted to celebrate, even though I was always full of ideas.

"You know what day it is tomorrow, don't you?" I couldn't stop myself saying in the end.

"The Japanese national day, or no, wait a minute . . . maybe it's the world day for protection of the ozone layer—goodness knows how you're supposed to celebrate that."

"I know you know . . . you're going to give me a surprise."

"Hardly. I've got an extra shift at work to do." He shrugged. We'd grown too big for having fun. Couldn't play games for evermore.

He had begun to work the night shift so that he had the house to himself while his father was at work. Lukas clocked off, rode home and slept for a few hours, and got up when Gábriel went off for his afternoon shift, the same time as I came home from school. The house was then ours until late in the evening, unless we went down to the pearl fisher's place. I did my homework at Lukas's, if I did it at all, while he sat and rocked on a chair, waiting. No matter how speedily I raced through it, he thought it took too long. That I went to school too often, read too much—not useful at my age, my brain wasn't fully developed. It was to be hoped that his brain wasn't either, I said, and how helpful was it to work every night in the chemical fumes of the factory?

I had no idea what I wanted to do with my life, only that factories didn't figure in my plans, and that being the case, school couldn't be given up altogether.

"What do you mean, not in the factories? You're not going to move?" Lukas looked utterly nonplussed. As if that thought had never crossed his mind.

I wait behind the gas station as he asked me to do when he phoned the evening before. After the night shift he comes past in the car I didn't know he'd bought, a blue Ford Taunus, far from new but not particularly rusty either. He can't hide his pride when he swings the car in and opens the passenger door and invites me to climb in with just a nod. Gábriel has neither a car nor a driver's license: this is Lukas's own thing, and he has worked a long time to be able to afford the driving lessons, keeping it a secret the whole time.

I have packed some essentials in an old military backpack, not sure what to expect. Left a note for Mama on the kitchen table: *Celebrating the day with Lukas. Don't worry.* Regret the last sentence, but it's too late now.

It is oppressive and tense in the car. Lukas has an air of determination rather than expectation. So clean-shaven, as though the hair on his face hasn't started to grow yet. A white nylon shirt in honor of the day. I recognize it, it is Gábriel's. My neck is itching with sweat, but Lukas himself looks completely cool, or rather cold. Coldness as another way of saying I'm on fire? The gift lies unopened on the dashboard, a minimal package with a curly ribbon that has loosened in the heat. He has forgotten to say happy birthday. It can only be a piece of jewelry, and to receive a piece of jewelry from Lukas seems quite remarkable. I am happy as long as he doesn't give it to me, just leaves it there.

"Where are we going?" I ask.

"Where have you always wanted to go?"

"The Atlantic?"

He must know that.

"Don't spoil it all now!" he answers, irritated. I should have guessed . . . He asked me to pack for one night, not for a week.

"Tivoli?" I say hurriedly. Now he doesn't reply, just speeds up along the highway, looking purposeful.

As soon as I climb out of the car I hear music from Tivoli in the distance, shrieks of panic and euphoria, the music of a barrel organ, speeded up. How long has he been planning this? Saving up to take the car over on the ferry and down the coast road to Copenhagen, paying for the entrance, the restaurant, and then the hotel. Neither of us has been so far away before, especially not him. Courage and money, where did he get them? He brings bill after bill out of his jeans pocket until I dare not point at anything I like, frightened of ruining him.

The only thing in the city we see is Tivoli, but that in itself is almost too much. I love it. Lukas resigns himself to it. Soon has had as much as he can stomach and is content to stand below and watch. The throng of people and level of noise seem to paralyze him.

I ride alone in and out of the demon's mouth, spinning backward in a terrifying whirligig, a whirlwind at a manic pace. The centrifugal force, the speed of the funfair, the cotton-candy kick: I feel as though I am an electrified giant baby with no control over up and down. It doesn't matter, no one knows me here. I let go and let my skirt fly, my laughter, my hair, faster, higher, more, climbing, hanging, shrieking. Then to be sucked backward out of myself, catapulted away from Lukas, to open my eyes and see him disappear.

I must have been born for this, to travel at speed and be flung out into a bigger place. Spin around among the deadly sins, ava-rice-arro-gance-lust-ful-ness. How am I ever going to be able to go back down to earth . . . be satisfied with firm ground under my feet again?

At long last I have to be. The lights of the amusement park are turned off and it is emptied, and we are tossed out into the world beyond, which I have forgotten exists.

Lukas looks resolute as we find our way to the hotel after midnight, until eventually we're sitting on the double bed after what seemed like an eternity of checking-in procedures and suspicious looks from the staff in the lobby.

"Like, what did they think?" I ask and drop, exhausted, full-length onto the bed. Lukas is silent for some time. Then:

"Shall we dance?"

He finds music on the all-night radio, produces two beers from the little cocktail cabinet and plastic glasses that he fills to the brim. Normally he drinks from the bottle, but this is not a normal occasion; he seems to have thought of everything. The beer looks as though it is made for children, with elephants on the label. I am cross-eyed with tiredness, and he must be even more exhausted because he didn't have time to sleep after his night shift. But he looks more tense than tired as he sweeps me around in the dance. I feel the music in his hips, feel him connecting with the music in a physical way that I don't. Seems to absorb it through his body while I listen to it at most. He is good at dancing, but nevertheless it is hard to stop myself . . . I am ready to burst out laughing because he looks so serious. Particularly when the music changes tempo and expression and becomes softer. Soon I lose control, the giggle grows into a fit of laughter. Lukas doesn't laugh, continues to look very serious, and I try to stop but only manage to half suppress it. He holds me harder. The music is slow, suggestive and sensual. It feels wrong, somehow doesn't suit us. I can't relax.

I've had the best birthday of my life, but now I just want to sleep. The beer and tiredness and music and ferry that is still swaying under my feet and the spinning top that I rode on seven times seven times, my ears are ringing, the noise increases every time I take a gulp of beer.

"Don't drink any more," says Lukas. But I'm not drunk. I feel horribly sober.

I'm woken at daybreak by the pigeons making a noise in the gutter outside the window. With the sensation of Tivoli still in my body, like giddiness between a dream and a nightmare. My lips are swollen, my head heavy. The clock radio next to the hotel pillow is showing ten past six, my back is cold, Lukas is no longer lying behind me. When I lift myself onto my elbows to listen for the toilet I see that his sneakers and his hoodie are gone from beside the door. He is always tired in the mornings, and I can't for the life of me imagine what could have tempted him out so early. Possibly he hadn't fallen asleep next to me last night as I thought, but got up again and went out, and . . . what then? He would never leave me alone here.

The presents are on the bedside table, the perfume Escape and the silver heart with two hands, barbed wire, and a burning flame. I'm still full of all the strange things I stuffed myself with yesterday. My mouth tastes of last night's cotton candy. My clothes are in an untidy heap on the floor. I have no memory of undressing, but I had been so beside myself with tiredness and still am. Pull the cover over my head, try to sleep while I wait. Let the hours go by.

At some time in the middle of the day I hear ringing, far away in another world; the ringing comes nearer and nearer as I gradually surface from unconsciousness to half awake and then at last shake off my drowsiness. I grasp for the phone and pull the handset toward me so fast that it hits me on the forehead, a real crack. It is not Lukas but a stranger who asks me in English to come down to reception. A hint of irritation in the voice. I quickly drag on my shorts and T-shirt, throw together my things and grab the giant panda that is leaning against the minibar looking at me, and go down. It was checking-out time almost two hours ago, says the young woman in reception, the same one as yesterday but with a different shade of lipstick, and she looks stony when she sees me come down alone.

"Where's your brother? Has he sent you to pay?" Pay? I don't have a single penny on me. The only thing I have is a headache and a giant panda that's big enough to carry me. My head is throbbing, I'm screwing up my eyes to ease the pain, rapidly need to come up with a lie to get out of here, but I can't find one.

"He's not here, he's gone," I say truthfully.

"Your brother?"

"No, the one who booked the room—he's not my brother." She looks at me, for so long that I begin to itch all over. There's something in the way she looks at me that stings. Little friend, she says, and it's impossible to avoid her eyes.

"Sorry," I mumble, for want of anything else to say.

"No, don't say sorry. I suspected he wasn't your brother. He behaved oddly. I should have realized."

I have no time to pull my head out of the way before she takes hold of my chin and examines my face under the light.

"What's this?" My forehead. No doubt there is an obvious red mark by now. "What a swine," she exclaims. "What else has he done to you?" Now she catches sight of the split in my lip, the spinning-top split, from the first ride when I wasn't prepared for the force and the speed. Swine? Done? I have no time to reply, my

mind as blank as an icy road. "Has he brought you here from Sweden?" I nod. "How old are you?"

"Fifteen."

"No, no, no. You don't need to lie to me. How old?"

"I was fifteen yesterday."

"You don't need to lie, I said. I don't want to hurt you. I'm going
to help you. Is there someone I can call? Your parents?"

That would be the end. Mama would report Lukas to the police
for kidnapping, if she hasn't already done so. Then she herself would
be charged with retaliation. Something with the ax. I just have to
try to get away from here, and then get home under my own steam
without a cent.

Exploitation of a child—he'd said it would no longer be called that
if he and I . . . if we. But we didn't, would I not remember, however out of it I was? The labels on the beer belied its strength and
Lukas was horny, I knew he was, but that sort of thing happened, it
wasn't the first time, he just used to hide it better. *This is a man's
world,* James Brown sang on the all-night radio. How could you
stop yourself being aroused by that? I was too, but more . . . kind of
mentally. Kind of mentally . . . Lukas bit my ear.

"*Kind of mentally?* For God's sake, Lo . . ." We were dancing, the
elephants were dancing, the froth was dancing, the plastic chandelier in the ceiling was spinning. Lukas pretended I wasn't stepping
on his toes. This is a man's world—but it wouldn't be nothing,
nothing . . . without a woman or a girl . . . I remember that, then I
don't remember much more.

THE DAY'S WARNING

After the year of the snake comes the year of the rat, the monkey, the dog. Let life run between your fingers like a red thread. Movement holds the promise of arriving one day, perhaps stillness does too, like here on Mama's doorstep. Home is where nothing smells strange. Papa's father could distinguish his trees by their smell. The cypress smelled of insecticide, the acacia of boy's sweat, the sequoia of cheap Russian cigarettes after the war. The war was just a strand in time for me, however much Grandfather talked about it.

I peer in between the trees in the arboretum. Mama is not there. I have waited, searched, called out. She should have been standing here in the doorway when I arrived home, when I swung the car in and parked under the white birch—she can usually tell when I'm approaching from miles away. The sun is strong but cold. I tuck my hands under my arms, my eye drawn down to Lukas's house. It looks just the same as usual, at least from a distance. No, don't think about Lukas now. Only good thoughts.

I shut my eyes and let the men in my memory slide along like rosary beads. Hard, smooth, they resemble pearls, without blemish. "Perfect" means complete and by extension dead. Not like Lukas— nothing perfect about him. And neither before nor after Copenhagen could we talk about what happened.

I must get up before I'm fixed to the spot, my backside numb as two deep-frozen ham steaks. I walk around the house, looking at Mama's miniature world from the outside. Seeing her life like a very big girl looking into a very small doll's house and wishing there was room for me inside. But there is no longer space for me here. Some things have shrunk and others have grown. All I can do is put my hand inside and touch the little velour sofa, the minute velvet lamp, the tiny radio, the miniature fruit bowl, the fringe on the rug, the hem of her skirt, the doll's house full of objects and habits that have become her life. Long for the past. It seems so strange that the same word, "longing," can be used for both wishing yourself away and wishing yourself back home.

When I met Lukas I was still a small child in Wellington boots that were far too big, a hippie youngster without hippie parents. The feelings of the person I was when I lived here are roused as soon as I return. Not exactly unpleasant, but remarkable that this person remains inside me.

I don't like going into the house when Mama's not at home. It's her life now, not mine. But in the end I can wait no longer; I go and fetch the key from the garden shed. The sound of the wind reverberates in the long hallways even though all the windows are closed. It was never cold like this when the house was full of people. The rooms smell white. Like Mama's almond soap, a tinge of scorched milk and the faint scent of new-fallen snow, though it is not the time for snow.

The world's smallest film festival. Two women and a guide dog. The hitchhiker I picked up on the way here laughed when I said where I was going.

"So . . . you and your blind mother have a film festival together, and you two are the only audience?"

"Yes, but we don't use that word."

"Film festival?"

"Blind." We behave as if nothing has happened. She wants

everything to be as it was, the same routines, that's all she wishes for now.

I can't say no. Of course I should be able to say no, but I can't. When Mama rings to announce that another film festival is coming up, I pack my bag and set off home, wherever I happen to be.

But this time she's not here. I arrive at a dark house, all locked up. Go around looking for a message, the north room, south room, east room, west room, even the attic that she never uses. I can still smell the sickly sweet scent from before that I didn't realize back then came from the grass Rikard used to smoke up here. After Mama's little sister drowned he was the youngest in the family and every-one's eyes were upon him. When I was born he was at last free from the nagging and scolding. Perhaps that's why he loved me so unreservedly. Called me his favorite jewel. Mama called me her fa-vorite worry.

In my memory this house is still full of people. Mama can't fill all the rooms with life on her own and I can't get used to the emptiness. The sound of my own breathing rebounds from the walls like faint sighs. I stiffen when I see the dog lying on the bat chair in the upper lounge. She can't possibly know that I'm the daughter here—daughters and mothers don't share an identical smell—and yet she doesn't even open her eyes as I pass on my way to Mama's bedroom. I lie down on the bed, numb because she should have been here and isn't. Tired after the long journey, I fall asleep.

I fall asleep hungry and awaken famished. Two headlights sweep over the faded cloudberry wallpaper. I manage to reach the bottom of the stairs and see Mama close the car door, before the stranger, whose face I don't catch, rolls away in a dilapidated old white Citroën.

Mama feels her way toward the house, up the outside steps, starts when she senses someone is standing in the doorway.

"It's only me, Mama."

"Lo! You frightened me!" A kiss on the cheek. An unusual greeting for her. In the hall she stumbles on my bags, pulls a face as she picks herself up, but waves away my offer of help. "Why have you got so much stuff with you? Everything's here. Clothes as well, if you need to borrow anything."

"I have to move on soon, Mama. I told you on the phone. Can't stay long."

She isn't listening. Her thoughts are elsewhere. Goes in with her boots still on, right up to the stove she uses.

"You could have lit it, couldn't you, it's freezing in here." The temperature must mean that she has been away for quite a while. An explanation would be in order, but no . . . she seems to be preoccupied. Who was he, the man in the white car? That she, after all these lonely years of "beware of men," might have met someone is inconceivable.

Maybe I'll be forced to get used to the inconceivable. Just have to let it sink in before I can ask her about it.

"That dog you've got," I say instead. "Isn't it the idea that you should take her with you when you go out?"

"She's a guard dog," Mama says. No, she's not, actually. God knows how long the waiting list is for such a . . .

". . . specially trained guide dog for the blind, Mama." I risk saying it; she detests the word.

"I don't want her. I've asked them to come and take her away. I'm not *that* blind."

That's what she wants everyone to believe, but she can't fool me. I can tell that she doesn't see me. She always used to have a special expression when she looked at me, like watching a favorite problem, with a sort of affection, however hopeless it might be.

Tales of blindness are just romantic stories about wisdom and a noble spiritual life. In reality it is bruises and spilled milk, burned
flesh, windows not cleaned, a constant searching for missing
items, and stumbling over everyday obstacles. Seeing her walk into
chairs and doors hurts me. Especially when she doesn't complain.

When I have made an effort to prepare some food, I receive a
mild telling off for not putting everything back in the right place
afterward.

"Knives, for goodness' sake, Lo, knives—go in the side drawer."
I have the urge to go up and put my arm around her and say, what's
the matter, Mama? She doesn't normally go on like that . . . as if
she's trying to stem a much greater chaos. Knives. Spice jars. Shoes.
Death. In the side drawer, Lo, the side drawer.

"I don't understand how you can look after your own home."
She sighs and sorts through everything that has been done wrong.
But I don't, I have no home, or none that I feel at home in. It's me
and the dogs.

Dogs? Mama turns her empty gaze toward me. Yes, dogs. I can't
explain.

Immortal, despite a life of hunger, despite the dogcatchers' nets
and traps, zigzagging through the traffic. In all the unfamiliar
towns I come to, the wild dogs are the least alien. They roam
where they want, do as they wish, crap where they like, don't care
a jot about anything they dislike. A free and perilous life. If I'd
been one of them, I would have died long ago, and yet it still at-
tracts me. A dog's only task is to be a dog, sleep in the sun, be
four-legged. Just to be a human, however, is not sufficient. Life
has to be lived inside the lines.

All those years I avoided my mother's eyes:

"Where are you going?"

"Out."

"When are you coming back?"

"Sometime."

"You're coming home for summer, aren't you?"

"Maybe."

All the long journeys and secret men, unanswered telephone calls, vague addresses, poste restante so-and-so. Those eyes that I avoided for so long, I miss them now. It is a desperately bleak feeling, being the only sighted person in the house. Now I'm the one who has to keep watch over her. If an atomic cloud started to grow on the horizon, she wouldn't notice. But at least she would die without being afraid.

I sense a pattern. Of love. Want to see her eating and sleeping to make herself strong, enjoy the sun on the steps, comb her hair, keep her safe. When she goes out alone she gets lost and has to be driven home by strange people in strange cars. Can hardly see her way around now, but that doesn't prevent her from chopping wood and cycling, and last summer she went down to bathe in the lake, lost all idea of where the shore was, swam around and around in circles until she almost couldn't keep on. At the last moment she felt the bottom beneath her feet and managed to find her way onto land.

"Close to the eye." She pulls a wry smile.

The feeling between us is changing. A new mixture of tenderness and irritation. I want to nourish and feed her, like a little child or a sensitive love. As she can't see I pour extra oil into the coleslaw and cream into the egg sauce. In my nightmares I see myself slowly being transformed into Nurse Ratched in *One Flew over the*

Cuckoo's Nest, the little white hat over the stiff hair, zealously conscientious, a witch in a starched collar who means well but does harm. Must be careful not to be like that.

I don't like the thinness around her hips and neck. Her jeans are loose. Sad to eat alone . . . but Mama never complains about loneliness, even though she stopped eating for a time when she was first on her own in the house, when Papa's father was no longer there. Later on she seemed to have made the decision that she had to survive that as well. To lose yourself is the most dangerous of all. She tried to teach me that when I was younger. If you lose something else you can always get it back—but if you lose yourself, who is going to search? While other mothers warned their daughters about rapists, unwanted pregnancies, and venereal diseases, she was always warning me about losing myself to someone.

THE DEMON'S MOUTH

Don't drink any more, Lukas had whispered in my ear, but I was already beyond that point. So sober that I fell asleep as soon as I felt his body against mine.

Afterward I just recall single moments, like flickering rays. Memories that can't be pinned down because they're too fuzzy, like the light in Copenhagen that day, swiftly changing September light over everything. Lukas and me. I remembered his body, his weight, the smell of bleach in the hotel pillow, but not the scent of him.

I had drunk as I had seen him drink on other occasions: quickly and with the deliberate intention of getting drunk. But that evening I don't recall him drinking anything at all, at least not as long as I was awake. The memory . . . too much bleach, too little oxygen, too much weight, too much flickering. Remember only a feeling of being alone, greater than any I had experienced before, like trash blowing along deserted streets in the morning. My loneliness or his? I didn't know—we were so close I couldn't see him properly, couldn't separate us.

His weight was enough; he didn't need to move a muscle. Weighed down by flickering lights, cotton candy, and Lukas, I couldn't move. Weighed down by loneliness. No kisses. I only saw the marks afterward. Long afterward. Like wounds on either side of the artery in my neck, still raw and tender. Perhaps it was the lifeblood he was lacking that he tried to suck from me. It had been going on so long, as if he had always needed what I had.

Under the swaying plastic chandelier we had moved toward the bed. Beer in every limb and hundreds of merry-go-rounds swirling and Lukas's hips against my ribs, danse macabre, strength and weakness evenly matched, his hand on the curve of my back. A place it hadn't been before, not like this, when it had no reason to be. His eyes turned away, but his hand remained.

I don't know why I didn't start to cry. He was crying, or something else was happening on his face. I don't know if he had lifted me off the floor or if I had lost the feeling in my feet. The dance of the devil until you drop, until your feet go numb and you've danced a hole in the floor, all the way down into the underworld, the unknown.

The whole of my childhood I'd danced on his feet, believing that I was leading. Now I was fifteen and it was he who was leading and I didn't know how to follow or how to resist.

Overcome by cotton candy and elephant beer, I disappeared into the mouth of the demon again and again. *This is a man's world,* even in my sleep. When I awoke he was gone and the first thing I felt was relief.

I was allowed to leave the hotel despite not being able to pay for the room. It wasn't my fault, the staff said. They seemed to assume the worst. They would trace him through the number on his driver's license and make sure they got their money; these things had happened before. Clearly relieved to be rid of me, as if they were watching a problem walk out of the door. A problem that could have been difficult for the hotel, a failure of responsibility . . . I was nowhere near fifteen, they were agreed on that, and he was so much older.

If the whole thing hadn't been about Lukas, I would have called Mama and asked her to come and fetch me. That was the last thing I could do now, but I had no other ideas as I stepped out onto the street, not even any notion of where I was in the city. No money, no map, no memory of the day before other than a vague feeling of soreness in my body. There seemed to be no solution, but none was needed—when I surveyed the street I saw the Ford in the spot where Lukas had parked it the day before. He was sitting in the front seat watching me, as if he had woken up at the very moment I came out onto the street, or maybe he had not slept at all that night. I slid into the passenger seat without a word. He said nothing either. First he had to wake up properly, pull on his shirt, and smoke a morning cigarette leaning against the car. Then he had to find a toilet and a cup of coffee and a piece of bread and some tobacco and go and pay for the room. I debated whether to warn him about going into the hotel, about the problem he might face with the staff. But I said nothing, and when it came to it they seemed to wash their hands of the whole thing, just wanted their money.

After that he had to drive around to find his way out of the center and north to the ferry. He had still said nothing. And I had said nothing. The silence became harder to break the longer it went on. We just drove.

"I didn't want to hurt you," he said finally, his eyes fixed on the line of cars as we drove up the ramp and into the gaping mouth of the ferry.

He stayed on the car deck for the entire crossing, while I went up and bought far too many candies, but I really just wanted to stand by the rail and watch the shoals of jellyfish under the oily black surface. Feel the force of the wind sweep everything away as I leaned far out over the water.

Only when the ferry had docked and I heard the irritated sound of horns from the car deck did I go down. Got into the Ford that was holding up the others behind. Lukas started the engine and moved off, saying nothing, but his last words hung in the air. And I replied that he hadn't. Hurt me. He never would, would he? But he just looked at me oddly, as if it were not something I had the power to decide.

On the road here I'd thought about him. My eye was caught by the hitchhiker's hands, the lad I had picked up by the ramp onto the highway. I had glimpsed his hands and couldn't stop staring at them. How they rested on the thigh of his jeans with the fingers spread out, in a way that reminded me of a game we used to play at school. A knife plunged faster and faster between someone's fingers, the bravest one or someone who couldn't say no, while the others watched, egging them on. I still had a scar on my left ring finger. It was Lukas who was holding the knife that time. Since then I've had a habit of looking at people's hands. My memory is full of them: first a quick look at the face, then the hands to find out what the face is holding back, because hands never lie. A woman I met on a train to Berlin claimed to remember every penis she had ever touched, and one could well imagine that was quite a few. I can only remember fingers, nails, knuckles, palms, backs of hands. A unique ability to remember hands and forget the rest. The hands of sleeping men with the smell of seawater, garlic, hash, perfume, lubricant, dog's fur, chlorine. I cup them over my face, watch the blood flowing, twisting in the blue veins just beneath the skin. Remember all the hands that ever touched me. Remember the ones I wished would touch me. The hands, the men, the towns.

The woman kept me awake the whole night talking about herself. It was that kind of night, caught in a trap, confined to a sleeping compartment on a slow train with a stranger who had taken life to heart. She was no longer afraid. Everything she had feared had already happened. Now she lived in a fait accompli. There was no point to her fear. Fear of what might happen is always the worst; that must be what it was the time Lukas stabbed me in the finger. It happened not because he was trembling, but because I was. Fear provokes danger.

Nothing happened the night in the hotel room in Copenhagen, and nothing was ever really the same again. I have never believed the myth about the butterfly beating its wings on one side of the earth and causing a hurricane on the other. But perhaps after all there is such a moment in everyone's life, a moment that spreads and grows until it changes reality. And for me it was a few seconds of that evening.

I wake up late to a day of unexpected warmth and the day's first warning from Mama: don't forget to hold your breath when you fetch wood, and wash your hands thoroughly afterward, vole fever is spread through fresh and old droppings.

She starts to prepare the meal, no surprises, the national food: sausages and potatoes, a beer, doesn't want any help, *just sit there at the table, Lo . . . sit in your usual place, as normal.* Everything has to be as normal, though nothing is. It looks dangerous when she handles the knife as if she could see it, cuts the potatoes rapidly in her hand like her mother used to do, fumbles when she lights the gas stove. What if the flame gets hold of her sleeve . . . I want to help set the table, but she waves me back to my place. Instead I look through a pile of books gathering dust on the windowsill, long ago forgotten. I pull out the one at the bottom, a well-thumbed *Anna Karenina,* the abridged version with stills from the film with Greta Garbo. I can't imagine the loneliness in store when you can no longer see to read. I started to read because I saw her doing it, because I wanted some of whatever it was that made her disappear into herself. Whenever we crawled into bed and I was warming my feet between her thighs, I would shut my eyes and listen half asleep to her turning the pages.

The sound of white birch being cut is like glasses clinking. Mama doesn't chop wood as effectively as she did, but she's just as obstinate. Then she puts the heavy ax on the chopping block and helps me to stack. The trimming ax swings from a strap on her work trousers with every movement she makes—the daughter ax I always used to think I would inherit. We have soon finished piling the wood, as long as she doesn't take it into her head to chop some more. This is the best time. To sit chatting after a job well done.

She takes off her gloves and the padded lumberjack shirt—not much left of her when she sheds the unattractive protective layer. She's a walking pair of collarbones, Papa's father used to say. Her hair has become thinner too, but still has its color, fair like the fields in the days before the crops are gathered. Clumsily she strokes the guide dog's head. Not used to patting dogs. Not used to patting anyone anymore.

"Do you remember the day of the fire, Mama?"

"In the field? Of course I do." She dries the perspiration on her neck, still looks good, just older. She has the sort of face whose lines aren't rubbed out by age and fatty tissue. If anything, the features become sharper. If only she would stop going around in Grandfather's old castoffs, his various sizes of large work trousers with the belt tied around her waist twice, the lumber jacket that is her second home. A waste of beauty. When I point it out she looks at me, amused.

"You've made so much more use of it."

"Your beauty?"

"No, your own." It isn't true, I have never been beautiful like her. My eyes are my only asset. Seductive, I sometimes hear. My mouth as well—of course it tends toward the generous, but generous with what? What does it promise and what does it hold?

"I haven't seen that Lukas for a long time," Mama says.

"Must you call him that?"

"What's his name, then?"

"His name's just Lukas. Not *that* Lukas."

"You always were oversensitive about him. I thought you had gotten over it."

Gotten over it? "It wasn't me who was oversensitive, it was all of you who were completely insensitive."

It wasn't an easy situation, she reminds me. "Whatever anyone said you got angry, Lo."

I don't want to spoil this precious moment, we have them so seldom, and yet I hear myself say, "You detested him."

"We didn't detest him, we loved you—there's a difference. We were scared of . . . It's not hard to understand, is it? The relationship was so lopsided, when you were at middle school discos he was at high school parties."

"He never went to high school parties, Mama."

"No, and you never went to middle school discos either. I know. That's the point."

I really don't want to fall out with her, have to be quiet, otherwise I know exactly what will happen.

This woodshed was one of our hiding places, a dark realm of spiderwebs and light filtering through the thin boards, the smell of newly cut wood drying out. The pearl fisher's house was our best place, but if we didn't have time to go there, we could come here. I had only the well-meaning concerns of the adults to escape from. Lukas had his papa, as unpredictable as a foxtrap.

"If anyone was inconsiderate toward him, Lo, it was you. He became so odd afterward," Mama mutters.

"Odd?"

"Odder."

We have never spoken properly about what happened. I have hoped that she has wrapped up what I did in some sort of all-forgiving mother love that can break down any sin at all into soft hairballs of the type that mothers, with a little goodwill, can swallow, as long as they come from their own children.

"Inconsiderate?"

She nods.

I know. Only I didn't think she saw me that way.

"Actually you have no idea at all about what happened," I say, shifting uneasily against the stack of logs. For certain conversations there is no good time. I just want to get out in the sun.

"Does he still live in the house?"

She doesn't know, but no one else seems to be living there at any rate. "It would've been easiest if he'd just disappeared after what happened," she says to herself. Where? Where would he have disappeared to? If ever anyone had nowhere to go, it was Lukas.

"He didn't ask about you once, Lo. Not once. That's how I knew something was wrong. Then I saw him less and less. But why don't you go down and see if he's there?"

How can she ask? She knows that I never go down there. That I don't want to. Certain things are simply impossible. Perhaps for him as well. If he has been aware that I'm at home, he has always managed to keep out of sight.

"All this woodcutting business, Mama," I say as a diversionary tactic.

"Yes?"

"Do you really think you should be doing it?"

"Why not?"

The word.

Full of shame.

A word I hesitate to voice. Her unseeing face is unreadable. She pushes the tin of mink fat into her pocket and fumbles for the ax again, tests its sharpness on her thumb, and takes the sharpening steel out of the other pocket of her padded lumberjack shirt. She has always cut wood, all the wood that was ever needed to keep this house warm; she has cut wood since the day we arrived here.

"Why not? Who else would do it? You?" You might as well stick the ax straight into me, she looks to be thinking. But make sure it is a deathblow . . . She hands me the ax, lingers a moment. "Why don't you go down there?" Turns her back on me and leaves.

Whenever I enter Mama's room I have to resist the feeling that it is out of bounds. Listen for her step in the hallway as I go around looking at her things. Sometimes I hope that she does the same, goes into my room and pokes around in my luggage, but I know that she would never do such a thing, never write, *Your mother who knows you,* like Jean Seberg did to her son.

I take a few books down with me. She has lit the stove in the drafty living room, where I fan the books out and let her fingers choose. I begin to read as I once read aloud for Lukas:

"I buy him cheese and yogurt and butter in Trouville, because when he comes in late at night he devours that sort of thing. And he buys me the things I like best—buns and fruit. He buys them not so much to give me pleasure as to feed me up. He has this childlike idea of making me eat so I don't die. He doesn't want me to die. But he doesn't want me to get fat either. It's hard to reconcile the two. I don't want to die, either. That's what our affection is like, our love. In the evening and at night, we sometimes throw caution to the wind. In these conversations we tell the truth however terrible, and we laugh as we used to do when we still drank and could only talk to one another in the afternoon."

The impossible balance of love. Don't become fat, overfed, blasé, too sure of yourself. But don't starve or fade, either. How do you sustain each other to just the right degree? I have no clue. I remember hearing about a pair of lovers who arranged to walk twelve hundred miles along the Great Wall of China to meet up somewhere in the Gobi Desert, a fantastic idea. But it didn't work out as planned. Love ran out along the way. The reunion was meant to cement their relationship, but when they eventually met, they decided to divorce, having been a couple for more than twenty years.

Mama asks to pick another, not happy with her choice. This is not a night for love. I set out the fan of stories again. Her fingers stroke them gently and she chooses a new one. I open it and begin again:

"It was a queer, sultry summer, the summer they electrocuted the Rosenbergs, and I didn't know what I was doing in New York. I'm stupid about executions . . . I knew something was wrong with me that summer, because all I could think about was the Rosenbergs."

I walk around the room while I am reading. Mama is developing the hearing of a bat—she tells me to leave the Venetian blinds alone.

"What are you looking for? You're making me stressed, your footsteps are echoing. You can't keep still for a minute . . . Must you walk around indoors in your shoes, as if you're on your way somewhere?"

I am always on my way somewhere, Mama. And I don't take off my boots for anybody. Perhaps by arrangement, but definitely not to order. These boots have walked many miles through foreign towns, boots that know what they want, even when I don't.

"Shoes," Mama says as I make an extra circuit around the room. "Is it a full moon? I've never understood what a full moon does to women. The rabbits in the field are on edge as well."

"Can you feel that?"

"Yes. The vibrations," she says.

She keeps the Venetian blinds closed most of the time nowadays, having become more sensitive to the light. Strange to be light sensitive when you cannot even see. I check Lukas's house, but there's no sign of life.

"Actually I don't think he lives there anymore," Mama says, sensing where my attention is directed.

"Are you sure?"

"No, but it feels empty down there."

A vague impression of absence—I can feel it too now. "And the house?"

Who would be interested in that? She sighs. Difficult to sell now that the factories have closed, everyone moving away, no one moving in. Always the same old story: foreign companies buy them out and shut them down, ignite hopes and blow them out again, until people give up and clear out, leaving their houses even if they can't sell them. Especially noticeable here in the outskirts—empty houses and overgrown gardens everywhere. The paradise my mother once migrated to has packed up and moved on.

"Perhaps he's waiting for better times," she says hesitantly.

Yes, if I know Lukas, that's exactly what he's doing.

Still, I can't imagine where he could have gone. He may not have belonged here, but he belonged still less anywhere else.

"Just try to think when you last saw him," I say. It must have been a long time ago, as it was a long time since Mama could see her own reflection in the mirror. If Lukas had moved away, she would hardly have noticed. Nor would anyone else. Did anyone around here know him? Apart from me. And his papa. She rubs a woodcutter's muscle in her neck.

"Never asked about you, Lo, when I happened to meet him anywhere in the village, isn't that strange?" She half turns, her silhouette slender as a boy's. "What does it matter anyway if he's still there? In all these years you've never been down to see him. It makes a person suspect the worst."

"The worst?"

"Yes. That something went very wrong at the end."

The last chore of the day: I wash the piles that are growing in the laundry room. Feel a warm breeze through the window while we fold the sheets. An acrid waft from the mink farm. The furs don't sell here any longer, but are sent to Russia and China where they sell like hotcakes, if Mama is to be believed. It's not appropriate for wild animals to be kept in captivity. The humiliation makes them smell bad. I recall how they used to climb up the mesh, chattering hysterically, when Lukas and I passed the low pens. One male or several females in every coop. Reminded me of the rat traps in Lukas's attic.

Only once does she cast her eyes straight at me, squinting like someone looking at the sun through grimy glass. "Lo, just think . . ."

"That I've grown so much?"

"That you're my daughter."

Mama was the woman who cut wood faster than her own shadow. Collapsed into bed at night, exhausted after the day's work. Now she needs to take a long bath each evening and listen to all the reruns on the radio, ritualize going to bed in order to cast out its demons. I go into the bathroom to ask her what films she'd like to see tomorrow, I've brought a few with me that I think she will like. *Repulsion*? She shakes her head deprecatingly.

"Something with Marlene Dietrich?"

"Oh, no . . ." she says as she lets the hot water run.

Breathless? Not that either. She hasn't watched that since Jean Seberg died, she says.

With the years she has become less sensitive to horror but more easily moved by sadness. You need to lay yourself open when you are young and shield yourself when you are older, says the person who warned me against everything when I was a child.

"You tolerate less. That's all I mean," she adds, as if sensing my objection. Because you realize how unfair life really is. What havoc it causes for certain people. Lukas, for example . . . She has thought about him from time to time, she admits. And about not being able to see, about being so worried about me, about him having a bad time. She rinses her face with the shower without shutting her eyes, and says no more.

The one cloud in my sky for a long time had been the cloud that hovered constantly over him. The pools of blood beneath his skin that subsided, only to be replaced by new. His problems were my problems, just not apparent in my skin. And the jealousy, I was frightened of catching it, the melancholy, as if he were filled with darkness, but there was something shining under all the mire, was I the only one who could see it? The way he saw the river rats was different from the way I did, and he couldn't bear to see them trapped and helpless. Gábriel nearly wrecked his face the time he found Lukas leaving the disposal of the rat cages to me. Lukas never recovered from the shame. Nor did his face.

PERIOD OF RAIN

After Copenhagen nothing felt straightforward and we couldn't talk about it. I looked at him. He looked back in that new way he had of looking at me since we'd come home. Black jewels nestling in their case behind bulletproof glass, those sorts of eyes. We were attached to each other without touching, on a fixed path, like the planets. Silence was his weapon, the only thing I have never coped with, the face turned away. Like Mama when I was younger, how she sometimes withdrew her love, to get me where she wanted me.

Childhood is a reverse telescope that keeps the world at a distance, but I was no longer a child. The railway was an enticing stream of silver that I wanted to float away on every time I saw it from my bedroom window.

To fill the emptiness that had developed between Lukas and me, I devoted myself for the first time to school. A little late in the day, according to the teachers, but Mama was relieved that, thankfully, I appeared at last to have realized there was life after being a child. I was at the age when it irritated me to do what she wanted, but it was so much more satisfying to shock the teachers. I improved my grades, raised them above shame and ruin.

"You can do it, you see, that was what we thought. If you keep on like this, then . . ."

Then what? The bright future would soon be mine? The reward for doing well in your studies was more studying. That much I understood.

———

The autumn I turned sixteen, the rainy period just starting—the windows misting up again, the road transformed into a deluge and all the trees in the arboretum up to their ankles in water—nothing drained away. The parasites had a whale of a time all through this endless period of wet. Grandfather was powerless. The arboretum was his harem. That poor army of trees was supposed to fulfill all his desires, Mama said.

Almost imperceptibly I was drawn back to Lukas and he began to look me in the eye once more. Time did something for us that we couldn't do ourselves. Nothing was as before, but we had to take what remained or lose each other completely.

After Copenhagen Mama had let go of me as if I were no longer hers, a young runaway animal who'd come home smelling unfamiliar. She stopped asking me where I was going and where I'd been. There was a sad feeling of freedom that should have been intoxicating. Whatever Mama thought we were up to before, at least it was no longer illegal. Even if she didn't approve, she could hardly stop us.

"I see how you look at him and it worries me," she said one evening. That afternoon Lukas and I had been sitting at home in the kitchen in full daylight for the first time. Mama came past and happened to see us, stopped abruptly, regained her composure, came in and took a drink out of the fridge, and went out again without a word. "And that's nothing compared to how worried I am when I see how he looks at you," she added. There was something about him that was weak, and weak people are the most dangerous, they drag you down. Strong people you can fight to free yourself from, but the weak get under your skin. After having warned me about Lukas's strength, now she was warning me about the reverse, as if it were the same thing. But "weak" was the wrong word. He wasn't weak. There was no word for what he was. When he slept, when he laughed, emptied the buckets of rainwater, ate bananas, when he said that ordinary happy moments are the best, I could see the pain in his face.

There's no such thing as fairy tales, he'd said, but perhaps it was just happy endings there was a shortage of.

Lukas's papa, Gábriel, kept himself to himself. In all the years he lived in the village he spoke to no one, mixed with no one. If he hasn't learned Swedish yet it must be because he is either stupid or stuck up, people said, and they didn't know which was worse . . . He was a steppe wolf at any rate, a recluse, odd, a rum one, as they said in my family. He went his own way in the community. It was alleged that he couldn't ride a bicycle. People alleged so many things, were so good at gossip. It was alleged that he had answered a personal ad. That was what brought him here, if you believe the rumor, and most people did. Things went well with the woman for a while, a very short while, and then they started to go wrong, so he took his suitcase and his son and moved to the wooden house that he'd bought for next to nothing. According to some, he hadn't bought this house by the lake at all. Just moved in because it was standing empty and no one laid claim to it. He made it decent, cleared the yard, fixed everything that was hanging off, and chased away the vermin. Soon it was one of the best-maintained houses in the district, even if it was jerry-built. He painted it a color like no other house in the area and it was difficult to know what to call it, when you spoke about it. Hungarian green, said my mother's sisters, who could not help spying on it every now and then. A color that was hardly going to meld with the surrounding greenery. At least Gábriel was particular about keeping things neat and tidy. And a good worker. Could have worked his way up, become a foreman, if he'd had the language, but he didn't—or didn't want to. There were different views on that.

Gábriel was most often seen walking beside the bicycle, which it was said he couldn't ride, on the road between his home and the factory. Like a dog walking alongside. What would a steppe wolf need a dog for, company or protection? He was good-looking, at least that was what my mother's sisters said, and his looks seemed to guard him from a worse fate. Despite everything, people were not as suspicious of him as they might have been. They talked about him, sure, but they let him be.

My fear of Gábriel wasn't logical. It was Lukas's legacy. I always felt awkward in his presence, and it was made no better that he was always kind toward me when we met. If my family treated Lukas like something the cat had dragged in, his papa seemed to view me as something unknown that you offered a chair to and treated with reserved respect. The unpredictable bouts of anger he directed at Lukas were never shown to me.

One afternoon when Gábriel was at work the telephone rang. Lukas was trying to do some repairs on the Taunus in the yard, though jobs requiring an adjustable wrench weren't his forte. It was raining as well. It had been raining the whole day, for weeks. The only progress Lukas was making was to become more and more greasy, more and more wet. He'd gotten it into his head that he could change the drive belt himself, because he couldn't afford to take the car in to the garage and he couldn't stand being unable to drive around. I'd been sitting perched with my feet on the bumper, watching his endeavors for a whole hour. I realized that he wasn't going to manage it; I had seen both Rikard and Katja do it on our cars, and Lukas was doing everything wrong. And he refused to listen to me.

He didn't bother about the telephone either, though I urged him to answer it. It must be something important: the telephone never rang in their house.

"You might have come into a big fat inheritance there and you've missed it," I said when the ringing had stopped.

"There aren't any relatives, you know that," he hissed, and knocked me so hard that I fell off. "Go and do something useful, rustle together a few leftovers or find something else you can do . . . answer the phone, for example, if it rings again."

That might happen in another year, I thought. But I was wrong. I had gone in even though I really wanted to go home, because when Lukas was in this mood it was like waiting for a time bomb to go off. When I heard the telephone again, I followed the sound through the house, until I found it in Gábriel's bedroom. A man's voice that didn't introduce itself asked to speak to Gábriel Puskás. Because Lukas's papa still didn't speak any Swedish, I went out to fetch Lukas instead. Reluctantly he left his fruitless repair work, went inside in his wet boots, and pushed me away to a safe distance before going into his father's room and taking the receiver.

From the monosyllabic, hesitant answers as his face stiffened, it was immediately obvious that something wasn't right. In the end he turned his back on me and stood silently with the phone in his hand. I was rooted to the spot by the door, trying hard to catch what was being said at the other end. But the conversation seemed to be over already, at least for Lukas. He stood with the receiver in one hand, propping himself up against the wall with the other.

"Fucking hell," he whispered.

I went up to him. Didn't dare to touch him.

"Lukas?"

"Go home," he said softly, but I didn't.

This is the sort of thing that happens when people are stressed and fail to pay attention—"a breach of confidentiality"—and this is how we learned, even before Gábriel himself, that he was dying. Bone cancer. Very advanced. Incurable.

We hadn't noticed that the illness had taken up residence in the house a long time before. Like an uncomfortably discreet uninvited guest, it had been very unobtrusive so far. None of us had been aware that Gábriel was ill—doomed, in fact.

Lukas's soundless and at the same time violent reaction surprised me. He and his papa had lived side by side for so many years in a strange silence, such an absence of words and feelings that even their body language was mute. When Lukas had grown too big for Gábriel to beat him, the last remnant of bodily contact between them ceased.

Gábriel was the only family Lukas had, and there was a sort of love between them, even if I'd never seen any warmth. Coldness, distance, and violent arguments were the only things their coexistence appeared to consist of. And in a way, it was the "almost" nature of it that was the most painful. Because every now and again there was a moment's contact, a smile, a glance between them that gave just a hint that under other circumstances, in a completely different life, they might have been close.

Winter passed and so did spring. Lukas worked the night shift at the factory, and Gábriel went down to half time and then was forced to give up altogether. The treatment he received was like sugarcoated pills in the face of death. April passed, its promises broken time after time. May the same. June—no more promises. We heard the nightingales. The area around the river was typical nightingale territory, and however alluring their song was, it still made me uneasy. The early summer slipped past in warmth, morphine sulfate, waiting, while the illness spread through Gábriel's bones.

We put a bed outside his room to be able to hear if he woke up in the night and needed something. I dreamed that a violent storm was tossing us apart, and when I awoke Lukas was holding me so hard I could scarcely breathe. Sometimes he murmured his own name in his sleep, as if he were already alone, the only one left.

Rice and cigarettes for breakfast. While he was waiting for the rice cooker, Lukas washed in the homemade shower that turned into an electric current in stormy weather. I followed his movements behind the nylon curtain. Suddenly he stopped. He was motionless for a long time, stood quite still in the jet of water until I was afraid and went up and pulled down the shower curtain. He was just standing there, as if he had forgotten that he was supposed to wash his hair.

"Fetch my cigarettes."

"Are you going to smoke in the shower, Lukas?" He'd gone mad, forgotten where he was, what he was doing. Lack of sleep and worry had eaten away at him and made his body sharper, more chiseled, as if death were attacking it as well. When I reached my hand forward to touch his chest, he fended me off quickly.

"Fetch them."

I didn't intend to. If we started to do more than one thing at a time, how would we make the time pass? If I were to go and fetch things for him while I had the sheets in soak, and he were to smoke while he was showering . . . then the days would be endless. The time we spent in the house to be there for Gábriel crept forward so slowly, even when we only did one thing at once. But he said, "The days won't last. The nights." And it was true, the endless days were numbered. For Gábriel and perhaps for us as well. We were on a narrow strip of ice, alone. There might be a thin band of ice that would bear your weight in a large area of weak ice; Papa had taught me that. We were standing on it now. If you walked out on a narrow strip and it broke, no one could help you.

It was clear that death wasn't going to take Gábriel quickly and mercifully, it was going to take its time. Bone cancer . . . the worst kind, Lukas had heard. His papa's body would soon be as hollow as the coral in the pearl fisher's house.

Did Mama guess what was happening, when one afternoon I said I was going to Lukas's and then didn't come home again? Or did she think that we were in the claws of love, that we spent all those days in bed, wrapped around each other, irresponsible, lazy, defiant, shirking school and work?

The first time she came and knocked on the door was twenty-four hours later. Lukas said that I was asleep, which made her suspicious, as it was afternoon.

"Have you been *drinking*?"

"No." He had. I hadn't.

"Why is Lo asleep at this time of the day, then?"

"Because she's been awake all night, we——"

"I don't want to know any more," Mama interrupted. Though of course she did, even though she thought she already knew.

I was sitting measuring out Gábriel's afternoon dose, following the instructions left by the district nurse. Through the door I could smell the sweet scent of ripened grain and heard Mama point out that even if I was not underage in one way, I certainly was in another. If Lukas was giving me alcohol . . . He made a sign to me that I should stay where I was, he could handle this, he was on his own ground now.

"It's cool, trust me," he said and shifted a millimeter in the doorway. Mama couldn't even peep around him.

"Trust you?" she said coldly. As if she ever had . . . ever would . . . "When she wakes up, send her straight home," she ordered, as if I were the common property of two foes and it was her turn to have me now.

"She'll do as she wishes."

"No, she'll do as *you* wish, that's the problem!" I heard Mama say, before she turned and left.

Whatever you do, don't lie to her, that never works, I whispered when Lukas came back in. He pulled me out of Gábriel's room so that we could speak undisturbed.

"Listen, it makes absolutely no difference what I say to your mama, you know. She's never liked me." I wanted to contradict him, but that would have been ridiculous. I caught sight of the two of us in the hall mirror. We looked wrong. Especially together. It was impossible not to think that our eyes should change places, he with his summer-bleached hair and almost black eyes, I dark and green-eyed. He held me a little too close, a little too hard. I wriggled away. Since Copenhagen he had kept his distance, but now it was as if he could no longer maintain that restraint. There was something insensitive about everything he did. He let both his irritation and his randiness spill over onto me and I was afraid of provoking in him what had become so easily provoked since Gábriel's diagnosis. Sex and sadness in a desperate mixture. I moved out of the way with a no. You always say that, I saw in his eyes. Love, love not, love, but what sort of love? Sex had always been the thing that couldn't happen between us. Mama would have detected it in me right away and then we would never have been able to be alone together—that feeling was still there.

"Must you go around seminaked? Can't you show my papa a little respect?" Lukas said, out of the blue. Seminaked? Skirt, pants, top, worn-out sandals, was that not enough? What did he expect? It was eighty-five degrees.

"What about you, then . . ." See-through, threadbare black shorts, that was all. Not that there were any secrets hidden under there, but at least he shouldn't complain about me.

"It's not a problem for you," he said vehemently, "if I go around like this."

I shrugged.

"No, well. Go and get dressed."

We had entered a time of constant fatigue, nights broken into small meaningless pieces by Gábriel's restless sleep. When Mama returned it was Lukas who opened the door again. He looked as if he had been living hard for days. His hair had started to form natural dreadlocks and his only article of clothing was hanging yet farther down his hips.

"I want to speak to my daughter."

I was on the point of going out into the hall.

"Where's your papa?"

"Asleep," Lukas said.

"You know—I don't like this at all." She insisted on speaking to Gábriel, but Lukas said it wasn't the time to wake him. "Fetch Lo," she demanded.

"If she wants to go home, she knows the way. Calm down!"

I stepped in just before it got out of control. Mama looked so alone standing out on the porch. We had never been apart as long as this, and as soon as she saw me she started telling me off.

"What do you think you *look* like? Have you been in bed all weekend? Has he turned your head completely? When are you coming home?"

"Soon," I lied. It was best that she didn't know. She was afraid of dead people, and dying was so much more frightening, and Mama had never been good at dealing with anything to do with death. "Mama, I just need to—"

"What?" she asked, looking out over the scorched sloping fields as if she were searching for storm clouds on the horizon.

"Stay with Lukas for a little while . . ." I didn't expect her to understand, and she didn't. She just said that she hoped I knew what I was letting myself in for. Looked at me as if convinced that I didn't have the faintest idea.

You know when a newcomer has arrived in town if he steps down from the train in slow motion, the last passenger, his eyes sweep along the platform, probing, squinting into the peculiar light that platforms like this are always bathed in, before he puts his bags down on the ground and suddenly he looks exhausted. He hasn't arrived yet, he doesn't even know that he is on his way to our village—first we have to place an ad. It is just a question of persuading Lukas.

"Everything's so easy for you, Lo."

"And you make everything so hard."

Always the same, waiting and hesitating. It's only an ad . . . A gamble.

"What do you have to lose, Lukas? Nothing." I slip away when he tries to keep hold of me. We've discussed it all morning, and I've run out of arguments. It feels as if we have been talking about this for half the summer and soon it will be too late.

He thinks it's a bad idea. Period. Mostly because it's an idea at all. Ideas imply change and Lukas's immediate response to anything that deviates from our normal routine is: no. When did he become like this? I don't remember him this way.

"You're going to regret it."

"Why the hell do you always think you know best, Lo? Especially things you haven't got the foggiest about." The questions he has . . . it is time to ask them now. *Now*—not later. There won't be a later. Gábriel won't live many more weeks.

It's not intended to be a truth commission, just a conversation. The last chance, the last conversation he will be able to have with his papa—and the first as well, for that matter. Interpreter required, for private case, that is all that needs to be in the ad.

"Private case?" He looks at me, distrustful. "Sounds like something dodgy."

"Oh Lukas, stop it . . ."

They've argued over everything, without understanding each other. Never spoken. There are so many things the two of them have never talked about, never overcome the short and yet insuperable distance of language. They've shared the same life, the same kitchen table, over which they could see but not reach each other, just enough vocabulary in common for everyday life, simple commands, and sometimes not even that. When Gábriel turned on Lukas it often seemed to be caused by some misunderstanding.

Something Lukas neglected to do, simply because he hadn't understood that he'd been told to do it.

This unwillingness to speak as well. Gábriel surrounded himself in silence as if it were a natural condition. Small wonder that Lukas soon forgot the language that was his when he arrived here. He quickly began to speak better Swedish than Hungarian. The new language became his only one, because that was the only one he heard.

Only when I've given up the idea, stopped believing in it myself, does Lukas unexpectedly give in. Before he has a chance to change his mind, I make the call. Half a minute, that's all the time it takes to dictate the ad over the telephone. Then it is just a question of waiting. We sit on their wooden porch, listening for the ringing of the phone, scratching at mosquito bites, watching the kites soaring with predatory elegance high over the late-summer sky. Bide our time—or maybe it is Gábriel's time we are biding; it is at any rate his time that is running out.

Every day he grows worse. Before it was every week, and before that it was every month. The irrevocable process of distraint and seizure has begun. Death's henchmen, some kind of execution squad, come and, bit by bit, remove his life and carry it away, and we can't stop them. As if it is no longer his, as if he has lost his right to it. All of a sudden they come and take away his ability to climb out of bed by himself. He could do it a moment ago, and we didn't even think about it—now he can no longer do it and we have to think about it all the time. For him it means immense frustration, for us it means that we can no longer leave the house together for more than a very short time. He can still manage to get to the toilet, but first we have to help him out of the bed and support him against the wall through the hall.

He's in pain when he walks. But he's also in pain when he's sitting and lying down. He seems to have reached the stage where he suffers with most things. It is merely a matter of how much.

A week passes without a single response. I had imagined that the telephone would start ringing immediately, at least not this humiliating silence. Another one of your bad ideas, Lo, Lukas appears to be thinking. Gábriel himself is luckily unaware of the whole thing. It's the only luck he has at the moment, so we let him remain that way.

Lukas seems relieved that there's no call. After all, it's not he who has been the protagonist in this. He acts as if he would rather be spared the trouble. But one day he will thank me, even if it just ends up as a failed attempt.

Sometimes it rains at night, but where does all the water go? A parched summer, as if the illness within the house were spreading out into the garden and the countryside beyond. Rustling brown vegetation. The trees around the house no longer cast shadows, having rolled up their leaves until they look like cigar trees that you want to stretch a hand out and pick from. We are careful about only doing one thing at a time—while Lukas rolls cigarettes, we are sparing with conversation—so we don't squander a pastime. He smokes instead of eating, and I have also lost my appetite, but that doesn't matter. We don't need any energy, we hardly move, we are in power reduction mode, don't even argue, lay all feelings aside. It's arduous enough to sit here on the wooden porch that has been our fixed point this summer, with the door open so that we can hear if Gábriel needs anything. It's almost too much to sit here watching the kites lazily glide over the field in quest of the characteristic movement of prey. We are the prey. They haven't discovered us yet, but soon the farmers will start to reap the crops and then there will be nowhere to hide.

Lukas needs to be held together and it is I who must do it. I sit right behind him on the step with my chin on his shoulder and hold him hard. And still I can feel how he is falling apart.

He murmurs strange things between sleeping and waking:

"I know you can't forgive me."

"Forgive?" I say.

He wakes up. "What?" Draws back from my touch, falls asleep again with his face in the pillow, begins to mumble:

"I didn't want to . . ."

"All right," I whisper, though I don't know what he is talking about.

The constantly gnawing worry has given Lukas's body a boyish frailty, as if he is regressing, like the lake—it has withdrawn too, dried up like a dead eye in the summer heat and left a circle of slippery gray-violet slime that you have to walk over barefoot to reach the water and cool down. But we don't do that any longer. There's an invisible line by the steps that we can't go beyond. We're anchored here now.

Life is like a fairy tale, cruel and cautionary, weee-oo ee ee ee ee ee-oo, sounds the hunting cry of the kites. I follow the steep drop as one of the huge birds of prey angles his forked tail and dives. Where did all the kites suddenly come from? I don't recall them as a child. They would have been etched in my memory with their long dark shadows. Lukas says that they were almost wiped out for a while. They stopped breeding—too much pesticide in their natural diet—then people started to put out scraps from the abattoirs onto the fields and the species fought back from the brink of extinction.

The vertical dive of a bird of prey is like a falling star: you should wish for something the instant you see it. I shut my eyes and murmur my hope into the sweaty curls on Lukas's neck.

"What?"

"Nothing. A secret."

Death rocks the chair in the darkness. And on the porch steps we sit and wait. The ad was cheap at any rate and we have at least tried, no harm done, Lukas says.

By the afternoon, the mercury has risen to ninety and all we can speak about is water. Lukas talks about the coolness of the Danube, something he is not likely to remember, while I spin refreshing fantasies for us of mountain streams, fjords, waterfalls, rivers, clear and ice cold. We have to go down to the lake and have a dip. Gábriel has just fallen asleep, and for the first half hour he usually sleeps without anxiety and sweating, so peacefully that he looks as though he will never wake up, and sometimes I almost wish he wouldn't, for his sake. We don't have time to look for bathing suits or even make our way to our sheltered bathing place, just rush straight down near the house and plunge in, naked, and forget for a little while.

I try to keep the sensation of cold as we hurry back, but we're already perspiring when we reach the house. In one way, leaving the house was not in vain. The first thing we see as we enter the kitchen is the flashing red light on the answering machine. I have a sudden feeling of unease. As if the message brings news of his death, as if someone has called to say that now it is over—the fight—Gábriel is dead in the next room and here is a very favorable offer covering all your death-related requirements.

Twice I listen to the message before handing the receiver to Lukas. The voice easygoing to the point of distracted.

"Hi, Yoel Farkas here, saw your ad and . . . yeah, if you still need someone . . . give me a buzz and we'll have a chat." There then follows a message of about the same length that according to Lukas is in Hungarian.

One bite in a whole week, so your hand mustn't shake when you reel it in. Afraid that Lukas will start to hesitate and make a fuss, I make the crucial call myself. The guy's voice is as smooth as it is on the answering machine, and he says yes without asking me to explain the almost inexplicable. He doesn't even hesitate when I'm honest and say that we have no money.

"I'm not doing it for the money," he says, as if he has already realized that this is a particularly deserving case that he can enter on the credit side of his karmic account. "I haven't done any interpreting for a while, so it'll be good practice. And besides, I can't wait to get out into the country. It's like walking on a hot tin roof in Stockholm."

When should he come? The sooner the better, I say. The doctors have said that Gábriel only has a few weeks left. They must be able to see that kind of thing. There's a risk that he will lose consciousness at the end, so we can't afford to waste any time at all. He has grown so thin that his bones are rubbing at his skin from the inside.

Lukas is circling around me as I speak, makes a sign that I don't know the meaning of, something about being careful, or maybe about money. I explain the unconventional remuneration we have thought of. Not sure that he understands at the other end. He's not listening very carefully, just says yes, seems pleased to be getting away from the city, just has one or two things to finish off, then he will pack and take the train down from Stockholm.

You know a newcomer has arrived in town when he steps down from the train in slow motion and suddenly has that look of exhaustion in his eyes. Him over there. No doubt. White shirt and kind of . . . optimistically large bags. What does he have with him? No one has asked him to stay for long. Have I gotten this right? What am I doing here? He appears to be thinking: should I really have come, am I going to regret this, when is the next train back? He has come to the end of the line and alighted there; no, it is not even the end of the line, the end of the line *is* something—this is a few stations before. An insignificant place where most trains don't even stop.

He's dressed as if he expected to land in another climate zone. The mercury is certainly as high here as in Stockholm, the asphalt is just as hot, he'll probably soon discover. Yes, look, he is already undoing a button at his neck. And another one. Rolls up the white shirtsleeves, wipes the palms of his hands helplessly over his face, as if the blazing heat were a bad dream he's trying to wake himself out of. At least it's the same for everyone. Except animals: it's worse for them. Two cats have already been caught like nightmare fish in the valves at the power station dam. No one has ever heard of cats drowning before. Desperate to quench their thirst in the devastating heat.

"Jesus Christ," he says, as I go to meet him and stretch out my hand. "I mean . . . sorry . . . hi . . . Yoel. How many degrees is it here? One-ten?"

Lukas doesn't take his hand, as if he doesn't understand what the gesture means. "We have stopped wondering," he answers tersely. It is true, we have. This is a heat that has to be ignored, like any other evil, in the hope that it might disappear. It will be better next week, the stranger says he's heard.

"They said that last week too, but it just got worse," Lukas says. But now it has reached the limit, it has to change, the stranger thinks.

"What limit? There is no limit," says Lukas. He has neither shaken Yoel's hand nor introduced himself.

"Of course. If you say so. Here in the country you forecast your own weather." The one who says he is called Yoel smiles.

I am relieved that Lukas doesn't hear the last remark, because he is clearly not in the right mood. Begins to fasten the luggage onto the old Yamaha that is his only vehicle now that the car is in for repairs. Once he has secured the bags and kick-started it he turns to hand it over to me.

"Are you riding with me?" I hiss. I'm usually always nagging about driving the old monster, without ever being allowed. It's not me he's worried about, he always assures me, but the motorcycle. Now he sneaks a glance at the stranger and I immediately guess what's going on. He wants to change our plan so that I drive the heavy luggage back to the house while he acts as guide. He hadn't reckoned on the interpreter who answered our ad being young and handsome with a captivating smile. I refuse to take the motorcycle when he passes it to me. A little while ago I had fallen off and nearly injured myself, and that was just in testing the seat. Now we're going to stick to our plan, and that's all we have. Without it everything will get out of hand.

He gives in, but makes his point by behaving like a lout and not picking up on the polite small talk on the platform. Just takes care of the luggage as if he was the anonymous footman. Halfheartedly he pulls off the accelerator and sets off for home.

"And that was . . . ?" asks our interpreter, who by now if not before must be regretting his decision to come here at all.

"Lukas. It's for his sake that you're here." I have no desire to apologize for him—I never do normally—but Yoel is someone we really need. Nothing should ruin that, not even Lukas.

All that Lukas and I used to need, to believe in the impossible, was each other. That we now had a plan too gave us a sense that what we were doing was feasible. "A long stay in a charming lakeside cottage," was what I offered the guy on the telephone in exchange for his services. Lukas had stood in front of me and rolled his eyes. We'll cross that bridge when we come to it, was my thinking. Now

I almost feel sorry for him as he walks beside me, full of expectation, as if he's really looking forward to it all. He doesn't yet know that the person he will be interpreting for is high on morphine most of the time and for the last few days has been more dead than alive.

"I didn't know he was *so* ill," is the first thing Yoel says when we arrive at the house and he grasps the situation. "I thought he was on a visit from Hungary. Have you really lived together your whole life without being able to speak to each other . . . I've never heard anything like it." If he hadn't broken off at that point, I would have been obliged to interrupt. Lukas has not asked for a sweeping analysis of his childhood and adolescence.

"You'd better go in now, while you have the chance. Gábriel sleeps more than he's awake," I inform him. This is deadly serious, if he hasn't realized that yet.

"Okay, so what do you want to know?" I fall silent and Lukas doesn't seem to know what to say either. We haven't actually talked about what the important questions are that he has to ask. This is Lukas's business now, I infer with a gesture.

"I want to know where I come from." His answer is almost inaudible. "And why we moved here."

Yoel raises his eyebrows. "Is that all?"

"And about your mama," I add. I see the effort Lukas is making, somewhere deep inside:

"As much as possible about her. I know nothing."

"And if you have any relatives left anywhere," I fill in.

"Yes. I don't want . . . don't want to be left alone," he murmurs. Alone? You're not alone, Lukas, I want to say. I'm here.

If Yoel thinks the whole thing is extremely strange, he doesn't show it. Lukas sucks in the last of the cigarette and stubs it out in a juice glass, listening to Yoel's quiet voice.

"Let me sit alone with him for a while. We'll try to take the most important questions first. But you'll have to reduce the morphine if we're going to get anything sensible out of him. He's delirious."

Merely by making an appearance and being present, Yoel is like soothing water washing over all the clammy anxiety. Not that he displays a great deal of empathy, but an ease, a sense that this whole thing need not be as impossible as it appeared to Lukas and me. I stand beside him and just breathe in the smell of clean shirt. It smells alive, I think. Fresh. And grown-up.

Lukas has been in the same clothes all summer, worn nylon shorts and a threadbare Bob Marley top. He doesn't even smell of sweat anymore, just smells of "that long hot summer when Gábriel was dying." Presumably I smell the same, in my not-so-white top and denim skirt that hangs like a sloughed snakeskin and itches around my hips day and night. I've tried taking it off, but it still itches, phantom itching. It's the heat.

Now and again I've taken a shower, washed and changed the bedclothes in the vain hope that some things can still be clean. A machine-load with Gábriel's sheets that have to be changed often. And so off with Lukas's T-shirt in passing and toss it in the drum with my snake skirt and a few underclothes, watch it all go around for an hour and then into the tumble drier, as if the wash were a little child that needed supervision. The laundry room has been my only refuge this summer, the coolest room in the house, the only place death doesn't reach. All is as it should be in here; all that has gone wrong outside is still as usual there—an exceptional state of equilibrium. I sit on the concrete floor until Lukas comes to fetch me with just a look from the door, a silent glance that says: come on, I need you. And I reply:

"Soon . . . just have to do the drier too." And so I switch the machine on one more time. Steal twenty minutes more of liberating, irresponsible solitude.

When I remove the laundry, it smells just the same as when I shoved it in. Perspiration and lingering panic.

To flies we're just another surface area. Salty humid dried flat curved bare fields of flesh. Open to invasion. So tired. No, much worse than tired—spent.

When Yoel arrives it's like a window flung open in a room that has been shut up for too long. A cold blast of oxygen rushes in and wakes us out of the torpor that has filled the house. He smells of summer, not damp and musty like us—no, he smells of bonfire and dry grass, brackish water, fresh air, aftershave. The house becomes more bearable when he is in it.

The outcome from the first session is meager, but it is at least a start. According to Yoel most of the time was spent explaining why he was there at all. You could have prepared this better, he gives us to understand. But how? That is precisely the problem, an almost insurmountable obstacle to communication. Otherwise we wouldn't have needed him to come.

"Do you think that we're . . . strange?" I ask when Lukas has gone out, indicating clearly that he wants to be left alone.

"Do *you* think that you're strange?"

"Yes. Or no. Maybe . . . but we're only doing what we've got to do."

"Well," Yoel says, "it's not that strange—to do what you've got to do I would say is quite normal."

Gábriel is not in fact as reluctant as I had feared. But it's a strain to speak and even more of a strain to remember. He answers in one or two words the questions Yoel puts to him from Lukas. I have the feeling that what Lukas gains from it is not worth the battle. Stop torturing him, I want to say. But what right have I to interfere?

They begin with what is important but not dangerous: places,

names, family details. Gábriel comes from a village outside Kecske-
mét. In the middle of the Puszta, in the Great Hungarian Plain.
From an area with many fruit farms and the apricot brandy they are
famous for, Yoel relates between rounds, seeming to put twice as
much into Gábriel's short replies each time. There's a special shine
in Gábriel's eyes when he hears Yoel mention barack pálinka. Yoel
can't help but laugh.

"It's really awful, barack pálinka . . . you need to have grown up
with it to like it," he whispers to us. There is a moment's levity in
the room, as if the pressure suddenly drops and everyone becomes a
little giddy. Gábriel smiles, Yoel laughs, and Lukas and I laugh as
well even though we have no idea what about.

Yoel seems to know most things. Has studied history at university,
traveled all over. Gives us complimentary mini-lectures between
Gábriel's brief and hesitating answers. About the Puszta, how the
people were driven out under Turkish rule, how the ground, when
no one was cultivating it, was reduced to a wilderness and for cen-
turies was just pastureland for cattle. From Gábriel he has learned
that his older brothers, Lukas's uncles, worked as *czikós,* cattle driv-
ers, when they were young. Gábriel was the only one in the family
they could afford to do without so that he could continue his edu-
cation. He had a head for books and got as far as studying medicine,
even though his studies were prolonged for financial reasons. He
was obliged to work at the same time, married and had children,
and then . . . Yoel pauses, searching for the best way to say it, the
gentlest way. But there is no such way.

Then—before he had passed his final exams—Lukas's mama died.
That was what happened.

A few years later Gábriel left the country with his son.

The conversation ends there. Gábriel indicates that he needs to
rest. It's frustrating for Lukas to break off, but there's no choice.

———

Lukas has always imagined that his mama died shortly after he was born. That has been his explanation for having no memories of her, not the slightest little tone in her voice, no blurred snapshot. That he was five years old and still can't remember her affects him deeply. He raises objections. Yoel must be wrong . . . But the next time Yoel asks, he receives the same answer from Gábriel, so Lukas has to concede.

Stop tormenting him, I want to beg him. But Lukas has a look in his eye that says, *You owe me this.* I have to hold him back now, instead of urging him on. And his papa is no longer capable of defending himself. If he speaks he knows that he will be left in peace afterward—so he speaks. What life gives with one hand, it soon takes back with the other. We learn that Gábriel finally succeeds in catching his teenage love, Lukas's mama, after several years of waiting while she was married to someone else. Mara worked as a nurse in a Budapest suburb and one day a week as a volunteer in a prison. Gábriel's greatest fear was that she would catch tuberculosis, as the infection often spread among inmates. But it wasn't tuberculosis that took her, it was fire. In a summer cottage they had borrowed from some friends, the last day of their holiday there, the fire that took hold in a pile of clothes on the bed. It happened so quickly. Gábriel had gone out into the woods to empty some partridge traps. He had actually gone off because they'd fallen out. They who argued so seldom had disagreed about some small thing, something to do with the children, the two sons. She, Mara, thought that he was too easy on them, would always smooth things over when she had reprimanded them. That meant it had all been to no avail and she was made to feel ashamed that she'd been too hard. They started to argue. After a short quarrel he went out. As he was returning he could see from far away that the little wooden house was engulfed in flames.

After a long silence Gábriel tells them about the other son, that there was another boy, Lukas's older brother. As the cottage was burning, as Gábriel was coming along the dirt road and saw the flames, Lukas had managed to get out. In spite of being the smallest. Or perhaps for that reason, because, unlike the others, he thought of no one other than himself and he ran. His mama and his brother were still inside. Lukas's burns indicated that he had been in the flames, but the only thing he could say was something about a candle in the bed. Afterward, when the burned-out house was examined, it was established that the fire had started in the bedroom. His mama and his brother, András, were found on the floor in the kitchen, presumably trapped in the noxious smoke.

Lukas is suddenly stricken with a splitting headache and goes out. A sudden flash of memory, like a migraine? Perhaps his brother, the memory of someone he shared a bed with, a name or a smell . . . He just pushes me aside and disappears. Yoel persuades me to leave him alone.

Gábriel has spoken about the brother as if he were certain that Lukas remembered him, Yoel tells us later.

"Are you sure that you don't—"

"No! I don't remember him. Maybe I knew about him, but if I did, I've forgotten. No one has ever said a word to me about a brother."

I had noticed something between Lukas and his papa many times without really understanding what it was—the remoteness in their way of looking at each other when one of them came into the room. A hint of disappointment in their eyes. As if they thought, *Oh yes, of course, you're the one who survived. It was you and me. Not the other two. They were left in the flames. It happened to be us* . . . So many years after the fire in the summer house, they still had that look in their eyes.

SCARS

I hear the music before I can make Yoel out through the tangled greenery, he merges in so well there on the veranda. As if he has already made the pearl fisher's house his own. He's sitting with his eyes closed, drinking a beer, in the last hazy light of evening, in Lukas's cane rocking chair, wrapped in our blanket with our cassette player on his knee, reggae disco. Lukas would hate this if he saw it, this picture of Yoel in front of our house. How handsome, how laid-back, how natural. How he squints into the sun and smiles at the fact that I am standing there—and the thought of what that might mean and might lead to.

"I was just going to leave this," I splutter, handing him the bicycle pump, which he accepts in a reflex action without taking his eyes off me. I have to brace myself against that look. Take a step back. That's not why I've come, if that's what he's thinking. He calls himself an interpreter, but I could see long ago that he's not.

He's an amateur who likes playing at being a man. *What's a girl like you doing in a dump like this* . . . He waits for my next move.

"What's this for?"

"Didn't you say you had a flat tire?"

"I don't even have a bike." He smiles. I hope that my flushed cheeks can't be seen in the red evening light.

"So what shall I do with this?" he asks again and swirls the pump around in one hand. "Bring a bike with you next time," he says. I go down one more step. "No, wait, don't go . . ." Yoel gently catches hold of my arm, stops me when I just want to slink away, mortified. "This is the nicest bike pump I've ever had. Truthfully."

"It's just an ordinary pump," I mumble, as the redness burns like wildfire from my cheeks to my neck, down between my breasts and farther on.

"I'll keep it as a reminder of you. Come and sit down for a minute," he says and sweeps his arm over all that he is offering: a leaky wooden veranda, a tattered cane rocking chair, and his own irresistible company. He's inviting me in as if this princely residence were his and not Lukas's and mine. "You're not in a hurry to go anywhere. You need to get out of the house for a while. A beer? No? Okay, I'll just have to switch to wine . . . no-oh . . . what about tea? That's what you'd like, I can see."

As a reminder of you . . . Does that mean he is about to leave? That was what I was afraid of. The job isn't finished yet.

"You're not leaving already?"

"Tomorrow."

"No!" I say, far too desperate. Yes. He has to go back to Stockholm. This evening is his last.

"Have you ever been to Stockholm?"

"Of course. I've been to Stockholm," I lie, as he shows me into the house, as if it really were his now. Hugely messy in the three rooms already. When he arrived it was spotlessly clean to hide the shabbiness. On the table by the window Mama's typewriter was sitting in state, waiting for his arrival. On the telephone he'd said something about a dissertation, thought that he might stay here awhile to finish it. The typewriter looked like a trophy, and it was, too, but when Yoel saw it he just said:

"What an old monster, cool! But I've brought my own with me, a new portable typewriter."

If only he knew what effort was required to bring it here—heavy as a small nuclear power station as I balanced it on the bike rack and

carried it the last bit in my outstretched arms. If he only knew what
risks I had taken to get it here. Mama would disinherit me when
she discovered it had gone. Papa's mother had given it to her. She
often repeated the story:

"When my father was seventeen he stopped working in the mine;
when I was seventeen I was given a typewriter. When you're seventeen . . . what would you like, Lo?" I didn't know yet. But there
were only a few days to go.

Scars are sexy, Yoel says. They mean that you've made a mistake,
that you've crossed a line. He runs his finger over the thin white
streak above my lip. He has a birthmark himself, a blue spot at the
bottom of his back—would I like to see? I shake my head quickly,
afraid that he will take off his shirt and that it won't stop there.

"Is it supposed to taste like this?" I ask to distract him and take a
gulp of the hot drink. Dust. I take another sip. Yes, dust. The tea he
has brewed must be several decades old, something the pearl fisher
brought home from one of his many journeys in the East.

Yoel assumes the air of a connoisseur. "Of course. This is green
tea, Japanese, have you ever tasted it?" I take the bowl with the
strange-smelling chicken soup instead, a mouthful, quite unpre-
pared for the heat that explodes in my mouth, green curry, red
curry, I think I'm going to die, my gums feel so much like open
wounds.

We do it. And before I have time to take in what we've done, we
do it again.

This secret will die with me, I'm thinking. Feel his birthmark
against my hand, rough like the devil's teeth marks in the curve of
his back. Think about Lukas the whole time.

I pulled up my skirt, he pulled down his jeans, it was over quickly.

It was a bit awkward, but it didn't hurt, no worse than being scratched by hawthorn bushes on the way here. The whole time I'm thinking about Lukas—not that it's him I'm with, I'm only afraid that he will appear, that I'll catch a glimpse of his face at the window, see him open the door and suddenly be standing there.

"Is it all right if I come inside you?" Yoel breathes in my ear. I don't have a chance to reply. He takes that as a yes. He fills me and it really smells of seed, exactly like grain ripe for harvesting in the fields around the house. I will have to . . . wash the sheets before Lukas comes here. I will have to rinse myself in the lake before I go home. Become pregnant—that doesn't even cross my mind. The least of my problems. A considerably bigger problem is that Lukas will die when he finds out about this.

I try to concentrate on how good it feels when Yoel caresses me. Fluctuate between enjoyment and fear at two-second intervals. I dare not take my eyes off the window. Yoel kisses my neck and around my breast, armpits, stops:

"Don't you shave yourself?"

"What?"

"Under your arms?" I feel his foot along my shin. "Not your legs either?"

"No. Do you?"

He laughs. "I like you. You're feistier than you look."

In the pearl fisher's house of all places, on the pearl fisher's bed. Afterward I take off my top and wipe away his semen, as naturally as if I had done it many times before.

"How long have you been together?"

"Who?" I ask absently, heavy with heat and tiredness.

"You and that Lukas, of course. You're safe with me, baby, I don't intend to tell him about this, it's best for both of us." We aren't together, I assure him. We have never been. Why does he think that? Because you act as if you are, he replies.

It seems that the only thirst Yoel focuses on satisfying is his own. He's been thinking about this since he got off the train and saw me—he claims. I'm not accustomed to compliments—if it is a compliment—and I squirm under his weight. Was that maybe what Lukas could feel, the scent of another man's lust over the platform? He lowered his horns at Yoel instantly. Is it really so simple? Laugh or cry . . . I can't decide. Marsupials. That's what Mama calls them when she's in the mood. Yoel lifts aside the quilt, pulls out of me, it hurts a little. He rolls off me, grimacing as he pulls his foreskin back into place, and with great vigor he leaps out of bed.

"Tell you what, we'll go down to the sea and have a dip," he says with a smile that turns into a laugh.

The sea? Just like that?

Laugh? Just like that?

I haven't laughed since last spring.

And the sea I've only been to a few times in my life. It was a whole-day affair for my family, who so seldom went anywhere.

"Just for a dip, Lo. It won't take more than an hour or so there and back. How far is it?"

"A long way."

"For God's sake, this is Skåne—how far can it be? Nowhere's more than a few miles from the coast? The water's going to be lovely this time of the evening. Come on."

Yoel just sort of . . . is. Just sort of does. Just takes. For granted. And me? I drift along.

"Can we borrow Lukas's bike, do you think?" Yoel pulls on his underpants and throws me mine. "I'm sure we can," he answers his own question.

Do you have to be so compulsively nice to him? Lukas had re-marked sulkily the very first evening. As if he guessed what was going to happen. Now I'm sitting next to Yoel in Mama's white

Volvo and praying to the gods that Lukas won't see us backing out of our house and driving off to goodness knows where.

I explained to him that borrowing Lukas's motorcycle was out of the question, not a chance.

"What do you mean? Are you together or what? But your mama's car, then? Can we take that?" Yoel had already taken enough . . . or that's what Lukas would have thought, at any rate. My virginity, my virtue, whatever you want to call it—my innocence, that word. What was it you were guilty of afterward that you were not guilty of before? Yoel took me in passing like a chocolate in a dish he couldn't help snatching for himself as he walked by. And soon I was sitting by Mama's bed telling her a sickening little lie—the car, we really need it, Mama—while Yoel stood outside in the darkness, leaning against the garage wall, waiting.

"I should really say no," Mama said as she gave me the keys, "but obviously, if Gábriel's so ill and needs to get to hospital quickly, and Lukas promises to drive carefully." I couldn't bring myself to look her in the eye. Took the keys without so much as a thank-you.

The worst deceit toward Lukas was not that I slept with Yoel, but that I slept beside him. Close, still—so much more intimate than lying under or on top of someone. I lay on his sweaty arm and tried to distinguish constellations in the microscopic flyspecks on the alcove's damp brown wallpaper. My own, the Lynx, should be there somewhere in the swarm of dots, but I couldn't find it. My eyes darted around among the flecks until they started to sting and I had to shut them. Yoel began to caress me again, but soon stopped, already satiated.

Now we're driving to the sea. Perhaps this is also a form of treachery. I have never been to the sea with Lukas. Yoel drives in the middle of the road, as if he owns it. Mama's Volvo usually causes trouble, but it obeys him. Obliging his every whim, fast for once and like putty in his hands.

"Isn't he a bit too old for you? Lukas. Bit too old, huh? How old are you?"

"I'll soon be seventeen."

"Seventeen," he says, surprised. "I thought you were younger." A hundred and eighty degrees of violet sky, curving above us. Yoel drives as if he owns both the road and the sky.

"We're not together. I told you."

"So you don't sleep together. What do you do, then? There's not much to do around here. Tell me. Catch grasshoppers? Count freight cars? Smoke? That Lukas seems a bit"—we shouldn't be talking about him, but Yoel doesn't notice when I try to interrupt him—"seems a bit stoned. Not just because he goes around in a rasta top wrapped up in his own world, but because he doesn't sleep with you, the sweetest chick in the village—it's obvious you like him. You seem to be prepared to do anything at all for him, at least. What kind of hold has he got over you anyway?"

Lukas is the last thing I want to talk to Yoel about. I have mixed blood with Lukas, with Yoel all the other body fluids, so much more transparent and easily combined.

"Why do you ask so many questions about him? I'm with you and all the time you talk about Lukas."

"Okay, okay," he whispers, smiling. "To hell with him."

I like Yoel because he is everything Lukas is not. I like him because I don't love him. Screw, chat, bathe. All at the same time, on the same day, and before the evening is over, he says:

"What do you say, babe, are you going to come with me to Stockholm? Life's just begun. For you at any rate." He's the same age as Lukas and is already beginning to feel old, perhaps because he has lived life at such speed, been everywhere, done everything.

Stockholm is so far away in my world, he might just as well have asked me to go with him to Ittoqqortoormiit.

That night I hear Yoel's words—this is no place for you, girl—while the river rats scuttle along the floorboards. Nocturnal animals, the most intelligent and sensitive of creatures. For as long as Gábriel was well, they didn't last long here. Why didn't they come down to the pearl fisher's house instead? We would have left them in peace there, like the Indian temple Lukas had seen on the television where rats were holy—free, quiet, well fed, unafraid. Rats aren't just rats, he tried to convince me, they run with the wind in their fur when they are free, scream like red-hot barbed wire when you drown them, hiss and splutter steam like green wood when they burn, have feelings like you and me. And the separation between body and soul doesn't exist. In the womb the skin grows out from the brain, Lukas explained, opening his hand and letting a drip fall, that's why it is so sensitive. It fell right on my back and my skin was so hot that a single drop gave me goose bumps.

The afternoon Yoel arrived on the train in the blazing heat was a day when everything smelled strong and burned and acrid and carnal, as if all the hay were flesh. An oppressive smell in the house was the first thing he pointed out to us. I thought it was the illness, but he said it was an animal smell. We had lived in the odor for so long we didn't notice it, but Yoel said that it stank. He was sure it was coming from the attic.

"The rats," Lukas said bleakly. When his papa stopped forcing him to empty the cages, he had forgotten them, suppressed the thought of them . . . the cages his father loved when he was well.

"I'll take care of them," I said quickly, because Lukas looked as though he would pass out at the mere thought of what it looked like up there. However disgusting I thought it was, I didn't harbor the same feelings for the animals as he did. I put on rubber boots, tied a kitchen towel over my nose and mouth, and fetched the hook for the hatch to the attic, before Yoel blocked my path:

"Are you mad, girl—we'll phone for Anticimex!" Stared at me as if he really were asking himself what loony bin he had ended up in. A few minutes later he'd had a telephone conversation, explained the situation, and persuaded them that they had to make an urgent call.

You know what people say—that girls who sleep with everyone don't want to sleep with the only one who loves them. It was only a line from a film, Lukas . . . from *Breathless*. I feel his eyes on me as we sit in Gábriel's bedroom. Yoel next to me. It's a strange way of getting to know your first lover, as observer at Lukas's papa's deathbed. On the last day Yoel is sitting quietly by the wall, prepared to be there but not to be seen. A stranger in their home, in the bedroom among the most intimate secrets of their life. Sitting in the darkest corner interpreting at a distance to show respect, or perhaps keeping a distance for his own sake. Because the situation upsets him.

He's not a trained interpreter, but his mother works at the embassy in Budapest and has found a few assignments for him. And the job is like this sometimes, he says: headlong into the life of strangers, vitally important events, sensitive conflicts, delicate situations. How do you make that all right? He explains that when he leaves he forgets everything that has been said. At the time he is concentrating so hard on the words that the content and context almost escape him.

Yoel sits with us until the end, ready to catch any last crucial words, but there are none.

Too late. Too late for me and Lukas too—something has happened this summer and it is not Yoel's fault. It would have happened anyway.

Lukas and Yoel. An incompatible chemistry. They even smell as though they have a totally different composition. Lukas slightly metallic, like water in storms at high altitude. He looks as though he was suffering from altitude sickness some days, something going out of control. Yoel smells of expensive perfume, even if he is broke. He doesn't want to smell broke, he reveals. But he's not poor in the way Lukas is, for a wealthy family always provides protection against the wolves. That way he can buy expensive eau de cologne with his last few cents.

I know that I have fallen for him. And I almost hate him for it.

MORTE

Should the eyes be open or closed? They are half open now. How do you close them without touching him? You shouldn't touch a dead person, should you? As a child I wasn't supposed to touch the dead birds in the garden, but I did. Always carried them in and laid them on a bed of cotton wool in clean butter dishes. Should we put a coin under his tongue? And his hands. What should we do with his hands? They are lying so haphazardly, one clenched, the other open, bent at a strange angle, as if he were trying to hold on to this life with one hand, though there is nothing to hold on to. Oedipus stabs out his own eyes with pins from a brooch, only I don't remember why. A desperate gesture from a grieving man because he can't weep? I've seen Lukas cry before, but not the way he is now, without tears, much more frightening. I feel like a hired mourner. I didn't have any strong feelings for Gábriel, at least not positive ones. Lukas's feelings weren't positive either, but despite everything there was a bond between them, and the line between bond and love, where does it lie? I look at Gábriel's hands. He was skilled with them, but I can't see them without thinking of all the times they hurt Lukas. Had Gábriel really deserved this summer of patient watchfulness, deserved Lukas's . . . kindness?

"Kindness is something people seldom deserve. That's why it's called kindness," Yoel says, when we've gone out to leave Lukas alone with his father for a while. We sit down under the roof of the porch in the rain and each drink a bowl of buttermilk, famished, haven't eaten all day. To think about your own hunger in the midst of it all felt so wrong. I let my stomach grumble while we sat by Gábriel's bed.

His last sentences had been incoherent. On one occasion he opened his eyes and looked at me. I felt like an angel of death, sitting there in my white T-shirt, pale after a summer indoors. I didn't know that dying was such a struggle, thought it happened by itself, without opposition. But when I looked at Gábriel it seemed anything other than simple. He was fighting and I couldn't decide whether it was to die or to live. At first I thought he was trying to cling on—you know it's the last thing you'll ever hold on to, this goddamn little life, the last wrung-out remnants of it—but perhaps he was trying to let go?

When he finally died I didn't even notice. It took some time before I realized that he was no longer breathing.

Failed miracle. The wisteria sways as if charged with electricity in the evening wind. It's been a still day, but now the wind is blowing up from all directions. The wind through Gábriel's hair gives me a start. Without my noticing, Yoel has opened the window and Gábriel's hair rustles like dry winter grass in the draft, as if he were coming back to life for a little while, but it's a false alarm. What did Lukas whisper in his ear before he died?

"Whispered? Don't remember," he answers absently. "I don't actually remember. Did I whisper something?"

The last thing that Gábriel told us was that Lukas was the cause of his mother's death. I thought it was so unnecessary to say it here and now, so harsh. I wished that Yoel had chosen not to translate it. What would Lukas do with this knowledge, other than bear it for the rest of his life? Possibly it could explain Gábriel's antipathy to him as he was growing up, the constant coldness. But did it bring any comfort to know the cause? What Lukas had now learned could never be retracted—that the fire he happened to start had robbed him of his mama. And the papa he loved. If it was a relief for Gábriel to unburden himself in his last conscious hours, it was now Lukas who would carry the load instead.

When I looked at Gábriel's hands, before they became slack and the blood stopped flowing through them, I thought of all the experiences they had in them. All the blows they had dealt and all the caresses, albeit long ago. All the thousands of hours at the factory, hand grips, muscle memory, everything you had to learn, only to die.

When he closed his eyes for the last time he had less than twenty-four hours to live. Something loosened inside me and was cast out when I realized that it was the end. A fear, a doubt. Now it was over. We had done what we could. It was not much, but we had done it. Now we could begin to live once more. Sleep and eat and laugh and touch each other as usual.

But for Lukas it was different. He had become less and less approachable, and now something in his eyes had withdrawn completely. His face was so haggard, it looked as though the whole summer had been one long all-night party. I stayed with him that evening, but when he refused to phone the hospital and ask them to come and fetch Gábriel's body, I left. Couldn't cope with one more sleepless night. Something had come to an end inside me too. For Lukas perhaps the body was still Gábriel, but for me it was dead.

"I'm going now," I said. He could have stopped me, but he didn't. He could have said, "I love you," or "Do you love me?" or "Hold me for a while," or "Come here and I'll hold you for a while." Whatever he had said, I would have said yes.

"Go," he said.

"Yes," I said.

"Well go then!"

"Yes."

I went. Home to Mama. Showered and changed my clothes and answered her questions as well as I could. Then I went down to the pearl fisher's house and spent the night there with Yoel. It was the last night before he returned to Stockholm. He was already late, had stayed longer than he had planned:

"For your sake," he said.

"You mean for Lukas's sake?"

"For all your sakes . . . You're the most remarkable constellation I've ever come across." Constellation? Like stars that form something together even though they are so far apart.

That night I dreamed of electric machines and legs of lactic acid that desperately resisted. Morphine injections, stained sheets over a dead body. Empty lungs, empty words of comfort. Don't comfort me, help me to shout, Lukas asked me in my dream, but in reality he didn't reach out to me, and I didn't dare approach him either.

I thought the whole time that he would knock on the door. I'd told him that when he had called for the ambulance, he should come and fetch me. When he had arranged for them to come and collect the body, he should tell me. But he didn't come.

It was as easy as that. Just to leave. I wasn't going to live and die in this village after all? In Mama's house, in Papa's absence, in Grandfather's arboretum, in Lukas's shadow. When you start thinking about childhood you know it's already over. Perhaps it's the same with love.

"We'll see how it works out. Not that it's ever worked before. As soon as anyone's moved in with me, it's gone wrong," Yoel warned, "but you're different." What do you mean, different? I didn't want to be different, I wanted to be the same as all the others.

"Well, you don't seem to have such high demands of life, I mean, and you're so damn sexy when you look at me like that—but be careful—I'm the sort that strikes back." So strange that it had gone wrong then . . . with the girls. I began to suspect that maybe it wasn't such a good idea after all. Reminded him that I didn't have a ticket for the train.

"Haven't you got a ticket? That means we'll have to steal a car."

". . . no . . ."

"Well, that depends on you. How much you want to come."

As if it were a game, a film, a *Bonnie and Clyde* remake. He sat by one of the open windows looking handsome, had packed but not cleaned, obviously intended to leave the house in the chaos he had achieved in such a short time.

"Besides, didn't Lukas say that he had a car in for repair and he couldn't afford to get it back?" The apple of Lukas's eye, the blue Ford—he will never let that go, I thought. "I've always wanted a cool old jalopy like that."

"Do you always . . ."

"What?"

"Well—do you always, sort of, get what you want?" I asked, provoked.

"Get? It's not a question of getting, Lo, it's a question of fixing."

Okay. But you'll never get the Ford. It was Lukas's pride and joy, the only dream he had managed to realize. Lukas's. When he was forced to put it in the garage at the beginning of summer to have the front axle changed, it was as if he had lost an arm. The garage had immediately found five other faults that they had taken care of, without asking him first, and now he had an unpaid bill of several thousand, more than he had paid for the damn Ford. If he didn't come and fetch it soon, they threatened to sell it. He couldn't pay, I knew that. I wished that I could help him, had turned over in my mind ways that I might wheedle the money out of Mama. And now Lukas had to pay for the funeral too. Thousand-krona notes would just flutter away, even if the undertakers agreed to an installment plan. He had no idea dying was so expensive. He'd thought that Gábriel had money in an account somewhere, because they always lived so frugally, but there didn't appear to be a cent anywhere. He must have sent money back home out of his pay all these years. Lukas just didn't know to whom.

"Maybe he won't think of it as selling the car to me, but as me paying it off for him," Yoel was calculating.

"Sure."

"Do you think?"

"No. Never! He would never do that."

"We'll see," said Yoel, as if he already considered the car his own.

Lukas looked as though he had fallen asleep in the sun on the wooden porch. Lay outstretched on our blanket, but rose hastily as if he heard our footsteps reverberate through the ground. I felt un-comfortable as soon as I saw him—as in the past, when I saw that he had been beaten but wanted to pretend he hadn't. It always gave me a bad conscience, as if it were my fault, which most often it was in one way or another.

I shouldn't have gone with Yoel to ask about the car. I wasn't his accomplice and the invitation to Lukas to be released from the car problem was completely Yoel's idea. It was like extortion. I knew how hard pressed Lukas was and when I explained that to Yoel he'd seen his chance—even if he did quickly turn it into us helping him out of a tight spot . . . It could mean debt collection, action for non-payment of debt, and God knows what, which would keep you in debt for ever.

I wondered whether Gábriel was still lying inside or whether an ambulance had driven through the village and I hadn't heard it. With sirens turned off, as always on that mission. I wondered if Lu-kas could see that I was holding my breath as we approached. That I had just been screwed and was ready to clear out. But how would he be able to see that? He didn't even look at me. Not one single time.

He just waited to hear what Yoel had to say and listened, expressionless. With every moment that Lukas did not look at me, I felt more and more transparent. Soon he wouldn't be able to see me even if he wanted to. I could still feel the sensation of Yoel's penis inside me; if I became invisible it would be the only thing to be seen, floating in the air like a raised finger at Lukas. I crossed my legs even though that would scarcely help. It was aching slightly and the rest of me was so numb that I couldn't help but focus on it. Lukas looked the worse for wear and worn out through lack of sleep, but at least he was standing up. Had he slept at all? He usually slept so lightly that he woke up if I wasn't holding him. Had he eaten? Spent the night out here? Was he cold? Had he drunk? Did he have a hangover? He was wearing my red socks. They looked out of place: the rest of his clothes were black for the occasion.

Yoel went through it all one more time, a deal where he paid the garage bill and a few thousand more into the bargain and took charge of the car. He didn't mention anything about "we," otherwise the chance of Lukas agreeing would of course have been zero.

"You're joking?" After an eternity I heard Lukas's voice.

"It's actually a good deal," Yoel persevered. "You'll get rid of a problem. And haven't you got enough problems just now?" Lukas gazed at him as though looking at a cheat and a traitor and trying to decide what category of swindler he was dealing with. "You should always ask for an estimate when you leave your car at a garage or call in a workman," Yoel admonished, as if Lukas hadn't understood that. Now there will be a fight, I thought. Now Lukas will take out all his frustration on him, wallop him.

"Take it," was all Lukas said. Yoel was caught off balance. An arsenal of arguments that he now wouldn't have use for. He hadn't reckoned on getting off so lightly.

"Take it."

"Okay . . . I don't have that much cash on me at the moment, but I'll send it as soon as I get to Stockholm. Okay? And we'll have to sign all the registration papers over to me, to avoid any hassle."

"Do what the hell you want," Lukas said and walked into the house. He knew. We'd always been so close to each other that one look was all he needed to see that I had been with Yoel. It wasn't hatred in his eyes, it was a kind of inverted love.

Yoel and I went off and recovered the car at the Loan Shark Garage, as Lukas called it. The dark blue Taunus that I had been in so many times with him—Yoel just pulled out a credit card and paid the bill and the car was his. The debt, which for Lukas was insurmountable, was settled in a quarter of an hour.

I traveled without luggage, didn't want to go home and pack, just to leave and phone home when I was out of reach. If my things were still at home perhaps Mama would think that I had only gone away for a while rather than moved for good. I didn't know how long this was going to last. Yoel had warned me that he was an unreliable, fickle type. It didn't scare me, quite the reverse; with Lukas everything had been in earnest and forever.

I rose to my feet and shook everything off. Went with him. Left a gaping hole behind me. Didn't look back.

Yoel's seed was still inside me. The one who sows, he shall reap, Lukas. God helps those who help themselves—it could have been you . . .

The relief when I left without saying goodbye was so great that it outweighed the shame. Lukas in the rearview mirror, carrying Gábriel's things out into the yard, the gas can on the steps, work gloves, the flames leaping up behind his body, stripped to the waist—he had grown so thin. The body I had always had so close to me that I never really regarded it as a separate part of reality, more an extension or duplication of myself.

Don't play with fire, Lo, Mama said all the time. It was Lukas who was the fire. The first one, when we met, was an accident. It must have been. A spark in the grass where it was extra dry along the railway embankment, a gust of wind that made it flare up. That spark was like a first meeting—you need to keep it alive or it will soon burn out. The one that was burning now, outside Gábriel and Lukas's house . . . Even if it was his papa's belongings he was setting fire to, I knew it was to do with me. He was burning what we had and what we didn't have. He was burning everything. Mattresses, bedclothes, blankets, chairs, shoes, books, piles of *Népszabadság* newspapers. Started a fire and walked right into it. I saw his frenzied movements in the mirror—a scene I had witnessed before, a circle that was closing.

Had Lukas not always had a dangerous combination of fire and madness to some degree? Throwing things into the blaze, everything he didn't know what to do with—it is possible to burn them and carry on. The relief in being powerless.

I saw that he could see that I was looking at him. And yet he didn't even lift his hand. Nor did I, paralyzed by a mixture of relief and shame. Lukas's hands were busy bringing out the last of Gábriel's things, all that had been his life, throwing it onto the fire and pouring gas over it all. And in my hands there was only lead, weighing down on my thighs while Yoel's fingers found their way up there in such a natural caress I couldn't stop him. With one hand on the wheel and the other in pursuit of pleasure, he pulled out onto the highway and put his foot down. It went like clockwork now, Lukas's car, money lavished on it and oiled. To me it would always be Lukas's car, whether Yoel had bought it or not.

———

It is the strong who remain behind, the weak who leave. I deserted, forced to go away to become myself. Hadn't I always said I wanted to see the Atlantic, Lukas? You could have taken me there, we could have gone there together, everything could have been different. I will never leave you; I am leaving you now.

You never lose the one you loved.

It takes two to tango, but only one to let go.

Words, words, words.

See you in hell, Lo.

His last line, never uttered.

PLAYED, LAID, BETRAYED

Yoel is in the sun, cooling himself down with a beer, looking at the view and from time to time at me. Now and then he shouts out something that must be an instruction, but his voice is drowned by the music from the car radio. It is going well all the same. I must have a natural talent. Around and around over the tacky late-summer asphalt, wider, hotter, faster circles. You need to be able to drive a car to feel truly free. Halfway up to Stockholm he'd thought it was time to stop and practice, at a rest area with a fantastic view over the highway and a sparkling stretch of water.

I want to slip out of the parking space without him. It isn't Yoel's car, it will always be Lukas's car, and the two of us never distinguished between yours and mine. When Yoel thinks my circles look perfect, he asks if I want to drive properly, nods in the direction of the highway—there are two hundred miles left and he's tired of sitting behind the wheel, wants to sleep the last stretch.

I focus on the road. When thoughts of Lukas intrude, I accelerate.

"You're a natural."

"I know." I put my foot down.

"Just take it easy. Stay in the inside lane until I say." Reluctantly I ease up on the accelerator. "You've got my life in your hands now, how does it feel?" It feels good. Better than it has in a long time, in fact. I want to pass. He laughs. "Not yet. When I say. You couldn't wait to get away, it's obvious."

He lets me drive until we arrive at the outskirts of town. We mustn't tempt fate. If anything were to happen he's the one who would be held to blame. He has both an American and a Hungarian driver's license. I have had a taste of driving and would prefer not to hand back the wheel, but the fun is over now.

"You're not even old enough, you're underage, aren't you? Not that you look as though you're not smart, but . . . inexperienced. Inevitable, growing up like that." In the shadow of the factories. That's what he calls it. He grew up in Stockholm, Berlin, and Budapest, studied in New York. He's the same age as Lukas, but so much more sophisticated and confident, and that adds years to his age. He's been everywhere, done everything. He looks good in neon and looks good without. We glide into a tunnel. I've never been in a car underground before, but I read *Alice in Wonderland* from cover to cover, and this is a darker version of the same thing.

When we have emerged above ground I roll down the window. The smell of the city is the smell of exhaust fumes, new asphalt, frying from the restaurants. This is the best present I could have had, I say, with my hair streaming in the wind and my eyes watering with the cold night air.

"What? Is it your birthday?" he asks, surprised, as he zigzags through the traffic.

Yes. Seventeen.

His apartment is in the Kasernberget district. A concrete block built in the seventies with windows the size of portholes. As we carry in his luggage I think that the ugliest house is the best location—that way you don't have to look at it. The street sign. I stare at it. Too much . . .

"What?" he asks.

"Strindbergsgatan? Did Strindberg live here? Really?"

He must have. At some time. He lived in lots of different places in the city, but it would hardly have been in this Berlin bunker,

Yoel says, displeased. In his presence you are always reminded that the English word "spoiled" has two meanings.

If Lukas could see us now—thank the good Lord that he can't—he would be beside himself.

"Don't think about him now," Yoel whispers. His stomach smells of ylang-ylang, sandalwood, a drop of semen. He slows the pace—to lead and to follow is a simple logic. Sex is about not thinking, he says, as if he knew it's the only thing I long for now.

It's so easy for him, not just in bed. Everything was so easy from the moment he opened the passenger door of the car, which a little while ago had been Lukas's prize possession, and asked me to jump in. Took my virginity in passing, then he took it again and again, before we had time to unload the car, unpack his things, before I even had time to draw back the curtains and look at the view.

Afterward: "Don't tell me that I was the first? But for God's sake, Lo, how could I have known? You should have said something, then I would have taken it a bit more . . ."

"What? Steady?"

"Maybe. At least I would like to have known. It's a . . ."

"Big responsibility?"

"No, but cool, like. Special." He looks at me doubtfully. "Do you mean to say that you and that Lukas never, not once, he didn't even try?" Now we are talking about him again and I don't want to.

Lukas would soon be twenty-four and I had thought that obviously he must do it sometimes. I couldn't imagine him with anyone else, but there must have been someone, sometime. Who could it have been? Someone at the factory? He never spoke about work when he was off, as if it didn't exist, other than a slight ache in his shoulders and hands. Perhaps that was why he was so secretive? Because he had someone there? I knew well enough that this wasn't so, but it was too sad to think that he had never had anything more than he had with me.

Stockholm the first morning: I release myself from Yoel's hold and launch myself at the window, tear the heavy white curtains apart. There it is. Sparkling like a glass of water in the sun. Stunningly clean and water everywhere with a perfect silhouette against the cyanide-blue late-summer sky.

While I slept I really must have landed on my backside in another world. The city is a forest of light and sound and motion. I can't remember when I last felt so small, perhaps the time Papa carried me in his arms over the field in the worst thunderstorm of the summer. He didn't dare carry me on his shoulders in case a flash of sheet lightning were to seek out the top of my wet head. Scared and with my eyes shut, I had rushed straight out into the field of grain—too small to be seen as I raced around in a vicious circle of panic. The movement in the grain revealed where I was. Papa caught me, comforted, scolded, saved, and carried me in a rough grip through the nightmarish thundering light.

Whether it is the world that has grown while I slept or I who has shrunk in my sleep—it has all taken my breath away. He laughs and kisses me between the eyes, a typical Yoel gesture. My fascination for Stockholm is clearly very moving, like a mole who sticks her head up for the first time and sees the light. He shows me the view from Söders Höjder. Just that I call it "Söders Höjder" makes him kiss me again between the eyes.

"It's just the most fantastic thing I've ever seen," I whisper.

"But you've never seen anything, honey: railway, lake, same old countryside, same old . . . what's his name now? Lukas?"

I lay my fingers on his lips. I can't rid myself of the feeling that I am a deserter, a heartless, heartless traitor.

"You know we live in the ugliest building in the whole city," he says, to bring me back down to earth.

"But I like it." That, according to Yoel, is because I was born between two factories. Four factories, to be precise. To be exact: four factories, a railway, an industrial park, and a hydropower station.

I don't know if he was a child who had too much love, but he must at any rate have had too much of everything else. Nothing is really good enough for him; the apartment is way beneath his dignity. At the moment he is too broke to live the sort of life he thinks he deserves. If only he hadn't made himself impossible with his papa. That is the risk with fine families—it is easy to be banished from them, he says. Monthly maintenance withdrawn. His father has taken his support away.

"What would've become of you if I hadn't come and rescued you?" I hear him say one day when we are eating breakfast in bed, so late in the afternoon that it's beginning to get dark again. The mud-king's daughter? A factory moth spinning an endless thread in the darkness of the wool factory? Eternal virginity? Shriveled up. The croissant in my mouth swells up like a ball of cotton wool the more I chew. I know that he's joking. But all the same.

"I don't come from the country. I come from the outskirts." It wasn't true countryside, because we had streetlights, but it wasn't true village either, because the road wasn't paved. It had something of a bad reputation, along with those of us who lived there. The houses weren't so well cared for, the gardens not so well tended, like the children. If only the railway hadn't cut through the view of the rolling landscape, if only the sound of the long freight trains hadn't shattered the conversations at the kitchen table. In late winter the lake always overflowed and the fields lay under water and the local flowers had ugly names like bog asphodel, frogbit, waterweed, water plantain, pod grass. The smallness of everything made it more noticeable that we didn't belong there, Lukas and I. If only our family circumstances had been normal, we might have given the illusion that we fitted in. But not even that.

"Factory moth," Yoel says, or do I just read it in his eyes? He himself is of a nobler species, without necessarily being more sensitive: a spinner of silk and satin, sharp and alluring features. Self-assured, unequivocal. The sophisticated type who has lived and traveled and knows his culinary French. In a restaurant he sends food back if it is not to his taste, and expects to be compensated for his disappointment. Loves everything ending in *confit,* which I eventually gather just means that it is cooked in its own fat. It sounds unappealing, but he maintains that duck confit is as near as you can get to heaven. And *coeur de filet,* the heart of the filet, is the thickest and best part. It is the part of me he will never have, but he doesn't want it anyway.

A playful and relaxed prelude, is that all we are for each other? If we make love early in the evening, he goes out afterward, seems to be hungry for something that isn't available at home. I'm too young to go with him, too young for the only places it is worth going to—he gets in everywhere, people know that he is no pauper, at least not in the pub.

Every time I try to imagine what Lukas is doing just now, I see him by Gábriel's coffin in his black mourning shorts, the only thing he wore at the end. Funeral for close family and friends—what do you do if the close family and friends consist of one person? A very simple ceremony?

It takes some time before I understand what the smell is. Only sense it at night, when I try to sleep and there is nothing to distract me. It is the smell of the summer in the house with Gábriel that has clung to me. Showering and washing my clothes doesn't help. It's embedded far up in my nostrils, inaccessible, until in the end it sub-sides, like a sorrow you can no longer bear.

The harsh light of summer has changed. Gentler and softer, like Yoel's laugh. *Mañana,* he says, and I try to learn from him. We will do it tomorrow, everything can wait, everything but the moment that must be enjoyed while it lasts. Now, only now.

Playing and caressing and deceiving. I straddle him in the Hiro-shima four-poster bed. Promise him eternal fidelity under a cloud of creamy white tulle. We laugh. Make love a bit more in the pale light from the Sodom bedside lamp. Order Chinese food in small white cartons delivered to the door. I have never eaten Chinese food before, never had food delivered to the door, only seen it in films. Yoel opens the door naked, but the Chinese man doesn't let his mask slip. It is called losing face in Chinese, Yoel explains, and he gives him a generous tip, "keep the change" . . . Money burns a hole in Yoel's pocket . . . We are on fire and make love and fuck behind the Gomorrah silk curtain. Love is like lighting a cigarette on a burning curtain, an exaggerated gesture, an excessive risk. Be careful, Lo, I hear Mama say . . . I like the kissing afterward with the taste of sweet-and-sour sauce. Even when I take him in my mouth he tastes of sweet-and-sour sauce. I have started to write down in my oilcloth-covered book the words you need to know when you are with Yoel. Sweet-and-sour. Fellatio. *Mañana.*

I am making love to a moth. He weighs nothing, lifts me off the sheet, we levitate, revolve, transpire. I give him a hard-on, he gives me goose bumps, I give him . . . well, what? He has everything al-ready. I can only give him the one thing he doesn't have—myself.

"People like you don't grow on trees, Lo. Or maybe you do, a very rare sort," he whispers, thrusting so deep inside me it hurts.

A man's penis is enlarged during dream sleep and on physical con-tact. I look at him to check and, yes, that is correct. On the other hand, if impotence can be cured with the smell of cinnamon, as they say on the radio, a scent from childhood, a mother's baking, that can't be proved with Yoel, he's not at risk. Sometimes he gets hard while he's frying eggs or when he's shaving or talking to a friend on the telephone, even when he's sitting staring at his dissertation.

"I want to have you, can't you see?"

"Put a bag of ice on it." I have promised to say no to him next time I distract him while he is studying. But I don't say no. If it isn't me, it will be some other craving that disturbs him. This thesis will never be finished, and it isn't my fault. *Coitus a mammilla*. The urge to play.

"Slowly," he whimpers, when I try to swallow him too fast. It is so powerful that we can hardly move, a blackout of pleasure, *la petite mort*. Yoel is fluent in the language of love.

"I love you," I say and don't mean it. It is so easy to say.

"I love you too," he whispers and doesn't mean it either. Storms and accidents don't touch us. I am naked apart from some black pieces of jewelry around my wrists and neck. Some cheap trash he has bought me for fun, magnetite, jewels for those on the way down—and I go right to the bottom with him, not deep, because he has no depth. He says that himself, and laughs with all his crooked white teeth.

He requires nothing of me. Not like Lukas. There are things Yoel wants, but it isn't a need, not dependency, just desire. He fills me up and at the same time he makes me feel lighter than ever before. But when I want to dance on his feet, he complains that I'm too heavy, and when I want to go out with him, he says that I'm too young. At least for the places he wants to go to. Kisses me between the eyes and goes.

When we're drunk we're useless in bed, but the day after we can keep going for hours. There's no greater aphrodisiac than a moderate hangover, I soon learn. The ease with which Yoel moves through his life, I'm waiting for it all to be overturned. Is there really no cloud on his horizon?

One of his former girlfriends seems to have the same unequivocal attitude to life as he does. She comes past sometimes and has a glass of wine on her way somewhere else. Treats me as if I were a home helper who is having a break between cleaning the toilet and ironing shirts and quite possibly sexual services that in her world are clearly part of that sort of job. She has always bought something incredibly expensive that she wants to try on and show off, after Yoel like a fool has helped her with the zip. It's the only time he ever appears to be an idiot; we all have someone who is more than a match for us, and she is his.

I start to feel very ill at ease when I see her through the peephole.

"You're such a loser still living here," she says and gives him an air kiss without touching his cheek. She never touches anyone, he says, except possibly when she has to lie with someone to . . . well. At least once every six months so that her boyfriend doesn't tire of her, and now and then with someone who can give her something she wants. The one-night stands seem to be reserved for what they can give her outside the bed rather than in it.

I listen, my ears like cupped batwings. She isn't bothered that I'm listening, perhaps that's the intention—just as the whole time she can obviously see me, though she never looks directly at me. She spreads disquiet with her mere presence in Yoel's kitchen, has the ability to use up all the oxygen in the room. Always the same pattern: she sweeps in, asks him to open a bottle of wine, takes three sips and leaves the rest, rapidly sums up everything that has happened to her since the last time. Her life is a triumphal procession and we have the honor of being the audience. I glance at Yoel while she's talking. Have the feeling that he is actually dazzled by her successes and that the apparently self-inflicted disasters awake his sympathy. Then she relates her human conquests—man or woman, it's not all that im-portant. However, it's never a question of sex. Sex is just the means, tried and tested, a win every time.

Several times a day I lace up my gym shoes and stuff a little money into my pocket, coins and small notes that I find all over in the apartment.

"Where are you going?"

"Out." Kiss him as I go past, taking long strides, eager to be moving. It's like having a dog, according to Yoel, a dog that takes itself out. I have nothing against being a dog. Adaptable, independent, always on the move.

"I miss you when you're not here . . . but you'll come home when you're hungry, won't you?" Yes. I'll come home when I'm hungry, but first I have to sniff around the whole town.

Stockholm is a dream from which I don't want to wake. The water doesn't smell at all like the lake at home, not fermenting sludge, if anything an acrid chemical smell of diesel and oil. At the beginning I managed to ignore everything that was ugly. In Yoel too.

Wallpaper with ominous eczema-colored flamingos in the bed-room, kitchen chairs in poison-yellow plastic that make me lose my appetite, on the wall above the bed Warhol's *Car Crash* in shocking pink. *The monotone repetition and the garish colors express a moral and an aesthetic emptiness that is a goal in pop art,* he recites. The mono-tone repetition and moral emptiness swim above us every time we make love; the cars crash at the same moment he twists my head backward.

The days with him float like music in a piano bar, hardly noticed. Neither of us goes out to work. He has money, so we manage, and if he has none, then he sorts it out one way or another. Yoel the fixer, trickster. Money is something to be handled with discretion, not something you talk about. If you have it, you spend generously on yourself and others. If you don't, you lie low for a while and don't grumble about it. Behave as if nothing has happened, it's just a downswing.

Lukas talked about money all the time. For him the downswing was perpetual, mental, or even in the blood. He was oppressed by it. Often talked about what he would do if he ever became rich, though we both knew it would take a miracle for him to become rich, and miracles never happen. That's why they're called miracles.

For Yoel the crises are never serious. He can afford to have a laissez-faire attitude to everything, can always call and bow and scrape a little and get his mama to write a blank check for him when the bills are piling up or he has found something expensive he wants for himself. Yoel the bon vivant, the dandy.

If there is a single cloud in his sky it is his parents, though it is more of a light cloud that at regular intervals passes by and is gone. The family meets twice a year, dispassionately. Gathers together in a large apartment on Riddargatan that's empty the rest of the time. His mama travels from Budapest, his papa from Berlin. To play at being married. The whole thing is topped off in a weekend, punctually and dutifully.

"Come home and sneak the wedding ring on again, just often enough to keep up appearances. They don't believe that we know they're separated, isn't that touching?"

He is the last shoot on some noble old tree, as high-class as he is poor. There's money in the family even if he doesn't think he has an adequate share of it. He has grown up in his brothers' cast-off clothes, and when he was a teenager his father was so stingy that Yoel was obliged to seduce his mother's friends for pocket money. He didn't tell me that, but he told his ex-girlfriend, who passed it on to me on one of her nighttime get-togethers in his kitchen. A middle-class objection to spoiling their children—you have to have a certain hunger to get anywhere in this world. Yoel's mama wants her sons to get as far as possible. So that she doesn't have to look at them, is his guess.

My mama didn't want me to get anywhere at all. All the others had gone. I try not to think about it—the reason—it is like a thousand-piece jigsaw puzzle, where most of the pieces are missing; you will go mad if you try to do it. The only thing I know for certain is that it all began when Papa left. That piece of the puzzle was in the middle, and even though the family was large, it only needed one person to disappear for it no longer to be whole.

I don't call her. Don't even open her letters. Reply to them unread. I miss you too, I write. But I can't go home, I can't cope with the feeling I would have standing in front of Lukas, even in my head. We met and parted against a backdrop of fire. Perhaps it meant nothing, but behind my eyes when I am asleep it is still burning, and in my dreams Mama calls and tells me that Lukas walked straight into the fire when I went. He left me a farewell letter, she says, but when she tried to read it the ink was smeared, completely illegible.

"But you'll definitely know what it said, Lo." I slam down the receiver as if it has burned me. Then I wake up.

I have begun to think like Yoel, *mañana,* I will do it tomorrow, anything less important than sex can wait until tomorrow. But tomorrow never comes. With every day that passes it becomes more and more impossible to contact Lukas. Likewise to call home, and the letters Mama sends I leave unopened in a pile.

"Isn't it better just to throw them straight out?" Yoel asks. He thinks it's reproach I'm afraid of, but it's not that.

In Mexico there's a volcanic mountain that hasn't erupted for three hundred years, and yet clouds of smoke can still be seen over the snow-clad peak. When I heard about that I thought of him, how sometimes time is of no consequence. I'd like to live in Mexico. I hear it's so lovely. If you don't love too much you don't love enough. Words, so easy to say.

What happened when I left with Yoel must have felt to Lukas like being overtaken in the last yards of a marathon. He had always expected me to race him at growing. He was an adult, but he couldn't live as an adult, must have felt castrated, seen the change in my face, sensed the teenage smell. To be starving and recognize the smell of something you want to have.

I know it's only words, but perhaps you have to stop trying to forget, so that one day you notice that it has worn off by itself, the cloud of smoke no longer hovering above the volcano.

It's hard to say what ruthlessness is, what insensitivity is and what just pure thoughtlessness is. Yoel's former girlfriend will never get away with it, I think, as she tells me how she does what she will with people to get what she wants. But the world around her seems infinitely forgiving. She does all right every time and Yoel does too.

When she looks at me her eye moves straight on, as if my face bores her.

"Don't take it so seriously. Look on it as entertainment," Yoel tells me, when she has finally gone. Entertainment? Is that really all she is for him? "You're just jealous," he teases me. Jealous? Never. Me? What is there to be jealous of? Well, yes, for that matter I am jealous of the way she gets him to look at her—it's the only time he shows a hint of vulnerability. At some time she has hurt him deeply and he knows that she can do it again.

While she leans against him and laughs at something only they understand, from the corner of one eye she looks at me: *I could seduce him . . . if only you were worth the effort, if only it didn't mean I would have to touch him . . .*

Why does she never touch anyone, I ask Yoel when at length she's gone. "Yes, why?"

He hesitates. "I don't know, because she thinks it's a waste of herself, probably."

When Yoel thinks I have gone to sleep he satisfies himself.

"Masturbation . . ." he says at breakfast.

"Yes?" I ask and hand him the deli liver pâté flecked with truffles like black demon eyes.

". . . comes from the word *manus,* meaning hand, and *stuprare,* meaning violate or defile."

"Mm, I know." Have started answering like this when he tries to enlighten me about the big world. It's starting to be tiresome. I have natural talent, all tuition is superfluous. And sex isn't as revolutionary as I thought it would be—certainly not more than staying awake all night with Lukas or swimming underwater with him the length of the lake. It's pleasant, it keeps your mind off other matters, you want to do it again, but that is the case with so many things. Perhaps because it's not quite as satisfying as you would like it to be.

It takes most of the daytime for Yoel to overcome his reluctance to grapple with his dissertation. Hungarian migration from the turn of the century to the Velvet Revolution. It's difficult not to be fascinated by his family's checkered past, twisting its way like a red thread though European and American history. My own family's history has looked the same generation after generation. If you know where you come from, perhaps it's easier to know where you're going. Was that why Lukas always seemed so lost? If you have no memory of a past you cannot imagine a future either.

Leaving everything behind you, emigrating like Yoel's relatives, the feeling of freedom imbued with guilt. A black vein running right through the relief—that you can actually leave . . . just go. Yet at the same time you have to live, perhaps forever, with the sense that you're a deserter.

He stays long enough to teach me how to handle the remote control for all the unnecessary electrical appliances, to make love to me until even that becomes a part of the everyday, and then he goes. The first trip is to Berlin and Budapest, where he has a parent in each city and an acute financial interest in a reconciliation with them. I don't know what I'm going to do in the flat. At home there were always jobs to be done, but here in the apartment there's nothing to occupy me.

The whole of the first night I spend in front of the television. The picture changes with the level of my intoxication. I have opened one of Yoel's expensive bottles and empty it slowly. Marsupials. Tasmanian devils. Completely normal kangaroos. Remarkable creatures with a highly unusual reproductive pattern . . . While other mammals carry their young until they are fully developed, the marsupial's babies are born soon after fertilization. I sit on the floor in front of the sofa with my glass of wine. Yoel has taught me to sit on the floor. It was unthinkable at home, where the floor was something you touched only with your foot.

I edge nearer to the television screen and watch the embryonic little baby crawl out of its mother's womb, creep blindly through her fur to reach the pouch. This particular female kangaroo is strangely like my own mama, more and more like her the more I stare at her. When the baby is born it's so small it consists of only a mouth and a pair of front legs. Under its own power it moves from the vagina to the nipple, latches on, and starts to suck. The nipple expands to become firmly clamped inside the mouth, and hanging there the baby accompanies the mother wherever she goes, the deep voice-over explains. Only after a few months have its jaws developed sufficiently for it to open its mouth and let go.

Sooner or later you have to crawl away from the great mother animal with her enfolding oxygen-deficient love-pouch. That's when you meet the other type, the ones like Yoel.

My life is entering a new phase. For the first time I am alone, all by myself, solo. One brief jaunt is followed by another: Yoel has been to see a friend in New York, Yoel has been to see a brother in Paris, a girlfriend in Copenhagen, a cousin in Zakopane. The apartment is full of suitcases that haven't been unpacked, because he doesn't like to dig around in the past. Instead of being reminded of old journeys, he wants to plan new ones.

I stop missing him, and he doesn't seem to miss me very much either, as the date of his homecoming is always being postponed, without further explanation, until I begin to feel quite used to the solitude. *The most beautiful place on earth is your collarbone,* he said not so long ago. As if he had been in every place, in every woman. *The skin under your arm . . . if I had to choose something to take with me to a desert island.* Silky smooth words about chiseled collarbones and soft skin. He slid inside me as if I were an icy street, as if it were never his intention, a pleasing mistake, that's all. And slid out just as easily.

However much I may dislike his former girlfriend and her way of marching right through his life as if she owned it, I find that I have taken one piece of advice from her for getting along in all situations: high heels. The higher the better. I buy a pair of sky-high calfskin boots secondhand and walk around in them all day in the apartment until Yoel comes out with:

"You look different. Have you had your hair cut? No . . . wait— have you lost weight? You have, haven't you?" He studies me as he sits fiddling with his newly purchased stereo. "It suits you. Not that you needed it, but you look fucking great."

"What about you, then?" I ask coolly, gripped with a sudden desire to deflate his self-regard. "Shouldn't you do something too . . ."

It doesn't work. His belief in himself is not shaken so easily. He stands up, slowly moves in, and then goes for the attack.

Make love. With a hungry Yoel on top of me. With the sky-high boots on. Afterward I try to watch *Breathless* with him, but he falls asleep in the middle of the long bedroom scene that is my favorite. You know that they have sex, but you never see it. They make love in French, with their mouths, speaking, almost without touching each other at all. Jean Seberg, cool and playful, intense and unapproachable, a mystery, like cats who allow themselves to be petted and tormented at the same time. I sit there with Yoel beside me, knocked out, and I know all the lines by heart without having anyone to play opposite:

"You don't even know how to apply your lipstick. It looks terrible," he would say.

"Say what you like, I don't care. I'll put all this in my book."

"What book?"

"I'm writing a novel."

"You?"

"Yes, why not me? Stop it—what are you doing . . . ?"

"Taking off your top."

"Not now."

"You're a bloody pain."

"Do you know William Faulkner?"

"No, who's he? Someone you slept with?"

"No way, José . . ."

"To hell with him then. Take off your top."

"He's one of my favorite writers. Have you read *The Wild Palms*?"

"Take off your top, I said."

"Listen. The last sentence is beautiful . . . 'Between grief and nothing, I will take grief.' Which would you choose?"

"Let me see your toes. Toes are important in a woman. Don't laugh."

"Which would you choose?"

"Grief's stupid. I'd choose nothing. It's not better, but grief's a compromise. I want all or nothing."

I keep my boots on until I tire of them and of Yoel's compliments. Take them back to the same secondhand shop and go to the hairdresser's, ask for a super-short Jean Seberg style. The hairdresser doesn't know what that is, but I have a picture from the scene where Jean Seberg is sitting on the bed and has just taken off the gangster hat.

"Are you sure?" he asks, looking at my hair that reaches almost all the way down my back. I think so. At any rate, I have never been more sure.

"It's a great sixties look, but it needs a film star charisma for this style to really work," the hairdresser guy says. I have that. "It needs the eyes," he says. I have them as well. All that's missing is a single dimple. I would really like to go blond . . . but I don't have enough money, so that will have to wait.

"What the hell have you done?" Yoel bursts out when I come home. "Your hair!"

"Exactly—*my* hair," I reply and stride past him on my way to the bathroom.

He looks at me as if I'm a stranger, as if he can't trust me with this hairstyle. Something in him cools down markedly when he's deprived of my hair. Was that all it was? The long dark childlike hair, was it so paltry that that was all it was?

INCOGNITO

Lukas's unattainable dream is just one of the many places Yoel has been to. Out of the blue one evening he asks me if I'd like to go there with him for the weekend. Budapest. Just like that? For years it had been like a mirage for Lukas, a distorted reflection of something he only vaguely remembered. How many times had we talked about going together? It would feel like a betrayal of Lukas to go there with Yoel.

I say I don't have a passport. Yoel the fixer can usually pick up the telephone and arrange anything at all with just one call, but this time he says absently, what a pity, perhaps he will ask her instead. At first I don't understand. Who? Her? His ex? He doesn't even like her. How can she behave as she does, be like she is, and still have his . . . whatever it is—love? Most people don't last long in her presence, only the very strong and the very weak, he had once suggested, without revealing which category he counted himself in.

Yoel draws back the curtain and looks out at the rain, one of many showers that have become one continuous downpour the last few weeks.

"We've got something going again. I don't know what. I, kind of, can't be free of her," he says, preoccupied.

As if he had tried.

He fancied girls like her. Leggy felines. With a squint, dangerous. So what was he doing with me . . . no idea. I wasn't going to cause multiple collisions when I went over a crosswalk, not even if I

walked very slowly with everything hanging out—that was clear
enough to see.

I left him. Or he left me. When he returned from his trip I was to
be gone. It was unspoken.

He hadn't specifically said that I could take the car, but I knew
where the keys were, I knew where it was parked and which tricks
were needed to start it, I had seen Lukas coax it into life so many
times. Yoel hadn't used it once since we arrived. Lukas's old Ford
wasn't a car you wanted to be seen in when you were in town. It
didn't look as cool here as he had thought, more of a sunken wreck
with circles of rust around the wheels and the watered-down lac-
quer that seemed to have lost its color on the way here. He thought
it smelled of fermentation from the bottom of the old lake, would
probably miss it as little as he would miss me, no deep void when
we both disappeared along with a few bottles of wine, bedclothes,
and a mattress from the attic. And a bit of cash. I knew where his
hiding places were and took what I could find, a mixture of crowns,
dollars, marks, and forints. He'd never lifted a finger himself to
earn that money.

Either he would be furious or he would understand. In any case I
wouldn't be here, so it really didn't matter to me. It's not a question
of getting, it's a question of fixing, he'd said himself. People with
principles rarely like to be treated according to those principles
themselves, but his money would go toward something important.
I would use it to forget about him.

A permanent loan. Exactly like the lifelong credit he had from
his parents. It wasn't a small amount that he had put away in his secret places that he thought I knew nothing about. His parents must
have been more generous than he acknowledged.

While I was searching I discovered an envelope in my own handwriting, the letter I had addressed for him so that he could send the

payment for the car to Lukas. It had never happened, even though I'd reminded him several times and even though he said he'd sent it. It was only a few thousand, Lukas's life did not depend upon it, but it was the principle. The envelope was empty. I put in some of the notes I had found but then changed my mind. Couldn't send them after such a long time; it would be an insult. As if it was all about the money, when in fact it was about everything but the money.

Later that evening I wandered up and down all the streets in all parts of town over all the bridges through all the parks. It was like stepping down into a purifying bath. It was still raining and I picked up all the apartment-for-rent notices I could find. Phoned around until I got lucky with a thirdhand rental in a district I had never heard of but sounded pretty, like the countryside, Hjorthagen.

At midnight I stopped at a little bar, just to see what would happen. Almost immediately a man came up and sat down on the stool next to me, ordered me a drink without even asking what I would like.

"I'm thirty-three, the same age as Jesus when he was crucified. How old are you, honey?" he asked.

Lukas's old car was my only fixed point, and in it I moved what little I had from one temporary address to another—most often in the small hours when the streets were deserted.

The smell of the lake that Yoel had complained about still lingered in there and made me feel at home. The smell of the fields, the factories, the familiar wildness. Sometimes I would sit in the driver's seat in a parking lot and let my thoughts wander from my house to Lukas's house to the pearl fisher's, out over the sloping fields, along the highway, farther, the Atlantic next. If I was between rentals I could sit there the whole night. As long as I had the car I was never really homeless. In the glove compartment and pockets I found things I had left there long ago, Escape perfume, my Lee shorts, a pack of my favorite chewing gum, an ugly yellow scarf that Rikard had gone to a great deal of trouble to send me, an earring I had lost and searched for everywhere except in his car. I found nothing of Lukas's. Not so much as a rolling paper. He never left any visible traces behind him.

I changed my job at the same rate as I changed my abode. Cafeteria, dry cleaner's, hospital cleaner, taxi dispatcher. Delivering papers was the worst paid, but it appealed to me. The routine and movement, rhythm, monotony, the turns in the stairs so easy hour after hour. The freedom to think in peace. The freedom not to have to smile at someone for money. The load that gradually lightened as I did my job was so simple and genuine. The good feeling after a day's work, although I did it at night. I mostly saw the dark side of town, didn't really have a plan, more like an undercurrent, an expectation of something.

"You can be whatever you want," Mama had said.

"I want to be someone else."

"No, you can only be yourself." Myself? Why would I want to be that? That is what I was already.

I used to come home from my newspaper rounds just as the morning traffic started up. The exhaust fumes seeping in through the window sent me to sleep. Yoel had shown me how to find pleasure, but through him I also learned that I needed no one. First a taste of sex, then of solitude, relished like a thirst I had suppressed and now could not quench. I began to guard it like stolen goods.

With every new place I unpacked my few belongings in, I felt less at home and more free.

One day at a time—that was what counted for the temporary contract I managed to get, on the corner of Vulcanusgatan. The rent was negligible as the house was waiting to be blown out like an egg and refurbished. Thirties standards with communal showers in a cellar so full of spiders that I kept hygiene to a minimum.

"View over the water," I wrote to Mama, though I lived where the Barnhusviken channel of water was at its narrowest, obscured by the massive concrete pillars of the bridge. Sleep was shattered by the sirens from the Sabbatsberg hospital and the noise of the trains that never seemed to cease.

I wasn't afraid of the dark. Shadows in the light frightened me more. And the throng of strangers on the subway was worse than loneliness. Lukas had been scared of quick movements: a caress could give him a start, and a whisper could wake him up. Cooped-up birds, fluttering, panic, the sound of wings against a pane of glass—those sorts of things frightened him. That someone might find our hiding place, that we should be discovered and exposed. He responded to sounds I couldn't even hear; he had the acute hearing of a blind person, could hear snakes swimming in the water. The snakes were the only things that made me feel safe with Lukas. He caught them with such lightning speed and flung them far away from me.

No snakes in this town, just the underground dragon that rattles in and out from beneath the earth. I let my memories of Lukas slip into fragile neglect, repressed just enough to be bearable.

TIME WEIGHS LIGHT

At first I didn't understand at all what Mama was talking about when she mentioned on the telephone something about a letter—by the way, in the middle of a conversation about something else entirely—that Lukas was supposed to have written to me. I was quite sure I hadn't received it. Oh yes, Mama insisted, a long time ago, a blue envelope, don't you remember?

She fell silent on the telephone as if she thought I was lying to her. The letter, she said again—she had acted as intermediary, folded it in two and put it in with one of hers that she sent at regular intervals.

She'd never referred to it before and now she wondered suddenly what Lukas had on his mind. As if conceding there may have been something.

For him to write to me must have been an almost impossible thing to do after what had happened. And besides . . . I couldn't remember ever seeing Lukas write anything, except possibly his name. It was one of the last things I saw him do before we parted, when he signed the devil's contract, leaning against the hood of the car that last summer. A letter from him must have required an almost insurmountable effort, not to mention the shame he had to overcome to go to Mama and ask her to send it to me. Without even being sure that I could decipher it. And the reply he'd received was silence.

The letters from Mama remained unopened. After all the moving and traveling, trips and years, I no longer even knew where the bundle of letters was. Just that I hadn't thrown it away. Gradually Mama and I had started to talk to each other again, in short conversations at long intervals about absolutely nothing—everything that might hurt was carefully avoided. And since we had started to phone each other, I'd forgotten all about her old letters.

It took forever searching among my unsorted belongings before I found the bundle, hidden and forgotten at the back of the trunk of Lukas's car. That's always the way, at the back, the last box, you know it will be, and yet you go through all the rest first, as if preparing yourself for the moment when you'll find it. I quickly ripped open Mama's envelopes with my fingers, one after the other without reading them, until I found the folded blue one from Lukas. She hadn't imagined it—it was there. There was nothing on the outside, but it still smelled of him.

I didn't open it immediately, thought: this evening. And when evening came: I will wait until tomorrow. And in the morning . . . tear it open quickly with my finger, skim through—a few seconds of temporary discomfort—how dangerous can that be? How difficult, how unpleasant? I already knew what must be in it.

To make it easier I tried to read it while doing something else. In the line for the car wash, by the freezer cabinet at the grocery, in the bathroom while the water was running. Sitting on the edge of the bath, brushing my teeth, I brought out the envelope without opening it.

Every so often I have to check that it's still in my pocket, as if a draft might suddenly whip it out like a chewing gum wrapper right up into the hot sun. It would burn like magnesium and be gone. That things can burn up, come to an end, is a relief as well as a dread. Each time I'm about to insert my finger, slippery with sweat, to slit open the envelope, I can't do it. For as long as I haven't read the words, they haven't reached me. It has been unopened for so long, it can stay that way a little longer. There's no rush. It's all too late.

I recall a story I heard on the radio a long time ago, a man and a woman, an extremely strong love between them, how circumstances forced them to part. The man had to travel to the other side of the world, but as soon as he had settled down there, sorted out the practicalities, and found somewhere for them to live together, he would write to her. That was what would have been agreed. She waited. And waited. No letter. Waited until her love had changed to bitterness, convinced that he had met another woman and didn't have the guts to tell her. The rest of her life she lived alone. After the woman's death some of her relatives were going to renovate the house to sell it. They pulled up the linoleum in the hall. There was the letter, wedged underneath by some careless postman. Fifty years had passed, and now, with her death, it was all irrevocably too late. If only she had swallowed her pride, written to him, tried to find him. If only he had swallowed his pride when he didn't receive a reply to the letter that never reached her, and written one more time. If only.

To have a weakness for someone is an expression I would rather not use, but sometimes there's no other way of saying it. To Yoel I was attracted, for Lukas I had a weakness. I remember his laugh, not because he laughed often but because he laughed so seldom. Time weighs so light in comparison; the letter in my back pocket is as heavy as if it were sealed with lead.

I can't imagine Lukas asking for help with anything at all, especially not from my mama. When I ask her how it happened, she says that a few weeks after I had gone he came up to our house. She

saw him coming from far away, so immensely slowly he stopped for
a smoke twice on the way up. She had hardly seen him after I left,
and now he was there asking for my phone number. When Mama
opened the door he had already gone down the steps, prepared to
be sent away.

She told him the truth, that she didn't have my number, that all
she had was a poste restante address for a post office in Stockholm.
He didn't believe her. But it was the truth.

The day I disappeared it was Mama who got Lukas down from the
blazing porch. A moment later the beams gave way and the burning roof fell in. She had probably saved his life, but at the time grat-
itude was not something he was capable of.

First, without understanding what was happening, Mama had
been standing in the bedroom when she saw Yoel and me driving
from the garage in Lukas's car, stopping at Lukas's house for a few
minutes to have some papers signed, carried out quickly against the
hood of the car. She wondered what was going on. Whether she
ought to go out. But at least at the window she had a general view
of the situation, if indeed it was one. It certainly looked like some
sort of situation, only she had no idea what it was about. She wondered even more when she saw Lukas begin to carry things out of
the house, throw them in a big pile until they formed a pyre, and
set fire to it.

Far too close, she was thinking. Far too close to the wooden
house, dry in every nook and cranny after so many weeks without
rain. The lighting of fires was prohibited after a summer so hot and
long that the days burned by themselves. When the fire had taken
hold he went inside and fetched more things that he threw onto the
flames. At the same time I came back along the path by the lake
with Yoel and the luggage we had collected. Mama had no idea
who Yoel was, as he sat behind the wheel in Lukas's car with me

beside him. And then we drove off. She had assumed that we would stay when we saw Lukas, try to persuade him to listen to reason, but we just drove past. The fire took hold on the steps. Mama had no time to think about me and where I was going. She saw Lukas get up on the porch, not to try to put out the flames—he just stood there as if he . . . had lost. She raced down to the kitchen, called the fire brigade, and ran.

Lukas was no slender thirteen-year-old now, as he had been when she'd used mild force to drag him out of the flames in the field fire along the railway line. She could only use words now to try to persuade him to save himself. She knew that there was a lack of oxygen near large fires and that lack of oxygen led to confusion, so she needed to act quickly to bring him down from the flames. She doesn't remember exactly what she said, something about me.

"After that? For God's sake, Mama, what happened after that?" No one has ever told me about this.

"You disappeared, Lo, and since then you've never asked about any of it," she answers, as if I have thereby forfeited my right to know. Then she tells me anyway: at the last moment Lukas came down from the burning porch, disaster averted, the emergency part of the disaster at any rate. The help Mama had sent for arrived and she let them take over. After that she didn't see him until he came and knocked on her kitchen door a few weeks later. He looked tired and black as if he had been rooting around in the charred remains in search of anything that had escaped the flames. Should she ask him to come in? He really looked as though he were in need of a bowl of broth, and she had cooked enough for a whole army, still not used to the minimal size of her reduced family. He looked so lean around the eyes. He looked like someone who could easily become emaciated, as if he only had his body on loan, like everything else that had just been taken away from him. But she couldn't bring herself to.

"He didn't ask about you, and what would I have said? I had no idea . . ." she says. "About why you, from one day to the next, had decided to leave everything behind. I knew even less than him—but it must have had something to do with the two of you. He didn't ask for any answers, either. Just the phone number. He wasn't satisfied with the address."

"He couldn't write, Mama," I interrupt.

"What?"

"No, he couldn't."

"But he wrote to you in the end. I sent that letter on myself . . . What did he want?"

When I don't reply she continues. Lukas had looked so dejected that she was afraid he would throw himself in the lake, so she tried to inspire some hope in him. Of what, I ask.

"Of you coming back eventually—if that was what he wanted." *Give her a little time,* Mama had said, when Lukas came back two days later with an unaddressed blue envelope that he asked her to send to me. And perhaps it was that hope that made him start to demolish what had been burned and decide to rebuild Gábriel's house. He set about the house construction in a sorrowful frenzy, as if something might rise up out of the ashes. Mama could see from our place how the work was progressing. When the first cold spell came, she saw him buy two propane heaters for the derelict house he had moved into, for want of anywhere else. It must have been cold and damp, so near the lake. Bit by bit, when he had the time and the money, he rebuilt Gábriel's house. The same house that he'd allowed to catch fire—as if all he'd wanted was to be free of it.

His spare time he spent building, single-handed, everything apart from the roof trusses that a framer in the village helped him with. As soon as the outside was finished the building work stopped. Lukas never set foot in there after it was finished, as far as Mama knew. This empty mausoleum at the end of the gravel road became a refuge for the river rats then, the ones his papa had forced him to catch and drown. It was at the point when he gave up hope of me returning, Mama says, that he also gave up building. After that he left it, one of many houses in the area standing empty since the lay-offs at the factories.

I never understood why Lukas didn't move away as soon as he dropped out of school and started work. Away from his papa, as soon as he could. There were cheap apartments near the leather factory. But maybe he couldn't imagine waking up every morning to any other view than the one over the lake, the highway, and our house up on the hill.

"Were you happy with that guy you left everything for?"

"Yoel? I didn't leave everything *for* him, I left everything *with* him. And yes, I was happy. For a while. What more can you want? Were you happy with Papa?" She doesn't answer, just says something about how it could have been anyone at all, that guy, couldn't it? No, not anyone at all, but certainly someone else. I was forced to go away to become the person I am. There had been a relentless breaking-up atmosphere for a long time. Papa and the other brothers and sisters who moved away, Mama's father with his burning lungs, and her mother with her heart embedded in the fat of grief, and Papa's mother with her cancer, and Gábriel with his crumbling bones. Death, death, death that summer. Good God, I was only seventeen and it felt as if life was over.

Just in time Yoel came gliding in over the disaster area and winched me up. I'm not lying when I say that I have thought of Lukas every day, but going away from here is the best thing I did. You shall leave your father and your mother, that is the way it is. It was not me who made it up. But maybe you could say goodbye first and clean up your messy room, Mama thinks. I don't know. There's nothing about that in the Bible.

It had been a summer to remember, water sprinklers going all night in the district.

Fire ban and watering ban, but this was a village for the quietly lawless, so everyone watered anyway, though no one got it into his head to start a fire, except for Lukas. Born under a falling star. He could have been prosecuted. If you start a fire in a house it is always considered arson, and what was worse . . . Gábriel was still lying inside, in the innermost room. Admittedly in a part of the house that escaped the flames, but there still had to be an inquiry and a postmortem to establish the cause of death and to rule out the possibility of his being killed by the smoke or the heat.

Even Mama had to make a statement about what she knew.

"But I wrote about that in my letters. I can't understand why you didn't come when I asked. You could definitely have given information that would have exonerated him—you were there when Gábriel died, weren't you? I assumed that you would want to help Lukas, but suddenly you seemed to be deadly enemies."

Mama put in a good word for him with the police, more than she really should have done—she didn't know how much he was to blame in all of this. Only that he must have been in despair that afternoon the fire started. For some people hell seems to have more than nine circles: Lukas lost his papa and me and his home and all his possessions and his car, and not long after that his job at the leather factory too. At that point, if not before, he should have left.

If it was anyone's fault, it was mine, but my crime carried no penalty. The worst seldom do. In the end Lukas was cleared of suspicion—he must have defended himself successfully, or else he wasn't considered responsible for his actions when he let the fire burn. Still, the fine for negligence was a minor disaster, destitute as he was. The only asset Gábriel had left behind was a house that had now burned down, without insurance. Lukas owned nothing. All he had was an installment-plan debt for the funeral, and his life, but who could call it a life? There was no collateral.

RIVER OF OBLIVION

I planned to leave, never to return. I haven't told anyone that. I was going to take what was left of Yoel's money and buy a ticket to somewhere. Where was less important. The main thing was that it should be far away. Mexico, perhaps. I'd heard it's so lovely.

I had a passport. Yoel must just have forgotten that he had helped me to fix that. As if all he did was fix passports for girls he thought hadn't seen enough of the world. You have to have a passport or you aren't free. Passport, money, car. Once I had set off, the rest would sort itself out, as it always had before. I had the sense that I could do anything at all as long as I was alone. As long as I didn't have to fulfill someone else's needs. I could manage my own, they were simple—just to live, that was the only thing I wanted. With no other weight to bear than my own.

I bought New York boots and a New York cap. Played *Porgy and Bess*. Took Yoel's money and went with the hope that the skyscrapers, dollars, and smell of frying would heal me. Heal me? That wasn't what I hoped for, exactly. New York is just a city. But if forgetfulness wouldn't come to me, I had to search for it, cross the river of oblivion, whatever it was called. I wasn't fully conversant with the geography of hell, just knew that I was right in the middle of it.

The city of dreams must also be the city of forgetfulness.

I had heard about the underworld river that formed the boundary between the world of the living and the world of the dead, and

I had a vague idea that you had to be able to cross the other way around, against the flow, back to the living—it had to be possible. I was in limbo, between life and death, the remarkable state you end up in if you deserve neither heaven nor hell.

I got on the plane and crossed the river of oblivion with a suitcase full of clean clothes and unread books. Nothing that smelled of him, or him, nothing either of them had even come into contact with or that could remind me of someone I knew. On the way in from the airport it was snowing. I felt a reluctant, frightening, provocative defiance. This city would make me forget, and I might as well start at once.

It's only a town. The leap to New York can't be any greater than the leap to Stockholm from the village where I grew up, and yet the first glimpse of the city takes my breath away. It's not particularly beautiful at the spot where I come up out of the ground, but it is New York. Exactly as you imagine it: even the street is belching out smoke and the dark façades push the sky so high up that you can hardly make out what time of day it is. I've been warned about strange forests where I don't recognize the dangers. You should stay close to home, know what's what, understand the rules. Here I have no notion.

A perfume. I try to visualize a face that matches the aftershave emanating from behind my back, where I'm sitting on a bench to regain my balance. A bitter aroma, something Yoel would never have used. But I recognize it, perhaps from one of Papa's brothers, their various bottles in a row on the bathroom windowsill. The advantage of old aftershave, I heard a friend of Yoel's once say, is that a girl feels safe with someone who smells like her grandfather.

When I stand up with my map to ask for directions, he doesn't look at all as I had thought. With his back to me on the bench, a slender-limbed Latino is sitting, not much older than me, deeply engrossed in his music. Long legs stretched out in front of him, T-shirt and jacket, gold chain. Eyes fixed on a far-off point. He shifts his attention from the distance, straight into my eyes, not so much as a muscle in his face moving. If it had been a competition, I would have lost.

As I open up my map of Manhattan, he continues to focus on me, not a single glance at the object I'm holding out between us. Map reading is a Swedish specialty, Yoel always said. Americans can scarcely decipher a map of their own city, but they are completely at ease with streets, districts, subway lines, bus numbers.

Who are you? Brut? Jicky? Équipage? Eau Sauvage? Hypnôse?

When he makes no attempt to help me, I start to fold up the map. Then:

"Where do you come from?" he asks, without removing his earphones. He looks surprised at my reply, as if he didn't really believe me. "You don't look Swedish. Swedes are usually tall, cold, and beautiful. I mean . . . well, you're not tall or especially cold." I give up folding the map and stuff it like a crumpled concertina into my bag, then ask for directions to the Lower East Side, having no sense of what is even north and south here. Now he says that he's going to tell me something I need to know to get my bearings:

"You see those towers over there, the two high ones, the highest in the city? You can see those from almost everywhere. As soon as you come out of the subway, you look for them. They mean downtown. The opposite direction is uptown. People would never find their way in this city without them."

When he finds out that I've just arrived and it's my first visit, he suggests a beer to celebrate landing. One beer won't be enough, but okay. I'm floating above the tarmac as I follow him along the wide streets, farther and farther from the station, as if he is trying to get me lost. Every neighborhood here is as large as a small town. Finally he stops at a surprisingly simple and anonymous place, the same as dozens of others we have passed on the way here. My eye wants to travel beyond the window to catch a glimpse of the pulsing streets out there.

"The New York sky gets electric just before it starts snowing. Do you know that?" he asks, lighting a cigarette. No. But I realize I have a certain weakness for people who tell me things like that. When I ask him what season this is, actually, he hesitates. He doesn't believe in seasons, he says—at least not in New York. It is mostly a question of weather.

"So you're one of those . . . reading types?" he asks then, with an eye on my bag, where a couple of travel paperbacks are sticking out. As though reading types would be a mutation of an otherwise sound human race. My response is a little evasive, as if it were an accusation I was trying to wriggle out of.

"I am too," he says unexpectedly. "Your favorite?" In his smile a gold tooth flashes like a portable life insurance. A gold tooth as well, I'm thinking, and pretend not to hear his question, but he asks again. I squirm, say cagily that I don't have one. I've read far too little to have any favorites, still reading everything for the first time, and anyway it is a very personal question.

"Sure you do. Come on, tell me."

Okay, Bukowski, I say in the end. He's the only one from whom I have read two books.

"Bukowski? You mean *the* Bukowski? Like *Charles* Bukowski?"

I nod, embarrassed that I feel embarrassed. Normal people don't find it more personal to reveal their favorite authors than their favorite cornflakes or their favorite air freshener. I'm quick to throw the question back at him.

"Plath," he says without hesitation.

"Plath? You mean like *Sylvia* Plath?" I say, because I know her name.

"Yeah." He smiles. And then we start to laugh.

We laugh until he wipes the froth of beer from my upper lip with his thumb. And then we stop at once.

DESIRE AND FEAR

We went back to his place. Or, to be exact, we took a taxi, because it was too far to walk to Spanish Harlem. On a street full of litter that was called Pleasure Avenue, Pleasant Avenue, or something, he asked the driver to stop. The air from the East River had an oily raw river stench, and the staircase reeked of mold, cement, and burned tostones. In the doorway a young woman stood as if on guard, half dressed, glaring at me when he said hello. Behind us as we were going up the stairs I heard her say something about *chica blanca, coño blanca,* white girl, white cunt. He leaned over the banister and hissed a warning to her.

"*Culo! Desgraciado!*" we heard her voice from below.

"*Puta!*" he shouted back.

"*Puto! Pato!*" she echoed, like cracks of a whip.

He clearly decided that could not be tolerated, and when he turned on the stairs I managed to grab hold of him and whisper:

"Come on, let's go, it doesn't matter, I don't understand Spanish."

"Yes you do! Do you think I'd let her insult us however she wants? *Carajo!* She'd never dare say anything if I was alone. She knows exactly what I'd do to her."

I recognized the swear words from Yoel's neighbors. When they thought their children were asleep they could stand on the balcony arguing for hours in a mixture of Spanish and Swedish. It was a nuisance, but at least I learned all kinds of foul words in the Spanish language.

Unsteady from the beer and his mood that exploded from one second to the next, I feel inclined to leave. Can I trust him? Do I have to trust him, is it at all possible to trust another person, or should you just make a practice of assuming the worst every time? If Mama had seen me now she would have said I was mad.

"Crackhead!" he screams at her once more, before we continue up the narrow stairs out of earshot of her filthy invective.

There's an elevator, but you can be trapped all night in it between two floors if you're unlucky, and he seems to assume we would be.

"This isn't a prime neighborhood, you know . . . But you don't need to be afraid of the rats, they're not aggressive, there's plenty of food here." We pass a floor in darkness. Sense how they move along the walls.

The rats never scared me at home. I had no feelings for them, neither fascination nor loathing. Lukas on the other hand never got used to them. Intelligent eyes, he said. "Do it quickly, for God's sake," he said, looking away as I drowned them. It was an act of love, I did it so that he didn't have to, but I don't think he could love me as much afterward. He may have been grateful that I did it instead of him, but he could never understand how I could do it at all, when it came to the crunch. "They're only rats," I said. "And you're only an idiot," he answered.

Thirteen flights I count, the lactic acid building up in my legs. He doesn't offer to carry my suitcase. I may have packed light, but it still feels heavy by the end. I don't have time to see much of his apartment before we reach our final destination, the moment when the whole world begins and ends in his narrow bed and the only air he lets me breathe is the air he has in his mouth.

"What's your name?" I whisper when he finally allows me some oxygen.

"Don't talk so much." He is in a hurry to pull off the dusty clothes I have been traveling in and his own. Kicks off his sneakers, wriggles out of his T-shirt and jeans, and bores his way in with no caresses or frills.

Smells are like memories, they merge with one another and create new variations. Lukas merges with Yoel who merges with Luiz, who merges with Lukas again. Like the smell of water mixing with sandalwood, cement, African myrrh, geranium, iron, smoke. He smells of . . .

"Brut?" I breathe in against his smooth brown jaw as I sample a little bite. He nods. How could I guess? My tongue runs along the nape of his neck, which is one of the most beautiful I have seen, and I am after all a collector of beautiful necks. I have Rikard's, Lukas's, Yoel's, and some others whose names I have never asked, and now Luiz's.

He doesn't object when I slide my hand into the gap between his groin and the mattress where his penis is resting semisoft and spent, and immediately it hardens again at my touch. Asks why I am here, in New York, and I tell him the truth: on the run. He looks surprised, a little worried almost.

"A jealous sucker?" he asks, as though he took it for granted it was a man. From far away I can hear how sad my laugh sounds, like an out-of-tune piano in a cold room. Jealous . . . if only it were so simple.

"*Dámelo duro*," I whisper. Somewhere in my dubious Spanish vocabulary I find the phrase, and he looks at me in astonishment as if I don't know what I am saying.

"Forget it, kid," he whispers disapprovingly. Rolls over onto his back again and in the same movement slides me up onto him. "I really like you—inside and out." In Swedish it would have sounded impossible, but when he says it, it sounds completely right. This city, everything that is new . . . it is so unreal that it doesn't even make me think twice.

We roll another half turn, our stomachs sticking together.

"You're such a beauty, do you know that?"

I nod.

And cocky too, I can see in his eyes that he likes that, as his long sinewy body presses me halfway through the soft springs of the bed, before we go quite still.

In the kitchen some time later he strikes a match and lights the gas stove:

"Be honest . . . when you were doing it with me, were you actually thinking about him? The one you're on the run from?" he asks, revealing his gold tooth.

"Yes," I lie, though for the first time in ages I had managed to forget him for a little while. "And who were you thinking about?"

He had no time to think, it was so quick. I was like a tropical cyclone in the middle of winter in Manhattan. Libido, the instinct for life. Thanatos, the death drive. Loving or dying.

In quick succession he breaks four eggs into a frying pan, the sizzling oil splashing up on his naked chest. He doesn't flinch. A liberal American layer of mayonnaise goes on eight slices of spongy bread, while with a practiced hand he flips the eggs over and fries the other sides. Salt. Tabasco. A few familiar movements. And the four egg-mayonnaise sandwiches are ready. Am I sure I don't want some? I shake my head. What he himself does with that amount of fat is a mystery that is solved when he tells me he only eats once a day. Mostly eggs, and eggs are practically vegetables, aren't they? I have no appetite; my mouth tastes a little of blood.

"Four double sandwiches a day, and I haven't been ill since the day I was shot in the shoulder on the staircase five years ago." I had felt the scar against my lips earlier in bed. "Women with guns . . ."

Luiz mumbles and examines me closely as he opens a beer for each of us. "You're far too thin. Far too thin. *Flaca* . . . But it's okay. I like thin girls." I look at my reflection in the night-dark window. Thin? This was a new accusation. But he's right, I hardly recognize myself, alarmed by how starved I look—lack of sleep perhaps, giving me that intense, slightly swollen look.

After the food he can't make love again. Doesn't even try. We just fall asleep together.

When I wake up he is no longer lying beside me. Out in the kitchen there is a woman with an intricate hairdo and a torn coffee-brown dressing gown, sorting out small change.

"*Gringa* . . ." she says when she catches sight of me in the doorway, giving me a measured look, as if I were an exceptionally pale specimen. Feeling awkward, I ask where he is.

"Luiz? He's up in the Bronx, of course. Where else would he be?" *Bronx?* Why there? And who is she, his mother, sister, pimp, spider woman—his fate? No, his ex, I realize. I try to cover myself, though she has already seen my winter-white nakedness. "He went out an hour ago. He'll be in his apartment by now, with his wife, and who are you, his new whore? How old . . . let me guess, seventeen?"

My cheeks red with shame, I scramble all my things together as I hear her say that Luiz, the dog, only sleeps here when he's had a fight with his wife and comes crawling back, has nowhere else to go when he's hit her and she's thrown him out. Then he comes here, and each time he has another slut in tow from the nearest bar, as if he thinks that will make him feel better. She gives me a look full of contempt, still counting coins with her two-inch nails.

"When he's calmed down—and the poor woman calls and forgives him—he goes back to her. He should be very grateful that I don't dish the dirt about his little comfort-fucks, then he'd find his bags packed outside the door when he came home . . . She has her limits. Just like I had once, when I still loved him. Now I don't care anymore."

The bastard, bastard, bastard . . . the stairs down will never end, and as I run I remember the sound of the telephone when I was half asleep. His wife must have called, forgiven him for hitting her, and then he went back to her without a word to me. Perhaps he liked sleeping with two different women within a few hours. I emerge onto the deserted street in pitch black at three o'clock in the morning, the worst possible time. It is snowing now as he predicted. The weather will protect me, I think—not even dogs are out in this. I just have to walk, start moving—fast enough not to get stuck, but slow enough to keep my balance.

I hurry down the wide avenue, speed up past the dark side streets without glancing in. After a while I discover that he has left a note in the pocket of my jeans. A telephone number on one side. On the other: "I never leave my number. Don't make me regret it."

I probably ought to sleep on it, but what you sleep on, you never do. I stop at the first telephone booth I see, and I call.

When he answers, it sounds as if he is on the other side of the world, not the other side of town. He doesn't apologize for his disappearance, doesn't even sound contrite, not a word of explanation about why he let me wake up in an apartment alone with his ex-wife. When am I going to see you again? he asks.

"Not as long as you're married," I reply.

"Married . . . Okay . . . to a certain extent married," he qualifies, after a few moments' silence. "A marriage of convenience. Haven't you heard of it?" He has lowered his voice a little now . . . Certainly, he is married, and certainly, they do live under the same roof, but they don't live as man and wife, they just keep up a front.

A front—for whom? I ask.

The authorities.

But how do you live so close together without something start-ing? That I have never understood. How . . . Luiz is silent on the telephone, and when he finally answers he speaks even more qui-etly. Not with her, he says. I only married her to help her.

It could have been a fictitious sob story, but if that were the case, he was very good at it. There's nothing wrong with her, he says, she's a great girl, at least when she's not being a pain in the ass—but she has come here in the hope of getting treatment for HIV; the marriage is just to help her and her two daughters. He tries to think of her as a sister—not easy, but he tries. You don't have to fancy your brothers and sisters to love them. That's how he feels about her. But lately . . .

He doesn't know if it's the illness, but recently she's changed. Has become temperamental and jealous, as if she believes he is thinking of leaving her. And he's certainly had that thought, increasingly. But he can't. It's not he who hits her, it's she who hits him, so they are doing their bit for equality of the sexes in this country. He says:

"Women know that men are stronger. But men know that women are harder." I stand with the receiver in my hand, my back against the glass, blue with cold. It has stopped snowing and now the wind is blowing instead, as cold as only wind in towns can be, through the wide empty streets. I'm obliged to ask, insensitive, but it has to be direct. And what about him?

"What?" he asks.

"Infected?"

"Of course not."

"You're sure?"

"Quite. And anyway we took precautions."

Did we? Not that I remember.

"No one in this city has unprotected sex, for God's sake, espe-cially not with a Swede," he bursts out.

But the violent kissing, blood on blood . . . I drop the receiver.

Go out into the cold. His words don't reassure me at all. I've been in New York for less than twenty-four hours and I'm sure that I have already exposed myself to a fatal disease.

You're mad, Lo, Mama would have said. It was also what Luiz said, as he distractedly caressed me.

"You're mad, girl. I thought that as soon as you started talking to me on the street, I could see it in your eyes. I know what mad girls look like, they look exactly like you, *nena*," he said and turned me over onto my stomach. "And I was even more sure that you were nuts when you came home with me without any persuasion . . . You must never—I'll say it one more time—you must NEVER go with strange men in New York, you should know that, for Christ's sake, didn't your mom teach you anything? You definitely must be kooky, babe, I was thinking, but okay, I like crazy girls, so why not? And if you hadn't come home with me, you'd only have gone with someone else—and you don't know what maniac *that* could have been . . . so it was better that you came with me. I happen to be a reliable guy, one of very few in this city. Then you got right into bed with me, when you were completely sober. I thought I'd have to waste at least half a bottle on you, but no, no . . . right into the bedroom, like a wildcat. I was speechless, and it takes a lot for me to be speechless, you understand, but that's the way it is with mad girls and me, they're attracted to me, I knew that before."

Paralyzed, I lay under a synthetic double quilt in a cheap hotel room in New York and thought about my own death. There are those people who can transform the most difficult experiences into something that strengthens them and helps them achieve maturity. Myself, I just wanted to be free of the pain. The quickest possible way out. Not to cling to sorrow—but now it was clinging to me.

I lay in my hotel bed and listened to Nina Simone singing in almost unidentifiable French, *ne me quitte pas,* don't leave me, her voice searing and pure. It hurt and then soothed—like a harsh big sister, like a winter bath, like a wound that is opened, emptied, disinfected, and sewn back together.

I took out an advance on death, and when I had done that, there was nothing else to be afraid of. The worst had already happened, so I had no reason to be worried about anything now. Safe and ravenous, hungry as a wolf, I climbed out of bed and went out.

I bought a pair of boots I had seen in a shop window opposite the hotel. They awakened a yearning in me. To walk. Just walk. Over the Brooklyn Bridge, the Manhattan Bridge, the Williamsburg Bridge, all the glittering bridges, cold and tempting, in the city that never sleeps. They were actually not my style at all, too sharp and too expensive—they made the rest of my clothing look cheap—but I was struck by such an inexplicable urge. A need to have them, like with some men, but with boots the craving is more compelling. All I have to do is throw enough money at them and they're mine. A pair of boots is a promise of movement—like a man is a promise, but of what you never really know. Make no demands of life, just go your own way, intoxicated with your own fragrance, however stale it may be.

Never stop: that seemed to be what this city was all about, perpetual motion, staying awake. Keep moving, it whispered, and I did. Until my money ran out.

When I reached home, Lukas's letter was still by the car windshield, unopened. Winter had passed as if it had never existed.

THE FIRST ONE TO LOOK AT ME

I have been on the road for a long time now. Looking for European deserts—there are supposed to be seven of them, but I haven't even seen one. I travel cheaply and slowly, preferably at night, on trains that convey so much sleep back and forth between cities and countries. But Mama never asks me about things like this—where I've been or where I'm going to—she quite simply never asks. Instead: if I have cut my hair, if the car is working as it should, if I have enough money to manage on, if I'm eating properly. Always the same questions, the same answers. Yes, Mama, I am eating properly, large quantities and infrequently. You save time that way. I have enough money to manage on, and if I haven't, I sort it out: casual jobs, bread-and-butter jobs, tricks. You don't need to worry. I live cheaply, most of all when I travel.

Sometimes I tell her even though she doesn't ask. About the girl in Berlin going up and down the platform on just one roller skate. She only had one leg, it must be a physical impossibility, but she did it anyway, gliding to and fro like the bubble in a spirit level. About the marionette museum in Nuremberg. A security man watched me, followed me through the rooms, showed me the storeroom in the basement where we could be alone, warm and dusty with headless dolls hanging everywhere. Afterward I thought—never again . . . was forced to go out into the town to buy new tights, black with red seams. That night I dreamed about the one-legged girl again. How she defied gravity and all the other laws of nature about the hellishness of everything.

Work hard, live cheap, travel light. Bohemian, Mama calls it. It sounds better in French, the simple life. However light I travel, I always have the letter with me in my luggage, but the opportunity to open it never presents itself.

I saw a butterfly whirling around like a shiny black chewing gum wrapper in the hot air above the rush-hour traffic in Warsaw. Then I stood on a train by an open window and smelled the same mixture of odors as in my childhood, caraway plants and wild cabbage, factory smoke, rotting toads, bonfires on the fields. At the station in Copenhagen a dog barked at me—not like dogs routinely bark at strangers, this one barked as if it really had something personal against just me. In Malmö I met a tourist, a young Frenchwoman who was laughing at the town. She kept repeating the word *mégalomanie* and I was uncertain what she meant. Delusions of grandeur? Yes, Malmö is a little town with a craving for status. A railway line that ends there like in the really big stations in the world. On the other hand: on vacation in Malmö in January? She must be slightly delusional herself.

Where do butterflies go when you don't see them, at night, in the winter, when the exhaust fumes and the sleet drape like a hangover above everything? They can't always be twirling over city streets, childhood fields, the hot railway line out of the village. Life is not a string of pearls made up of lofty moments. It is only like that afterward when you have kept the best pictures and deleted the reality between.

When the gods want to punish you, they answer your prayers. If you knew how many times I have wished him dead, she says.

Now he has been dead for three weeks, I find out when I call home. His weak point was his heart. I sit on the edge of the bed and wait while Mama weeps.

He hasn't lived with her in the house for a long time, not since the heart attack he had when a storm passed through the arboretum and he tried to save the sequoia. Gale warning. There wasn't even anything special about that tree, other than that he liked it, but he liked all the trees. He remained in a hospital bed after that, didn't get up again, didn't come back, not as himself. Then he had one more attack, Björn's weak point . . . Mama's tears subside and finally cease. The funeral? Have I missed it? No, not yet. The day after tomorrow, Lo—are you coming? No one can be so far away on this earth that they don't have a chance to get home by the day after tomorrow, not if they really try. Is Papa coming? I ask. Of course he is coming. Everyone is coming.

"Not me," I say.

"Do as you wish."

"Yes." She is silent.

"I love you, Mama."

"I know."

We sit in silence for a while. She is the only person I can do this with. The morning air is cold in the room. I pull on my white skirt, the receiver tucked between my shoulder and my ear, rinse my face with the strongly chlorinated water. I have never been good at funerals, and this is one funeral I would definitely not have been good at.

I can't find my underwear, or my wallet with the pain relievers either. The room is very small—only you could lose something in such a small room, Mama would say if she could see me now. For a second, when she asks where I am, I don't know. I have to take half a step from the washbasin to the window and draw back the net curtain. Don't remember the name of the street, but it is spring here, the silver birches in the rear courtyard of the hotel are coming out. Grandfather would have liked this town, full of trees, the air smelling of Russian cigarettes after the war.

"Lublin."

"Dublin?"

"No, Lublin, between Poland and Ukraine. Lublin, L as in—"

"Lo," Mama says, "come home."

I will come. But not until after the funeral. When you wake up, I will be there, Mama.

"Then I can't wait to wake up," she says, as if it has been a long time since she felt like that.

She won't be alone. People will be coming from all points of the compass, mostly from the north. And Papa. A long time has passed since they last saw each other. He moved back north to the others a long time ago. I've really never been good at funerals and they will have to do without me—Mama and Papa on either side of the aisle, who would I sit beside? He has lost his father, she has lost . . . well, who understood any of that, in fact? I'm afraid that Mama will start to weep during the service, not like the others, no, she will cry like a dog, between her teeth. Like she cried just now on the telephone when she told me he was dead.

Not wanting to reach home too early, I make an unnecessary detour via Stockholm to get the car and drive all the way down. It's so late when I eventually arrive that it's already light. I fetch the door key from the garden shed and go in through the cellar, creep up the long cold steps. My old bedroom is cold too. Mama has forgotten to turn on the heater, or else she didn't believe I would come.

Freezing, I go up to the attic for a couple of blankets that are always on top of the water tank. The scent of summer games and birchwood smoke reminds me of how we used to sneak up here and play the princess and the pea, a game that Lukas never seemed to

properly understand the point of, but his was only a supporting
role: the footman who had to stuff the pea between the thick layers
of blankets. I was made of genuine princess material, writhing on
the wretched pea, more hollow-eyed with every night I was forced
to sleep on the miserable bed. Lukas helped me put a streak of soot
from the flues under my eyes to show how I grew more and more
worn out by the discomfort.

Once he pretended to be the budding prince who crept into the
chamber to seek the princess's warmth—things had been shaping
up for that, he had been forced to sit in the dark bored to death for
far too long, waiting while I tossed around in a theatrical lamenta-
tion over insomnia. But a princess who can't tolerate a golden pea
underneath her can hardly put up with a 125-pound prince on top
of her. I panicked, tried to knee him as he had taught me in self-
defense, but didn't succeed and grabbed hold of a sharp, rusty im-
plement instead, hit him right on the forehead with all my strength.
He dropped onto me like a stone. If the blood hadn't looked so re-
alistic, I would have thought he was joking. But it was pouring in a
very lifelike way out of a bottomless gash and I had to wriggle free,
tear off my dress, and wrap it around the fountain of blood before
running down to the adults wearing only my underwear.

The unconscious prince was hauled down from the attic, driven
to the hospital, and stitched back together. Afterward he was
dumped back at Gábriel's and threatened with the police. I don't
know what Gábriel did with him next, but by the time I was allowed out again, he had started to gather moss.

And for me: lengthy interrogation until I nearly fell asleep from
exhaustion standing up. Only if I admitted something would I be
allowed to go to bed. Was I sure that *nothing* had actually happened? If I thought about it. Really thought about it. Papa's mother
was making hot chocolate and warming up meatballs, and it made
me feel sick. Did he touch you, did he touch you . . . He must

have—why would you have hit him otherwise, that's not like you. My aunts fixed their blue eyes on me until I told them the truth, that Lukas lay down on top of me when I was not expecting it, that I couldn't get any air, that I got hold of this thing . . .

"Thing? What thing?" Mama asked, alarmed.

"The what-do-you-call it? That hard thing . . ." They all stared at me. "The rusty thing. That I hit him with. I didn't mean to."

It wasn't your fault, Lo, he's the one responsible, they assured me.

The scar on his forehead afterward. L-shaped with stitches that first reddened and then paled in the sun. Each time he looked at himself in the mirror he would see the initial of both our names.

A few hours later a panting noise wakens me, fully clothed under double blankets. When I wake up I never know where I am. I'm tossed out of sleep with the sensation of colliding against something hard—another new day? It is always like this. Wide awake, with no idea where.

It's the guide dog Mama has unintentionally acquired as her final companion in life. It sniffs at the dust on the trousers I was traveling in. I must smell of wild dog—they always rub against my legs, as if they want something. To belong, perhaps. Domesticated dogs unnerve me, and I push this one aside and climb out of bed. The house is silent. Everyone hurried away as soon as Grandfather was lowered into the earth. I had hoped that at least Rikard would still be here—it's been such a long time since we last saw each other. But his room is empty and Mama's too.

Mama, bitten by frost, is sleeping on the veranda in one of the dilapidated summer chairs that ought to fall apart but holds together at the seams just for her, so that she has somewhere to sit and nurse her urine infections, her bronchitis, freeze her fingers, dream deep-frozen dreams. She looks as though she is no longer part of this world. It's only when she opens her eyes that I know she's not dead. No emotion in her face—she doesn't even seem to be able to distinguish my silhouette. Snow-blind. It's a hideously bright day.

"Were you sitting there asleep? In this cold? There are quicker ways to die, Mama."

She gives a start. "Lo?" It's nothing, she says, and pulls her hand through her hair, brittle with frost and static—nothing at all—she was born in much worse. Outdoors, where the cold belongs, she can enjoy it. Indoors she can't endure it.

"Don't tell me you've been sitting here sleeping all night . . ."

Mama makes a dismissive gesture, but it looks as though she has. There are no footprints up to her chair. The snow must not have been forecast, often the case here in the remarkable south. You can go to bed on a warm spring evening and when you wake up the world has turned white during the night. I'm cold in my flimsy dress under the thin jacket. It was spring in Lublin, spring all the way to Warsaw, and it was spring all the way to Berlin too. In Copenhagen spring was beginning. Here it's winter, but starting to warm up with a smell of fresh green timber and newly fallen snow that is already melting. I sweep the snow off the cane chair beside Mama and sit next to her without touching. She looks as though she could fall to pieces, not from frailty, but from cold.

The summer before I was born they slept out here on the veranda, she has told me many times before. Because it was so hot, because Mama was so big she could scarcely move from one chair to another, couldn't spend the night indoors, couldn't tolerate Papa's brothers constantly pointing at her stomach and asking when she was going to produce this . . .

"How was it? The funeral?"

Mama squints into the light. Doesn't know, she says. Yes, she was *there,* but not quite with it. But it was nice. Rikard said it was nice. So it was.

I nod. So it was.

Even if she just sat and waited for the service to end, right at the back of the church—right at the back even though she ought to have been sitting right at the front.

There's no obligation, I say. And Papa?

He had aged. That's what the priest whispered to Mama, who obviously couldn't see for herself how he looked. The priest was the same one who buried Grandmother Idun, the last time Papa was here. Mama didn't remember the priest, but the priest clearly remembered Papa. She had thought he was handsome when she saw him at the last funeral, and now he had aged even though he wasn't so old, but what does age have to do with old at all?

Mama had just waited until it was over. It was a short service, but it felt very long, with the children who had traveled down from the north and some old workmates from the factory. The coffin decorated with fresh branches from Grandfather's various trees in the arboretum—he wouldn't have liked that, in fact he would have hated it—that they broke boughs off the trees. It was like breaking the arms off children, but he was dead now and had no say in the matter.

Anyway, it was good to see the others again, even if she couldn't see them now. They'd all come, but no one stayed long. Rikard and Marina stayed the longest, had left on the night train a few hours before I arrived. Rikard looked just the same, hadn't changed at all, according to him anyway. A few more sun- and laugh-lines around the eyes, that was all. New girlfriend, young, sweet, pregnant. They were all young, sweet, and pregnant, Marina told Mama— but no one ever saw any children. They obviously took them when they left, because Rikard was one of those men women want to have children with, but not necessarily anything more.

I had bought a few packs of Silk Cut for Mama on the way here. When I take two out and light them, she sniffs at the air. Is it . . . yes, you can't mistake the smell of light, mild tobacco.

"I don't smoke, haven't smoked since before you were born."

"Me neither," I say, "but with you I'm prepared to make an exception." She smiles.

"Well. That's all right then," she says and reaches forward with her hand ready for the cigarette. Still smiling, she cautiously inhales the smoke. But as it escapes through her frozen blue lips she becomes serious again. The trees in Grandfather's arboretum have a snowy side and sunny side, a brittle cracking sound when the ice slips off the branches. It's when something thaws from a frozen state that it breaks.

"Lo," she says hesitantly.

"What?"

THE SLOPING CEILING

"Two weeks outside time and space and everything I was used to,"
Mama tells me. Two weeks is nothing, two weeks is everything.
Put up with it until it passes, Björn had said. But it didn't.

She liked being alone with him in the new house as they waited
for the others to follow with the vanload of furniture. As far as she
was concerned, they could take their time. Perhaps she liked it too
much; the new light made him look different, smell different,
stronger. She looked different too, she could see it in his eyes.

Björn taught her how to cut wood. She had an energy that she
had to channel into something sensible, he thought, and she learned
quickly, as you do when you learn something that in fact you already know.

More than anything she liked doing nothing with him. They'd
never done that before—at home you always did *something*. But the
new house was perfect, needed no attention at all, required nothing
of them. They picked up snails in the arboretum instead, fat and
shiny silvery green. He'd heard that they were edible, at least in
France, and here in the south they were already halfway there, pity
to let them go to waste. Boil them, or what? Butter? Salt? Mama
had no idea, but they had a try. It turned to glue. They laughed
about it the whole evening. Seeing him laugh was an unusual sight
and she liked it very much.

After she had taught him to laugh she wanted to teach him to
swim, but he wasn't interested in that.

"Only animals swim," he protested.

"Aw, come on." She went first to show him. Up to her waist in the water. Turned around.

"Watch me—it's not dangerous." But Björn looked as though he thought it was dangerous to watch her.

"Are you scared?"

When she said that, he was forced to go out into the dark water. The words were a trap that had already closed around him.

"Lean back, I'm holding you. You have to relax, otherwise you'll sink."

He sank. As heavy as a black oak. As taut as a gun with the safety off.

But she held him.

She was strong and the water made her stronger.

The whole of his weight rested in her arms. His white underpants filled with water so he looked like a drowning Ophelia, and she had to laugh at him—she'd seen him more or less naked so many times in the old house, where they lived in such a cramped space, but this sudden diffidence was something you had to laugh about.

Nothing could happen. The existence of a possibility didn't mean that it was a real possibility. Not because Björn was like a father to her—the paternal type was the last thing he was—but Idun had always been like a mother to her, even more than her own. She had to put up with it, whether or not it passed.

After two weeks they were no longer alone, people in all the rooms. Karenina became Katarina again and Björn returned to his normal self, slower to laugh and other nonsense. He had to forget the swim he had taken with her and be content with viewing the lake from a distance. The lake that he thought with a little goodwill they could count as their own, like the barley fields and even the silver curve of the railway as it swept so assuredly through the countryside bearing its promise that the world carried on forever.

They were no longer alone, but the tension between them continued, soundless as a bird of prey. That someone might notice it, that it might suddenly strike with no chance of them stopping it, had been a nightmare. They had to avoid each other sufficiently to avert disaster—but not so openly that anyone had cause for suspicion.

With Idun leading the way, the new arrivals walked through the house, absolutely silent, struck dumb, until the children started to fight over the bedrooms on the upper floor. The upper floor for the children, the floor below for the adults, two pretty bedrooms with doors out onto the veranda. Veranda, it was like being in America. There was no limit to it all. *Three* toilets . . . Rikard, the youngest, ran around like an excited puppy and squirted into all three and flushed them so that it sounded as though an almighty torrent was running through the whole house. Björn shouted at his son, but Idun just laughed. Before they'd had to manage with a communal dry closet, so this was a luxury to laugh over every day.

The furniture was unloaded and carried in. It looked meager in the large bright rooms. That was the disadvantage of trading up so dramatically, Björn said—not without some pride, because the move had been his idea from start to finish and this was the house he had found, crowned by the universe of exotic trees that spread out right to the edge of the fields of barley.

The shared bank loan, which had been much bigger than they had anticipated, was what held the four of them together now. Forever. As well as the past, of course.

Children, memories, origins. And the fact that they were all now strangers in this new place. Björn, Idun, Anna, and Aron.

And the bird of prey. The one that never struck. Doomed to keep circling.

"Love is a folie à deux," Mama says. What she has just told me is floating somewhere above my head, finding no point where it can sink in.

"Papa, then? Why Papa?" I whisper.

Mama is quiet in the brightness, hesitates so long I think she has changed her mind and doesn't want to tell me any more. Then she gathers herself—the first one to look at me . . . she had thought.

The first time Mama saw the pearl fisher's house it reminded her of a room decorated for a party that never took place. The feeling of an extravagant life. It was in such an inaccessible spot, it must have belonged to a person who wanted to avoid contact with others at any price. Even though it was cluttered from floor to ceiling with things from distant journeys, the house was echoing and desolate, as if everything had been hollowed out by time and vermin, like a walk in a dead forest. The way Mama describes the place reveals that she doesn't know I spent my entire childhood there. As if I didn't know every joint in the damp wooden floor, every flyspeck on the wall in the alcove with the bed, exactly how the light filtered through the branches of the coral tree, the sour scent of the larch trees outside and the humid smell of incense and secret sleep.

In the alcove, in the middle of winter, bitterly cold. They must have kept their jackets on. Mama was sure it was that particular winter afternoon that I was conceived, because she had only been in there once and not returned.

That my life had been created in there, in the iron bed where Lukas and I often slept our secret sleep, is an unreal thought.

No one knew the pearl fisher, but everyone knew who he was, and Mama had decided that she would find the deserted house she had heard about. When she finally did, her first thought was that she would share the discovery with Björn. If anyone would

understand, he would. They shared something that the other family members didn't, whatever it was, perhaps only a determination—
for something more, something else, new, a striving, a dream, or
several. And this was a house built by a dreamer, possibly a little
mad, but he may not have been. Whether you are mad or not is
measured by how successful you are, Björn had said, so when in
the end, after much searching, she found the place, she went to
fetch him.

He was the only one she wanted to show it to and she wanted to
be alone with him there. Nowadays there was never the opportunity. It was perhaps best that way, because her feelings for him
hadn't passed—quite the reverse, they had grown and tangled
themselves up in a knot of misery, no deliverance, no peace. She
was twenty-one so it could hardly be seen as a harmless passing
crush. No, nothing felt harmless any longer. They never spoke
about it, but sometimes . . . he would cast a glance across the room.
Only a glance, but if you know, a glance is enough.

It was a cold and beautiful day. She took a shortcut over the winter fields and met him in the arboretum. He was standing there in
his blue work trousers, no coat, but wearing a leather cap so ugly
that you had to look like Björn to get away with it. Standing there
doing something, as usual she didn't know what, she supposed
mostly standing and enjoying being between the trees. That was
what he liked most about the arboretum, she'd realized—not the
trees themselves, but the space between them. The silence and the
tranquillity that she could long for too.

Now he was watchful as he saw her approaching in the distance.
Even more watchful when she came up close to stand in front of
him, twisting and turning her mittens and her request. He shook
his leather cap when she had finally managed to formulate the
question that was so difficult to ask. No, Karenina. Don't call me
Karenina . . . It is still no, he said. He didn't want to. Without fur-

ther explanation. Just no. Even though she could see he was not busy with anything. A sheath knife in one hand, that was all, a pretext in case he was caught red-handed doing nothing.

He didn't want to. Not interested. Or perhaps terrified, she wasn't sure. Terrified? Yes . . . or whatever it might be called.

Her hopes were turned to disappointment. Sudden, strong, crushing disappointment. Without a word she turned and walked away.

The first one to look at me, she said to herself, without really understanding where the idea came from. The thought just appeared in her head, unexpected and powerful, obvious and quite defiant, not to say insane, but nevertheless . . . appealing, yes, liberating, at any rate less impossible than other thoughts she'd been having lately.

The first one, she thought as she walked up toward the house, her hands throbbing with blood and cold.

They were all there, Björn's four sons, busy with various things in the yard, the first sunny day for a long time. As it happened it was Rikard who looked at her first, from the open kitchen window where he was changing the weather stripping. Not Rikard . . . he was too young, the youngest of all the sons, no, not Rikard, she thought, slightly embarrassed. The next one to see her was Jon, but he was taken; he and his girlfriend were sitting on the step enjoying the winter sun. And then Isak, on the way to the compost with the day's slop buckets. But he didn't count, he was her brother. She went up to Erik, who was bending over the engine of the broken-down Volvo, the eldest of Björn's sons and the one who resembled him most. But Erik was irritated and said, "Can you not see that I have my hands full? Where have you been anyway? You need to cycle down to do the shopping . . . milk, minced meat, soap, cigarettes . . ."

She pretended not to hear. She had already turned to David.

There was only David left, the son who resembled Björn least.

David with steam coming out of his mouth in the cold, on his way out to the winter fields to shoot small game, standing by the garage cleaning his gun.

"Come on," she said.

"What for?"

"Don't ask so many questions."

"Okay, okay, stop nagging, I'm coming."

Everyone was used to her waywardness, and perhaps David should have had his suspicions when she told him to come without any why or wherefore. But he had no objection to accompanying her. Help her with whatever it was she needed help with. He liked her, she was easy to like, and he was the only one who did, but that just made him more convinced. When they passed the arboretum, Björn watched them go. All the way down across the frost-covered fields, the same way she had just come and wanted him, Björn, to go with her . . . she was now walking with David.

"I don't know what he thought. I really don't know what he thought when he saw me go off with his son. And I've never asked."

At least she was no longer nervous, not with David. Not at all as she would have been if Björn had been at her side. What she was feeling and doing and why, she couldn't have explained, but she didn't need to, because David asked no questions.

In the end she was the one who asked why he was taking his rifle with him. He didn't need it where they were going. Surely he understood that they weren't going hunting. He was already caught.

"You never know," David replied, excessively vigilant. It also felt a little excessive when he suggested that they shoot off the lock when they reached the house and were unable to open the door. She took out a small pocketknife instead and worked it open. As if she had spent her life entering places that weren't hers.

The chilled hideout was full of remarkable things, but instead of paying closer attention to them or perhaps lighting a fire in the stove, she guided him into the sleeping alcove and disarmed him.

The gun she propped against the old propane burner beside the bed.

"What's gotten into you," he breathed when, still wrapped in her woolen scarf and without even taking off her mittens, she started to unbutton her cardigan. She had nothing underneath. He'd seen her naked many times, but never like this, never for him, only him.

"Shhh . . ." she whispered, snuggling up to him in the creaking iron bed. She was quite calm and confident, sitting with her woolen hat and her white breasts. He was mortified and bewildered. How did she think they could keep this secret from the rest of the family?

"Shhh," she hushed him again.

He'd always liked her, she knew that, maybe he looked up to her slightly. She was a few years older and had a way of making the age difference seem bigger. She was the one who always said what she thought, who even dared to stand up to Björn, something the others were wary of, with the exception of Idun.

When she tried to undress him she discovered a small home-tattooed star on one shoulder, newly done, not particularly attractive. She hadn't realized that there were things about him she didn't know. Here. Now. Him. That was all she wanted, she couldn't explain it any better than that. David pulled his shirt back on, didn't want to let her take his clothes off. No naked skin, perhaps it was too cold for that, and she had kept most of hers on too. His lips were dark with the cold, his pupils had contracted. She didn't know what that meant—excitement, confusion, bedazzlement, all at the same time?

The quilts had a pattern of strange flowers she didn't know the names of. And in David's eyes something else she didn't know . . . a mixture of disquiet and lust verging on terror? He was probably a virgin. She was not. But she wasn't as experienced as she tried to appear.

David against Björn was like David's fight with Goliath. David was a boy compared to Björn, but he made her feel like a woman. On the sloping ceiling in the alcove over David's head hung the silhouettes of two Japanese dragons, cut out with edging scissors. She saw them only that one time, never forgot them. What sort of battle they were engaged in, whether they were mating or fighting, it wasn't possible to see. But they could keep on indefinitely, they were so evenly matched.

If Mama could see me now she would ask me what the matter was, why my eyes . . . I wouldn't be able to reply, but I wish she would ask. The love Mama used to warn me about, I always wondered who it was she had loved with that sort of passion. There was never the right opportunity to ask.

"Lo, I love your papa, but I can't bear to think about him," she answered whenever I tried. Her voice had a tone that didn't invite further conversation. I pictured them as two animals equal in strength and wounds, who avoided each other so that they weren't forced to tear each other part.

When Mama hears the familiar sound of the lighter, she holds her hand out automatically. Fingers poised for a cigarette. Her unseeing eyes sharpen. She listens to the sound of paper. A shadow of anxiety passes over her face. The sound of paper being ripped.

"What is it?" she asks. "Is it for me?" I hand her the lighted cigarette. No, it is for me, Mama. I am opening it now.

Lukas's letter is as short as it is illegible. I stare at it and can't understand what I'm looking at. Unintelligible signs all mixed up together. It is obvious how hard he tried, how important it must have been, how impossible. His handwriting used to look as though he wrote up and down with his left hand and he never managed to get the letters in the right order.

The only feeling I have is of relief. Unbelievable relief.

No recriminations, at least none that I can interpret—there is no chance that I'll be able to decipher this. I didn't know that you could be so dyslexic, a whole page of illegible marks. Now at any rate I have done what I could, made the effort to look for the letter, found it, taken it with me everywhere, waiting for a place where I could open it, and in the end torn it open and read it, or at least tried. Only to find it impossible.

The muffled call of the bittern has been inside my head for so long, and the moment I skim through the letter it glides out over the lake. Deathly quiet and a little heavy at the front. And my head is empty, light, and calm.

TOMORROW NEVER COMES

When I have stared long enough at Lukas's incomprehensible words, I see . . . at first only one word that stands out from the rest. Written with extra effort to make that at least legible. A simple word, and nevertheless I don't understand it—why is he saying that to me? A feeling of disquiet spreads through me, just as when the bats in the attic unfold their dry wings after the winter and wake each other up, one after the other, until everything is fluttering. I rise out of the cane chair, tell Mama that I have to take a walk, give her my jacket so that she doesn't freeze to death, and leave her there.

The cold bites into my face and makes my eyes water. From a distance everything looks as usual, as I remember it, though I haven't set foot anywhere near Lukas's house since I left. See you in hell, Lo. Hell could be here, on the steps of the house where he grew up, or it could be where we used to sit with a bowl of rice and his hand-rolled cigarettes and nothing special to do. It required intelligence to love like that, quietly and with no props. We grew up so understimulated, filled each other's field of vision so completely, breathed the same air, heavy with toads rotting in the rain.

He isn't there, hasn't been for a long time, Mama said, but I have to see for myself. No trace left of the fire. The exterior looks as though it has been restored, but only from a distance. When I come closer I see that there are no details in place, the interior crude and unfinished, bare partitions, no furniture, a façade, that is all. The river rats must have their own empire here now with their own laws, move around as they please. If they stay here and keep each other in check, they'll be left in peace. I look in all the windows and the toolshed and the garage, but everything seems to have been abandoned. I go down to the lake, imagine the boom of the bittern on a certain sort of evening, like the time Lukas had drunk too much and wanted to go home even though he was already at home. I haven't been to the lake since then either. The last time I walked along this path was with Yoel, a stranger on a chance but momentous visit. I didn't want to leave, but nothing held me back.

The dead forest and our hiding place. Yet childhood is not a place to which you can return. Why Lukas? How many times have I asked myself this? Because he and I were the people we were? The dead forest has risen up again, but the tender green shoots are just brushwood growing healthily between the trunks. I continue along the shore without finding our hideout. Was it really so inaccessible and well concealed? There are no fixed points for my memory, everything indistinguishable, like the vegetation. I must have walked too far, gotten lost. Stop and look out over the lake, and there . . . with the lake water halfway up the broken windows, there it is. It is either floating or perhaps sinking, a little way out in the mirrorlike water, about to be dragged even deeper. From a distance it looks like a rotting, half-sunken barge. Wherever Lukas is, it can hardly be here.

The sheltering trees around the house are gone. The beautiful little larch grove felled. Good timber, I remember Papa's father used to say. After the war he had traveled through Finland, and when he came home he talked about the delightful larch forests and the impressively strong women, in that order. Grandmother laughed about that. Tall trees and hardy women, a longing for something that could compare with him.

I stand at the water's edge and see the light divide the lake, split it into the silvery surface and the dark depths. Giddiness, now or never. The water is deadly cold and muddy with sludge from the bottom, but I have to do it. Take off my clothes and wade out. When the water reaches my thighs I begin to sink. The bottom of the lake is so much marshier than I remember, or is it just my adult weight that pulls me down?

I should have left the seal of time and silence intact, had respect for it. The letter wasn't as unreadable as I had hoped it would be. After turning it over in my mind, in the end I could work it out, even though with every word it became harder to interpret, as if he took so long over each character that darkness descended while he battled with something that was impossible, too much, too awful. *Forgive me.*

It was the last thing I had expected from him.

An accusation or a declaration of love or both, that was what I'd imagined. Not this. *Lo . . . Copenhagen . . . forgive me . . . answer . . .*

The letter had traveled a long way. Lukas must have been waiting for an answer—fearful to begin with, then impatient, in the end resigned—no, in the end nothing at all. My silence taken for a no, I don't forgive you. It only takes one to let go.

That explains why he never came up to Mama's house when I was at home. When he saw his old car standing there under the white birch. Not because he couldn't forgive me for going away— but because he thought that I couldn't forgive him.

The lake water is halfway up the peeling door to the pearl fisher's house. I'm forced to enter via the broken window, haul myself up and clamber into the cold hall. A dull stagnation fills the rooms. The moisture dampens both the light and the rustling in the winter reeds outside. The rooms aren't submerged. The floors are damp, but the wood seems to have swollen with water from underneath and become watertight like boat timber. At first sight everything seems to be as usual. I find no food in the cool cupboard that might indicate someone's recent presence. At first I think I can feel a faint warmth coming from the cast iron of the stove, but it must have been my imagination.

It is impossible to go back. The place I pictured existed only as long as we were here. The rest is just dead coral trees, an impression of wandering around in an artificially lit display.

I had slept the sleep of an inebriated child—an overtired youngster who has eaten far too much—and Lukas couldn't stop himself. Was that what he was trying to say in his letter? *This is a man's world . . . even in my sleep . . . but it wouldn't be nothing, nothing without . . .* intoxicated for the first time, teenage-drunk, sugar-scented, available, out of it, amid the dark brown sheets. Dark brown, I remember that, have always had a memory for useless details. The curtains at the window were also dark brown, the entire hotel dark brown, like a bat, cheap and yet, I suspect, a fortune for him.

A memory for details. But I've forgotten what it is he's asking me to forgive. That he might have done something against my will. Surely I would remember that forever? You couldn't even drown the river rats, Lukas.

A few short seconds, that was all it took. The moment when I felt your weight and the knowledge that I wouldn't have had a chance—if—and for a moment you did too, enjoyed the advantage before you regretted it. Held me like a dog holds a piece of meat he is prepared to fight for. I remember the sense of being at the mercy of your desire not to hurt me. *I didn't want to hurt you,* you said afterward. For me it meant that you could have if you had wanted to. *I could have hurt you, but I didn't want to*—that was what I heard.

After that I saw the vice inside you, inside all men. But it provoked me more than it scared me. You know it, I know it, therefore it doesn't need to be said. And if we do say it, it changes nothing. I don't hurt you because I'm not able to. But you don't hurt me because you don't want to.

What happened next?

How could Mama have told me?

Tell me what happened next, I asked, and didn't know what I was asking for. If there had been such a thing as fairy tales, there would be just a few for adults only, like the one Lukas used to tell me about the nightingale that sang most beautifully in captivity after its eyes had been poked out.

All Mama knew about him she had heard from the doctor in the village. How she managed it, patient confidentiality and all that . . . But for the doctor Mama was just a lonely blind middle-aged woman she could unburden herself to without risk. At any rate, after the fire Lukas had visited the village health center, with wounds that had become inflamed and needed to be dressed. He had eye problems caused by the smoke and the heat. He had a wear-and-tear injury from the factory. And some old injury that from time to time gave him headaches. After a while pain in his shoulders too with the toil of building the house and a chronic respiratory infection. The pearl fisher's house that had become his temporary home was wet with damp and drafty and winter was approaching. He suffered such a serious loss of appetite that he was not eating any food at all. Insomnia. And then the fire negligence prosecution hanging over him and an inquiry into his mental state. The only thing Lukas could thank his lucky stars for, if he had any, was that the house was uninsured. At least he was not under suspicion of insurance fraud. And the fact that his papa had neither life insurance nor a krona in the bank meant that Lukas escaped accusation of increasing the morphine dose too quickly.

It was as if his body had suddenly seized up, all at once. Perhaps he just wanted to be looked after, the doctor thought. But not touched. Not that. No eye contact. He didn't even want to take his shirt off in front of her when she needed to examine him. Difficult to talk to, unwilling to provide information about history of illness in his family, didn't want to fill in any forms at all. He winced at any physical contact. A very reluctant patient, and yet he came and continued to come, with old injuries and new, his immune system destroyed, the degeneration of a human being—it happens sometimes. As a fellow human being, the doctor had followed it with horror; as a doctor, not without fascination.

Then Lukas stopped showing up, suddenly and unexpectedly. Either he had been released from all his afflictions at once or, more probably, he had gone under. Possibly relocated, like so many others. At the leather factory where he worked there had been more layoffs. The doctor figured he was one of the many who left.

A long time passed. When one day he was sitting in the waiting room again, it wasn't because he was ill, but to ask for a certificate of health. He requested it for a job he was going to apply for elsewhere. Visibly changed—or just more his old self—that was something the doctor could not determine because she hadn't met him before he became ill.

Specimens taken and routine tests. Everything was as it should be. He had regained not only his health, but also his physique. The doctor didn't believe in miracles, but maybe . . . everyday miracles. When Lukas came for his next appointment to get his test results, she signed the health certificate and handed it over with the feeling that she was delivering a present. He should have a good chance, she said, of getting the job he was hoping for, on an oil rig somewhere in the Atlantic.

I looked at Mama imploringly, as if she could turn back the clock. But no, even she can't do that.

"*On an oil rig?* When you've been accused of arson?"

"That investigation was dropped," she reminds me.

"But—fire negligence . . ."

Well, if they did a check, Lukas managed to slip through regardless. He got the job. That was the last the doctor heard from him.

Lukas on an oil rig sounds like an evil fairy story, but there are no fairy stories, he said.

"Mama, I don't know whether I want to hear the end."

"We can save it for tomorrow, Lo."

Tomorrow never comes. But I suspected anyway.

They say that a factor leading to pyromania may be homelessness during childhood. You and your damn hand-rolled cigarettes, Lukas, only a lunatic would smoke on an oil rig, did your mistakes teach you nothing? Did you not sign a contract about fire safety when you got the job, had you not promised me to stop smoking, had I not promised you never to start? To whose lot does it fall to cast himself into the flame of guilt and put it out with his own body? An uncontrollable impulse. How often do you not think I have wanted to do it too? But it can't be—you can only forget and carry on, forget and carry on. It's a blessing to be able to forget, but for you the blessing was that everything could burn.

I can still feel the tenderness around my midriff when I curl up in the alcove in the pearl fisher's house and shut my eyes. It was sunny on the highway, the first light of day, as I was driving here at dawn at eighty miles an hour—too fast, too slippery, too bright—and suddenly: the oblique shaft entered through the windshield and transfixed me on the driver's seat. I was veering across a no-man's-land, straight into the light. Within its dazzling force was silence, the world was in slow motion, playing backward, moving away. Not a sound, no metallic smell of blood, only something that was closing, my lungs emptied of air. There was no pain, it was beyond good and bad. If I survive this, I thought, if I survive, I will give our story a happier ending.